READY

READY

LUCY MONROE

BRAVA

KENSINGTON PUBLISHING CORP.
http://www.kensingtonbooks.com

BRAVA BOOKS are published by

Kensington Publishing Corp.
850 Third Avenue
New York, NY 10022

All Kensington titles, imprints and distributed lines are available at special quantity discounts for bulk purchases for sales promotion, fund-raising, educational or institutional use.

Special book excerpts or customized printings can also be created to fit specific needs. For details, write or phone the office of the Kensington Special Sales Manager: Kensington Publishing Corp., 850 Third Avenue, New York, NY 10022. Attn. Special Sales Department. Phone: 1-800-221-2647.

Brava and the B logo Reg. U.S. Pat. & TM Off.

ISBN 0-7582-0864-2

First Kensington Trade Paperback Printing: July 2005
10 9 8 7 6 5 4 3

Printed in the United States of America

For my sister Diane. You are such a special part of my life and I love you very much.

And with special thanks to my friend David Counard, a former Army Ranger, who patiently answered hours worth of questions for me. Thank you!

Chapter 1

Lise was used to running into walls, but falling into traffic was another matter altogether.

So, in the split second before her hands connected with cold concrete in an attempt to break her fall, she knew she had not imagined the hard shove between her shoulder blades that sent her sprawling forward. No more than the squeal of tires from braking cars, or a woman's shrill scream behind her.

She shoved herself up from the pavement to her knees, but her body kept going as someone yanked her back to the curb. She landed against a wall of bodies.

"You need to be more careful," came a burly, deep voice.

A woman dressed head to toe in Seahawks green and blue said, "You've got to watch yourself after a game—the sidewalks are crowded and so are the streets."

Lise forced her lungs to suck in the frigid November air and wheezed out, "Somebody pushed me."

She almost fell off the curb again, trying to turn around to see the people behind her. "Somebody pushed me," she repeated, her voice high-pitched. "Did any of you see who did it?"

"What are you talking about?" This from an older man, his expression disbelieving.

"I didn't see anything," a woman in a red parka said.

An older black woman patted Lise's shoulder. "I think you're mistaken."

"She's probably disoriented," the woman's companion said to her.

The voices went on, a cacophony of sound in Lise's head, but one thing came through clearly.

No one had seen him.

Again.

The light turned and pedestrians surged onto the street around her.

Shaking with reaction, she stayed where she was, but watched the mass of people pass by. No malevolent stares were directed toward her, no undue attention focused on the woman who had almost gotten hit by a car. Nothing that might indicate who *he* was, the man who had shoved her off the curb.

Or had it been a man? She didn't even know that much, and the not knowing was the most terrifying thing of all.

She had no clue where to look for her enemy, or how to recognize him. However, she'd thought she was safe here in cold and rainy Seattle, thousands of miles from the small Texas town of her birth.

She'd been wrong.

Lise stared at the anonymous e-mail, her stomach churning.

It was the third one in as many days. Combined with the nuisance calls and the blood-red rose she'd found lying on the driver's seat of her locked car, it was enough to make her sick with fear.

Ms. Barton, I hope you enjoy your Thanksgiving vacation in Canyon Rock. The flight from Portland will be crowded. They always are on big travel days like

that, but family should always spend the holidays together. I'm sure your brother, sister-in-law, and new
niece, Genevieve, miss you. That pretty little baby
will grow up before you know it, not knowing her
aunt. Are you sure moving so far away was a good
idea?

The e-mail wasn't completely anonymous. It had been signed.
Nemesis. Not the stalker's real name, Lise was sure. She was
a writer. She knew who Nemesis was—the goddess of vengeance. Although the longer she was stalked, the more convinced she became that her stalker was a man.

Not a goddess, but a devil.

She shivered in her desk chair, chilled to the very marrow
of her bones. She'd already turned the heat up, but she knew
it wouldn't help.

This cold came from the inside.

Why had Nemesis mentioned Genevieve? It wasn't the first
time he had brought up her family, but it was the first time
he'd mentioned one of them by name.

Was this e-mail some sort of threat against her baby niece?

All thoughts of going home for the holidays crashed and
burned in the face of her stalker's certain knowledge of her
travel plans. There would be no sneaking out of Seattle and
driving three hours south to fly out of PDX. Not if her stalker
would just be waiting for her at the other end of her journey,
ready to do who-knew-what to her family.

Joshua stopped in front of the door to Lise's apartment.

He had not planned to fly into SeaTac before going to
Texas, but he'd had no choice. His baby sister's emotional
well-being depended on him talking some sense into Lise
Barton.

Bella was a wreck because Lise had called to cancel her
visit for Thanksgiving. His sister believed *she* was the reason

her new sister-in-law had moved to Seattle and refused to come home for the holidays. Bella had spouted some baloney about being afraid she'd displaced the other woman since she married Lise's brother, Jake.

According to his sister, Lise had said she had a cold that she didn't want to expose the baby to. That had sounded reasonable, but then Bella told him that Lise had said she wouldn't be able to make Christmas, either, because of an unexpected deadline.

Bella was sure the excuses were phony. She said that Lise planned her deadlines a year in advance. He didn't know about that, but the sexy but shy author of kick-butt women's fiction would not put work ahead of an important family event. That much he knew. He was still reeling inside from the shock of her moving across the country from them. She was too attached to Jake, Bella, and the baby for the move to make any sense.

When Bella had let slip that Lise had cancelled her arrival *after* discovering he was going to be at the ranch for the holidays, he'd known what the real problem was. Lise didn't want to see him again.

He was here to fix that.

He knocked, glad to see she at least had a peephole in her door. Her so-called *secure* building had been so easy to get into, he was embarrassed for the agency that installed the security measures and the guard at the front desk in the lobby.

A crash came from inside the apartment. Then silence. He knocked again, louder this time.

Again there was no response.

He called out her name, but absolutely no sound came from the apartment.

Had she fallen and hurt herself? She wasn't always completely aware, and he'd seen her walk straight into a wall when her eyes were hazy with a certain look she got.

His fist against the door made it shake within its frame.

Still nothing.

He surveyed the locks on the door. They were too basic to be of any real use at keeping out the criminal element. He didn't even hesitate.

He had the door open faster than if he'd had a key.

A slight *whoosh* of air to his left sent him into immediate battle-ready mode. Reflexes honed by six years in the Army Rangers and a decade spent as a mercenary took over. He swung toward the faint sound, his hand coming up to block the blow.

He grabbed the poker before it connected with his head and had his assailant in a headlock before he realized it was Lise.

He tossed the cast-iron poker aside and spun her to face him, her dark blond hair flying around her face. "What the hell are you trying to do?"

Big hazel eyes stared back at him with a glazed look he'd come to know all too well in his profession.

Terror.

Her breath came in shallow pants and her sweatshirt-clad arms were trembling.

What the hell was going on?

"Why didn't you answer the door?"

Her mouth moved, but nothing came out.

He shook her gently. "Speak, Lise."

Her eyes blinked and then filled with tears.

"Damn it." He hauled her against him and wrapped his arms around her.

He'd really frightened her when he forced his way into her apartment. He hadn't considered that possibility when he picked her locks. He should have.

She was a small-town Texas girl living in the big city.

Obviously, she hadn't acclimated well.

Her body shook against him and he felt like a real heel.

"I didn't mean to scare you, little one."

Lise's fingers were digging into his shirt, holding the denim so tight, he'd lose the shirt before he lost her grip. She pressed her face into his chest as if she was literally burrowing into him.

"Joshua?" It was the first recognizable sound she'd made in over a minute.

"Yeah?"

"What are you doing here?"

"You told Bella you weren't going to Texas for Thanksgiving."

Lise shuddered. "No. I'm not going."

She didn't sound like she had a cold. Her usually soft voice was strained, but not in a way that could be caused by a scratchy throat.

He rubbed her back.

It just seemed like the right thing to do.

She responded by relaxing her hold on his shirt just the tiniest bit. He kept it up, talking to her in the same tone of voice he'd used to calm the little boy he'd liberated on his last mission. He used similar words, too, telling her it was all right, that he wouldn't let anything happen to her, that she was going to be okay.

It took almost as long as it had taken him with the boy before she relaxed enough to step away from him. When she did and he got his first good look at her face, he winced.

He'd seen snow with more color than her skin, except the purple bruises under her eyes. Her bow-shaped mouth trembled.

"Lise, you don't belong in Seattle."

"H-how . . ." She blinked, made a visible effort to gather herself in, and her quivering lips formed words. "How do you figure that?"

"It's pretty damn obvious to me you aren't settling into city living. You get an unexpected visitor and you're practically crawling out of your skin."

She shook her head and laughed hollowly. "Trust me, moving back to Texas won't help."

"Why not?"

"My problems travel with me."

"What is that supposed to mean?"

She didn't answer, but this time he didn't wait around for a reply. He propelled her gently toward the bedroom. "You can tell me about it on the plane. Get your stuff together. We've got an eight o'clock flight."

"No." She twisted from his guiding hand and stopped, wrapping her arms around herself, covering the Dallas Cowboys logo on her sweatshirt.

"I can't go, Joshua." Her southern drawl was very pronounced, her voice on the ragged edge of hysterical.

"Why not?"

She swallowed and looked away from him, her body stiff with stress. "I'm afraid."

"Of what?"

"I don't want my family hurt because of me." Her eyes were both pleading and wild. "If I go to Texas right now it could put them all at risk, even little Genevieve."

He bit back an ugly word. "Explain."

"I'm being stalked."

Lise flexed her fingers, feeling the tension in her body clear to her fingertips.

Joshua had reacted to her announcement with absolute silence. He stood there, a formidable dark shadow in her hallway, his brown eyes trying to see into her soul. His stillness was as complete as his silence, which unnerved her, but at least he wasn't telling her she was crazy, or imagining things.

"Do you know who is stalking you?" he finally asked.

"No."

"Why do you believe you're being stalked?"

"I don't just believe it, I *know* it." As simple as his questions were, it was hard for her brain to form answers in her current stressed-out state. "I've gotten anonymous e-mails that make it obvious I'm being watched."

"Did you try to trace the e-mails?"

"Yes." She stopped, having lost the train of conversation, and then she remembered again. "It didn't work."

"Is that all that has happened so far?"

"It's enough." Which wasn't the whole answer, but was as much as she was willing to share right now.

"Yes, it is," he said, surprising her.

The fact that he had believed her when no one else had, not the sheriff back home, and not the Seattle police, was just sinking into her sluggish mind when he spoke again.

"You can tell me the rest of what's got you so scared on the flight. No way do I believe you're this out of control over a few e-mails."

She didn't have time for explanations. She had to get him out of there, then she had to leave. She didn't know where she was going to go, but she wasn't going to sit around waiting for Nemesis to show up on her doorstep like Joshua had.

She grabbed his arm and started shoving him toward the door. "Thank you for stopping by. Tell Jake and Bella I love them."

Her words were coming in short bursts and she wasn't completely sure what she was saying . . . whatever it would take to get him to go.

He stopped in front of the door and didn't budge. "I'm not going anywhere, Lise."

"Of course you are—you're going to Texas."

"Not without you." He put his hands on her shoulders, their warmth and strength making her feel safe, but that was an illusion she couldn't afford. "I'll watch out for our family. I won't let anyone hurt them, or you."

In any other circumstance, she would have believed him, but her unknown enemy had the advantage. The minute they stepped on a commercial flight, Nemesis would know where she was. He could beat them to Texas, or follow them. Either way, the risk to Jake, Bella, and little Genevieve was too great.

"Even you can't stop a bullet shot from a sniper's rifle, or a brake line being cut on a car, or—"

"Are you saying those things have happened to you?" he asked, breaking into the litany of fears that had plagued her conscious and unconscious mind for days.

"They *could* happen and I won't be around my family if they do."

Her mind was splintering again, trying to figure out the best escape route least likely to alert her hidden tormentor, while grappling with the problem of getting Joshua out of her apartment.

She yanked the door open. "I'll call Bella and reassure her, okay?" Just as soon as she stopped somewhere with a phone.

Right now, all she wanted was to get into her car and drive forever, leaving her life careening out of control behind her.

Joshua said nothing; he just pushed the door shut again with his heel, his coffee-brown gaze never once leaving hers. He leaned back against it, crossed his arms, and waited with an attitude that said he'd wait there forever, but he was going to have his way.

Something snapped inside Lise.

Fine. He could wait there until hell froze over, but she was going to pack. She was leaving—not with Joshua, and not to Texas where she would put her family at risk, but she was going. She spun on her heel and rushed into the bedroom, a jumble of things she needed to take with her filling her fractured thoughts.

She was throwing clothes willy-nilly into a duffel bag when a beeping sound scared her, making her drop a pile of underwear onto the floor.

She stared at the multicolored cotton for several seconds

before she latched onto the fact that the beeping sound was the phone ringing.

She grabbed the cordless phone from its base. "Hello?"

"Lise, your visitor left without taking you with him."

Her already madly beating heart climbed into her throat at the computer-digitized voice she'd come to know much too well. "*Who is this?*"

"You should have gone with him. Family is supposed to be together on the holidays."

"Why are you doing this to me?" she shrieked, feeling what was left of her control slipping away.

"An eye for an eye, Lise."

"What are you talking about?" None of this made sense. Her life didn't make sense. "I don't know what you want from me!"

A strong arm settled around her shoulders and she screamed before realizing it was Joshua.

"You sound upset," the inhuman voice taunted.

Joshua's lips settled next to her ear. "Is it him?"

She nodded her head violently, making her neck ache, but no sound would emerge from her throat.

"I guess it will be you and me together in our lonely solitude on Thanksgiving. I can't spend it with my family, either." The phone clicked in her ear.

A hand tapped gently on her cheek. "Lise."

Joshua's voice.

He was there. She wasn't alone.

How long had she stood in paralyzed fear? She didn't know.

"The phone . . ." she croaked out, her throat unaccountably dry.

"What did he say?"

"Something about spending Thanksgiving together." Stupid, weak tears filled her eyes. "He thought you'd gone and he taunted me about being alone."

Joshua's eyes narrowed at that. "We need to get you out of here."

She looked at him, unsure of what he was saying. Was he still harping on her going to Texas?

"Pack some clothes. We're leaving."

Fine by her. Joshua could get her out of the apartment and then she could disappear. "Okay."

"We'll go to a hotel," he said, even though she hadn't asked.

That sounded so good, the tears burning her eyes spilled over. "Yes. A hotel. *Away from here.*"

He didn't answer, just picked up the pile of cotton panties off the floor and shoved them into the duffel bag. "What else do you need?"

"I'll do it." The overwhelming relief of leaving her apartment galvanized her brain enough to allow her to tackle the problem of packing. She was ready in less than five minutes.

He looked at the small burgundy leather duffel bag and then at her. "Let's go."

Nemesis slammed his listening device down, rubbing eyes reddened and bleary from lack of sleep.

He hadn't been prepared for her to leave the apartment. *She wasn't supposed to leave the apartment.*

He would not tolerate interference in his schedule.

Fury filled him, tightening his stomach into knots, and the urge to lash out overwhelmed him as he turned and slammed his fist into the wall beside his computer, picturing Lise Barton's face there as he did it.

Pain radiated up his arm, filling his stomach with bile.

He cradled his bruised hand against his heaving chest and forced himself to think. It was difficult. His thoughts kept scattering, chasing memories he could not afford to dwell on.

She had left the apartment, but she would not dare go to Texas for the holidays, not while she feared him following her.

She wanted to protect her family.

His lips twisted cynically. Sure. More likely she wanted to spend the holiday writing her treacherous books. Either way, she would not go far. She had to come back to her apartment and when she did, he would be waiting . . . watching, just like always.

No, her leaving with the man was not a showstopper. He had said something about staying the night in a hotel. Nemesis could find them. He was very good at finding information on the computer, although his abilities had not kept him employed after what Lise Barton had done to him and his family.

He shoved aside a half-eaten sandwich that had gone dry and stale while he listened to the discussion between the man and the home-wrecking bitch. Pulling the information file out from where it had rested under his uneaten meal, he flipped open the manila folder and started going through the list of people she had regular contact with.

She'd called the man Joshua, but there was no Joshua on the list.

Frustration gnawed at Nemesis.

He couldn't look for the man if he didn't have a last name. He would have to do more research before he could start searching credit card records to find them.

When he did, perhaps he would visit his vengeance on the man who dared to take the bitch's side.

It took Joshua thirty minutes of evasive maneuvers before he was satisfied they were not being followed.

During that time he did not speak and neither did Lise, but tension continued to emanate from her side of the car. Once he pulled onto I-5 North, he flipped on the radio, letting the low-volume classical music fill the car.

"That's nice." They were the first words Lise had spoken

since they'd left the apartment and she said them in an almost normal tone of voice.

"Music helps calm nerves."

She gave a short, humorless laugh. "I guess I seem pretty stressed-out to you."

"A little," he said dryly.

She hugged herself as if she was cold, but the car's heater was keeping the interior warm despite the low temperatures outside. "I feel stressed, to tell you the truth."

"How long has he been stalking you?"

"I got the first e-mail six months ago." She tugged her gloves off, affirming she wasn't really cold, just upset. "I don't know how long Nemesis was watching me before that."

"What did it say?"

"That I shouldn't buy so much junk food. I'd just made a chocolate run to the grocery store. My current work in progress was giving me fits and I didn't feel like cooking, so I bought a lot of easy prep meals and snacks, too." Her soft voice echoed with pained vulnerability.

"He was watching you pretty closely, then."

She shuddered. "Yes."

"What did you do when you got the e-mail?"

"I shift-deleted it like I do all my junk mail. I thought it was weird, but it didn't occur to me that it was the beginning of something sinister. He didn't say anything about why he was writing me." The now flat and unemotional tones of her voice were at odds with the near hysteria she'd been exhibiting earlier. "He never does . . . not in his e-mails, not in his calls. He just makes sure I know he's watching me."

"When did you realize it was a serious problem?"

"When he called. I got good and scared then. He talks through a computer digitizer and it was really eerie, you know?"

"Did you go to the sheriff?"

"Not then." She sighed. "I still thought I could handle it. He hadn't threatened me or anything."

"What happened to change your mind?"

"How do you know I did?" she asked, sounding curious.

"You wouldn't have moved away from your family and home if there was another solution open to you. So, I figure you went to the authorities, but they couldn't do anything for you."

"It was more like a case of *wouldn't,* but you're right, something did happen that made me realize I *really* wasn't safe."

"What?"

"He broke into my apartment. I came home after visiting Bella at the ranch to find the things on my computer desk altered just enough for me to know someone had been there."

"What did the sheriff say when you reported it?"

"He thought I was being a publicity hound, that I was making it all up to get media attention."

"Why in the hell would he believe something so stupid?"

"He used to work for the Houston police force, and a woman did that very thing. She was a self-defense instructor and the free publicity got her a boatload of clients, I guess."

"He refused to take you seriously because he'd been burned once by a false report?" Joshua had a hard time believing it.

"A lot of manpower got wasted and it left the detectives involved looking stupid, not to mention really jaded about the whole stalker issue. The sheriff ended up leaving his job and moving to Canyon Rock. He wanted concrete evidence I was being stalked before he would open an investigation and I couldn't give it to him."

"Idiot."

"I thought so at the time, but I've got to admit I didn't push too hard. I didn't want Jake to find out, and things get around in a small town. So, I went home and had my locks changed, but Nemesis managed to break in again."

"Did you report it?"

"Yes, but this time the sheriff was really belligerent. He told me he didn't have the manpower to stake out my apartment and I still didn't have concrete evidence. After all, nothing had been taken."

"Bastard."

She shrugged.

"So, you moved across country to get away from the stalker."

"I'd researched the problem and read about several cases where stalkers had hurt the family or loved ones of their victims. It disturbed me." Her hands twisted together and her face averted to look out the side passenger window. "I started having nightmares. Then, during one of his phone calls, Nemesis mentioned seeing me with my sister-in-law and baby niece. That's when I decided to move."

He understood her choice, but it hadn't been the smartest one. Moving away from the small town where she was well known had actually made her more vulnerable to her stalker.

Chapter 2

Lise smothered a yawn as Joshua led her into their hotel room. Exhaustion was catching up with her and pretty soon she'd need toothpicks to prop her eyes open.

"I'm sorry," she said after a jaw-stretching yawn took her by surprise. "I'm just so tired all of a sudden."

Joshua dropped his bag on the bed nearest the door and shrugged out of his coat. "When was the last time you slept a whole night?"

She crossed the room and plopped down on the end of the other bed, her legs so tired they didn't want to hold her up anymore. "The night before the last Seahawks game."

His dark eyes glinted with curiosity. "What happened?"

She told him about the incident on the street after the game, reliving the fear and frustration of that night while she took off her own coat and tossed it onto a nearby chair.

"You could have been killed."

"I don't think he meant to really harm me at all." She'd thought about it a lot. "Traffic moves pretty slowly after a game. I think he just wants me to know what kind of power he has over my life."

The word Joshua said was one she didn't even use in her writing. "Did you go to the police?"

"Yes." For all the good it had done her.

Joshua went to the window and slid an expandable bar into place so that it could not be opened; he then shut both the privacy curtain and the drapes. Each movement made her feel a little bit safer, a little more protected.

"What did they say?"

"The sergeant who took my statement didn't believe that I was pushed, but he filed a report anyway. I insisted."

"Why didn't he believe you?"

He'd thought she was an ignorant country bumpkin who could not tell the difference between being shoved in the back and jostled by the crowd. It still made her angry. "There were no witnesses to corroborate my story. No one else saw Nemesis push me, even though there was a huge crowd around me."

Joshua opened the door and put the DO NOT DISTURB sign on the outside before turning back to face her. "Probably *because* of the crowd."

She nodded, trying to swallow another yawn and not succeeding. She'd been scared for so long, the relative safety of being with Joshua had released her body from the constant adrenaline rush of fear. The inertia of total exhaustion was taking over.

He dug something out of his bag and put it on the door under the privacy lock. "Has Nemesis been in your Seattle apartment?"

"Not that I know of, but he left a red rose on the seat of my car. It was locked in the parking garage at the time."

"Did you report the incident?"

"Yes, but it was the same story as before. I didn't have proof and wasn't taken seriously." The same sergeant had taken the report, and the fact that the doors had been locked had convinced him she was some kind of kook. "I think the police sergeant and the sheriff back in Canyon Rock are related."

Her attempt at humor fell flat. Joshua's handsome face

didn't even crack in a smile. "So, you cancelled your trip to Texas and decided to deal with this on your own again?"

He sounded less than impressed by the possibility, but she nodded. "I didn't have a lot of choice. I'm not putting my family at risk, no matter what."

"You'd rather face your stalker with a fireplace poker." The derision in his voice irritated her.

"Not really, but it's what I had on hand."

He measured her with his eyes. "You're pretty damn independent."

She supposed she was. The one person she knew would not let her down was herself.

"You need my help."

The blunt statement took the breath out of her, but she wasn't about to deny the truth of it. She'd passed that point about when he'd disarmed her and gotten her in a headlock before she could even scream. If he had been Nemesis, she could be dead, or hurting badly right now.

Joshua watched the play of emotions across Lise's face. Denial wasn't one of them.

"You're right," she said. "The authorities won't take me seriously and I'm afraid Nemesis will have to do something pretty awful before they do, but what can *you* do?"

"I can keep you safe, for a start."

There was no mistake about the expression burning golden in her tired hazel eyes. It was relief. "Thank you."

"I plan to nail the bastard, too."

"Do you think you can?"

He wasn't offended by her expression of doubt. "Maybe not alone, but I've got a couple of buddies who will help. Hotwire's a computer expert and Nitro's great with explosives, but he's got other talents just as useful."

"Interesting names—are they mercenaries too?"

"We were in the Rangers together." Evading direct answers had become a way of life for him ten years ago. "When did Bella tell you what I do?"

Had Lise run from his profession as much as she'd run from the primitively passionate man he'd become with her?

"She didn't."

"Then how did you know?"

That vague look settled over her, the one he identified as her *writer look*. "It's the way you move, the way you are hyper-aware of everything and everyone around you. It's just like the other mercenaries I've met. Special Forces soldiers are that way, too, but there are subtle differences."

"You've met other mercenaries?"

"Sure."

"Right."

She frowned at his disbelief. "I interview a lot of people for my books. I like hands-on research. It's how Jake and Bella met, or didn't they tell you?"

His sister had said something about it, but attending a few fashion shows was not in the same league as getting into personal contact with the men who peopled the shadowy world he lived in. "What did you do, contact *Soldier of Fortune* magazine for a reference?"

"Not the first time. I'd learned about a mercenary from a retired Navy SEAL I knew. The man he hooked me up with wasn't hero material at all. He was cold, and so calculating. You could just tell he'd kill his own grandmother for the right amount of money."

"Who was it?"

She said a name.

His heart about stopped in his chest at the prospect of her spending five minutes alone with such a predator, much less the length of an interview. "Are you crazy? You don't chat over coffee with men like him."

"Yes, well, I figured that out. The next man I interviewed

was the one who worked for one of those companies advertised in *Soldier of Fortune* magazine. He was a total phony."

He was getting a pretty intimate picture of the type of research she did to write her books and he didn't like it. He'd
read most of them since meeting her the year before. If she
talked to the types of characters she wrote about, the list of
stalker suspects would be as long as his mother's grocery list
the week before Christmas.

"So you went looking for another merc to talk to?"

"Yes. He was retired and I liked him."

When she named the man, Joshua had to bite down on the
urge to curse. It was the same man who had drawn him into
the gray world of being a soldier for hire. He had ideals, even
if the average civilian wouldn't understand them. Combat
had retired four years ago, turning his business over to
Joshua. That's when he'd taken Hotwire and Nitro on, the
two men in the world he trusted.

"You live damn dangerously for an introverted writer who
shies away from mingling in crowds."

Soft pink tinged her cheeks. "I'm not that shy."

"Apparently."

"I know you didn't ask for pay, but I will. Pay you, I mean."

He stood up, rejection pounding through his veins. "I
don't want your money."

"You're a mercenary. This is what you do." She licked her
lips nervously and his gut tightened for reasons that had
nothing to do with their discussion.

"I've done a lot of things I wouldn't want to put in a mem-
oir, but no way am I taking money from you to help you."

"That's a ridiculous attitude, and I would feel better keeping this on a professional basis."

"Tough."

Her eyes widened, highlighting their reddened condition.
"There's no reason for you to refuse to let me pay you."

She spoiled the severity of her tone with another yawn.

The woman was seriously ready for bed.

Too bad it wouldn't be one she'd willingly share with him.

"There are a couple of reasons," he ground out, forcing his mind away from a path it had no business traveling down, especially since she'd just become a job.

"Name them."

"One, you can't afford me. Two, you're family."

"I'm not your family."

"Close enough." What he didn't say was that if she'd had no connection to him at all, he'd want to help her.

Lise Barton got to him in a way no other woman had since he was a naïve new recruit to the Army Rangers.

Joshua heard the water stop on the other side of the privacy wall while he listened to Bella's latest *cute baby* story about Genevieve with half an ear.

Lise came into the main room, her hair wet from her shower and looking more alert than she had earlier, not to mention too damn appealing.

That was going to be a problem.

She sat down on her bed and started brushing her hair out. Damp, it looked more brown than blond, hiding the gold highlights that rippled through it when it was dry.

"Isn't that just the sweetest thing?" Bella's voice reached him even as he watched Lise's movements with entirely too much interest.

Her pajamas were a pair of men's boxers and a well-worn t-shirt that molded her delicious curves when she reached up to run the brush through her hair. She wasn't big-breasted, but she wasn't small, either. She was perfect, her firm breasts jiggling just enough to make him crazy with every swipe of the brush on her hair.

He wanted to curse as his body reacted with pain-filled intensity to the sight. It had been too damn long . . .

He forced himself to answer his sister with a mild, "Yeah."

"So you'll be here in time for dinner and you've talked Lise into coming with you?" His sister sounded like she was having a hard time believing that.

"Yes, Bella. *We will both be there.*"

Lise's eyes snapped up at that, their gold-and-green depths asking him a question.

"I told Lise babies are more resilient than she thinks," Bella said in his ear, "Genevieve is not going to end up with pneumonia because she's exposed to a little old cold."

"You're starting to sound like a Texan," he teased his sister, while wondering how much of a fuss Lise would put up about his travel plans to Texas.

He hoped none at all when she heard his arrangements.

Bella laughed. "You know what they say about us trans-plants—we end up more Texan than the natives."

He chuckled at his sister's exaggerated drawl before saying good-bye and hanging up.

Stretching his legs out in front of him, he crossed them at the ankle and waited for Lise to say something.

She didn't disappoint him. "You told Bella we'd be there for Thanksgiving dinner tomorrow."

"Yes."

"Why?"

"Because we will be."

Eyes narrowed, she drummed her fingers on the bed-spread. "Has anyone ever told you that talking to you is like talking to a fence post on the shy side?"

"No, I can't say they have."

She huffed, shaking her head, and then smiled, making his pants feel a size too small in the crotch. "I guess I should have asked *how* rather than *why*."

He liked the measure of sass she'd managed to recapture since arriving at the hotel. "Hotwire is flying my plane into Arlington Municipal tonight. We'll meet him at the airport at o-six-hundred tomorrow. Then, I'll fly us to the airstrip on your brother's ranch and Nemesis will be none the wiser."

"You have your own plane?"

"Yes, a small Learjet." He'd wanted something fast, that could fly above thirty thousand feet, avoiding most weather-based turbulence, and a plane that did not need refueling for a cross-continental trip. "It comes in handy in my line of work."

"But you were flying commercial . . ."

"I was out of the country."

She tucked her rapidly drying hair behind one ear, exposing the feminine column of her neck and a shell pink ear he could remember tasting. Once. Definitely a memory better left on the junk heap.

"On a job?"

"Yes."

"What kind?" He raised his brows and a blush spread across her cheeks. "I guess I shouldn't have asked that. Sometimes I don't think."

He remembered how frequently she had asked probing questions before. He'd deflected most of them, leery of her pursuit of personal information.

"Must be because you're a writer."

She shrugged, the blush intensifying. "Maybe. My father always said I asked too many questions and all the wrong ones. I don't mean to offend people."

From what he'd learned of her father from Jake, Joshua thought the man had been a pretty useless parent.

Which for no accountable reason made him want to answer her question. "It was an extraction, and your question didn't offend me, but I don't normally discuss my jobs with anyone."

"Not even your friends, Hotwire and Nitro?"

"Not unless they're on the job with me."

Which was an answer to her earlier question if his buddies were mercs, too.

She looked like she wanted to ask something else, but was literally biting her tongue to hold the words in.

"Spit it out. I told you, your questions don't offend me. If I don't want to answer, I won't."

She smiled again and this time it warmed his insides. He liked seeing her relax with him.

"What kind of extraction, a person or a thing?" she asked.

"A little boy."

Her gaze glazed over with that vague look. "You saved him, didn't you?"

"I returned him to his family for a very high fee." She would do better not to romanticize him. "Do you have any problem with flying out tomorrow?"

"No, and thank you for making it possible. I miss my family. I haven't seen the baby in two months. I bet she's grown so much I'll hardly recognize her."

The wistfulness in her voice stirred something inside of him. "They miss you, too. Tell me something."

She picked up the brush and put it on the nightstand before climbing under the covers. "What?"

"Why didn't you tell Jake?"

"About being stalked?"

"Yes."

"He'd insist on helping, try to get me to move to the ranch or something, and he'd worry."

"If you lived on the ranch, no civilian would be able to follow you around without Jake, Bella, or one of the hands noticing."

"Civilian?"

"Nonmilitary."

"You aren't military."

She had a strong tendency to get lost on conversational tangents. "I'm a soldier, just a private one."

"It's not right that Jake should have to pay for my problems."

It took him a second to follow the conversation back to the question she was answering. "How would having you there be making your brother pay a price?"

"I told you, *he'd worry.*"

"He's not a little old woman with a bad heart, Lise. He's a man." A strong one, whom Joshua respected. "He can handle a little concern on his sister's behalf."

"He spent my whole growing-up years worrying over me, trying to make life better for me. He deserves his own happiness now." Her tone said she wouldn't budge on that belief. "Besides, as much as they'd all watch out for me, they'd be at risk as well."

And she'd made it clear that really worried her.

"From now on I'll be with you. You'll be safe and so will the people around you."

"Thank you, but what about your job?" She bit her lip, looking worried again. "It could take weeks, months even, to catch the creep messing with my life. Some stalkers remain unidentified for *years.*"

"This one won't."

"You're not short on confidence, are you?" She didn't sound bothered by the fact.

"Why should I be? Believe it or not, honey, this kind of thing is child's play compared to some of my assignments. Our perp is already too escalated not to get caught. He's not watching you from afar—the night he shoved you into traffic proves it."

"You're right." She fluffed her pillows. "He took a pretty big gamble that night. He'll make other mistakes."

"And I'll be there to catch his sorry ass."

"As much as I want to see Jake, Bella, and the baby, I wish we were starting the investigation now."

He liked the enthusiasm and hope lacing her voice. It was a big improvement over the hysterically frightened woman he'd taken out of her apartment.

"We are. Hotwire and Nitro are going to sweep the place for bugs while we're in Texas."

She snuggled into her pillow, planting impossible images into his head he'd do best to ignore.

"I'll find a way to pay you back for helping me, Joshua."

He could think of one right now, but figured he'd get slapped for suggesting it.

He already had one over-the-top incident to apologize for; he didn't need another.

Lise could not breathe.

Nemesis was there, right behind her. Impenetrable darkness surrounded them, but she could hear him breathing, *feel* his malevolent presence. Terror paralyzed her limbs and she could not run, froze her throat and she could not scream.

"Lise, I told you that you would never be free of me." The digitized voice tormented her with its certainty, with its inhuman inflection.

"No," she moaned, forcing the word out.

"You will never get away."

She shook her head, her mouth opening in agonized denial, and this time she managed to shout. "No!"

"I will always find you." The words beat at her as relentlessly as Nemesis himself. "No one can protect you from me. No one wants to. Joshua will leave you. They will all leave."

She covered her ears with her hands and cried, "No," over and over again.

"Lise, wake up, honey." A different voice. Tender, caring, human.

She turned toward it and a single shaft of light penetrated the darkness, illuminating a tanned masculine hand. "Come on, honey . . ."

She reached out for the hand, but she couldn't touch it, no matter how hard she tried. She whimpered in frustration as connection remained just out of reach.

Then suddenly her hand was engulfed in the strong, warm fingers. He started pulling her toward the light, toward safety, toward ...

"Joshua?" She hovered between consciousness and her nightmare.

"It's me. Are you awake?"

Her eyes opened to the shadowy darkness of the room, so different from the dense blackness in her dream. The sensation of Joshua holding her hand woke her completely.

"Are you okay, Lise?"

"Yes," she croaked out past a dry throat. "It was just a dream."

"More like a nightmare."

"Yes."

He got up and tried to pull his hand away, but she could not let go. She wasn't a clinger, and since the end of her marriage two years ago, she'd done her best to avoid any semblance of relying on a man, even Jake. But she did not want to be left alone with the aftermath of her dream.

He stopped tugging on his hand and turned it over to squeeze her fingers instead. "You sound hoarse. I'm going to get you a drink."

She didn't want water, she wanted comfort. His presence. However, she let him gently disengage their fingers. He was only gone a few seconds, but it felt like a lifetime as she lay in the bed, trembling from the mental remnants of her nightmare.

"Sit up so you can drink this."

She pushed herself up, surprised at how difficult it was. Her arms felt like they'd turned to Jell-O. He reached out with one hand and helped her, then sat down beside her on the bed, keeping the arm around her.

She put a trembling hand out for the glass of water. "Thank you."

He helped her drink it, their fingers brushing together as

they both held the glass tipped to her lips. He coaxed her to drink almost the entire glass before he set it on the nightstand between the beds.

Her head rested against his chest. He was wearing a t-shirt, but the heat of his body radiated through it. "Were you dreaming about him?"

Joshua had not turned on any lights and the darkness felt intimate, not frightening like the pitch black in her dream.

But intimacy was another kind of scary, and she forced herself to push out of the comforting strength of his arms. "Yes."

"You said before that you had nightmares. Do you have them every night?"

"No." Just most nights.

"Lise, you aren't alone anymore." He stood up. "I'm not going to let him hurt you or anyone you care about."

She desperately wanted to believe him, but to rely on another person so completely was scarier than being stalked. No matter how good he was at his job, he was still a man and men could betray you. Even good men.

Joshua's hand halted midair above Lise's shoulder. She looked like a fairy all curled up under the covers, her porcelain features relaxed completely in sleep. She hadn't had another nightmare last night and he'd been glad. If he'd been forced to get out of bed again, he would have crawled into hers.

He wanted her.

And the feeling would not go away

He'd spent months trying to forget the taste of her lips, the feel of her resilient flesh under his fingers.

He had not succeeded despite the fact that she'd made it clear she wasn't interested in pursuing a sexual relationship with him. He'd been sure his wild sexual reaction to her had been the result of not enough downtime after a mission, but he'd been with her less than twenty-four hours and he was back to where he'd been the night of his niece's christening.

So horny he could barely walk straight.

Only this time he had a job to do and sex and work did not mix. Not ever.

Chapter 3

"So, you ready to explain the real reason you moved to Seattle, Lise?" Jake's words fell like mini-explosions into the companionable silence around the Thanksgiving table.

Instead of looking at him, she glared at Joshua. What had he told her brother?

Okay, he hadn't agreed *not* to tell Jake, but she'd thought she'd made her feelings clear on that. She didn't want her brother worried about her, or trying to get involved with catching her stalker.

Joshua's impassive expression gave nothing away. "I didn't say anything, but I think *you* should."

"I told you I didn't want to." Not that her desires were going to count for squat now.

Jake had the scent and he'd be on it like a dog on a bone.

"He deserves to know."

"Didn't want to tell me what?" Jake asked.

She tried not to clench her teeth. "Nothing important."

"I'm not buying it."

Big surprise. Not. "Nobody asked you to *buy* anything," she pointed out, even as she had to acknowledge part of her *was* ready for the secrecy to be over.

"Don't be a smart aleck."

Bella pushed silverware away from Genevieve's little quest-ing fingers and settled the baby further back on her lap. "Was it me marrying Jake? You didn't have to move from the ranch. I didn't mean to displace you."

The look of uncertainty and hurt on her sister-in-law's face tore at Lise's conscience.

"My moving had *nothing* to do with you." She took a deep breath and let it out, accepting that the time had defi-nitely come for the truth. Joshua had promised to protect her family and she was going to have to trust him to do that. "I moved to Seattle because I'm being stalked and I hoped the move would get me away from my stalker."

"The hell you say." Jake's eyes burned with unmistakable concern and anger.

"Like a fatal attraction, or something?" Bella asked, her tone incredulous.

Before Lise could answer, Genevieve put her hands out to her daddy and Jake took the now yawning baby.

"I don't think Nemesis is attracted to me," Lise said to Bella. "He wants retribution for something I've done."

"What?" Jake demanded, his voice quiet so he wouldn't startle his baby daughter, who had snuggled into his lap and looked about half-asleep already.

"I don't know."

"How do you know he wants retribution?" This from Joshua.

She'd forgotten to mention that part of the call to him. Which was not surprising, considering how muddled and ex-hausted she'd been the night before. "When he taunted me about being alone for the holidays, he said something about an eye for an eye. That implies vengeance to me."

She looked at the other adults at the table, wishing they could answer the questions clamoring inside her head. "I don't see how I could have done something heinous enough to invoke such a reaction without knowing it."

"Chances are, you didn't." Joshua leaned back in his chair

and rolled the sleeves of his dress shirt up to expose muscular brown forearms. "This is not about rational reality—this is about perceptions in a mind disturbed enough to fixate on a woman and stalk her."

That made a lot more sense than her having done something horrible and not realizing it. She smiled her appreciation.

He smiled back, and she lost her focus for just a second.

"What kind of behavior are we talking about here?" Jake asked, reclaiming her attention.

So she told them about Nemesis, watching as her brother's outrage grew with every incident she outlined. At one point, he asked something in a voice that startled Genevieve, waking her up. Bella took the baby from him and soothed her back to sleep.

"He's been stalking you for months?" Jake asked with a forced but deadly quiet.

"Yes."

"Why didn't you say something?"

"She wanted to protect you."

Her gaze flew to Joshua, who had been silent during her explanations. He wasn't looking at her; he was looking at her brother.

"I didn't need protecting." Jake frowned at Lise, his emotion closer to the surface than she'd seen it since he told her Bella was pregnant with Genevieve. "You did."

"It was my problem, not yours."

"I'm your brother, for heaven's sake. Of course I have a stake in your problems."

She shook her head.

"Instead of telling me about your stalker, you lied to me and to my wife." Jake sounded baffled and hurt. "I could be the one who told Nemesis where you live now. I didn't know it was supposed to be a secret."

The self-condemnation in his tone hurt her.

"Nothing happened and if it had, it surely would not have been your fault."

"That wouldn't have been a helluva lot of comfort if something had happened to you because of it."

"I didn't want to risk any of you being hurt."

"Well, that backfired, didn't it?"

"What do you mean?"

"Bella has been in torment for months because she thought she'd done something to drive you away from your family home."

"I'm sorry about that." She looked at Bella, whose expression was filled with concern, not censure. "I wanted to keep y'all safe, not hurt your feelings."

"*Torment* is really overstating the case." Bella frowned at her husband. "I was worried about your sister, not wallowing in obsessive guilt."

Jake grimaced and turned away from the reproach in his wife's eyes.

"How was I supposed to look out for my family if I didn't know the threat was out there?" he asked Lise, his grievances taking another tack. "What if Nemesis had decided to get to you through Genevieve or Bella? Something could have happened to them because of my ignorance."

She knew the angry words were spurred by Jake's own sense of protectiveness, both toward her and his wife and child. But they still sliced straight into her heart. Because he had a point, one she had not even considered.

"She did what she thought was best, Jake. She believed moving away would remove the threat from you, Bella, and the baby." Joshua's expression dared Jake to disagree.

She'd never known her brother to back down from a challenge and could predict his next words with one-hundred-percent accuracy.

"She was wrong to lie to me," he said, fulfilling her expectations.

Suddenly, Joshua was standing, leaning over the table toward Jake. "Get over it. She's telling you the truth now."

She hadn't realized that when Joshua said he was going to protect her, he meant from her brother as well. It was an odd feeling. Even her ex-husband had never stood up to her family on her behalf.

"Don't tell me how to deal with my own sister." Jake was on his feet, too, and looking ready to hurt someone.

She thought he might be considering Joshua as a likely prospect. She knew in Jake's macho mind, the other man made a better target for his frustrated anger than she did.

But she wasn't about to let the confrontation get worse. "I'm sorry, Jake."

Joshua turned his laserlike gaze on her. "You have nothing to apologize for. You weren't acting out of selfish motives. You gave up everything familiar to you to protect your family. If your brother is too stupid to see that, I'll gladly set him straight."

"Joshua!" Bella's voice was distressed.

Jake looked one step closer to violence and Joshua's jaw was as hard as quarry rock.

Soon Genevieve would be awake and crying.

So much for a warm family dinner.

Lise stood up, not terribly impressed with either man and feeling sick inside for ruining Bella's first Thanksgiving as a married woman. "I'm sorry I've upset y'all so much. Maybe it would be best if I leave. I didn't mean to spoil everyone's holiday." She looked at Bella with a sad smile. "And I definitely didn't mean to hurt anyone."

Jake's face clenched and pain flashed in his eyes. "You aren't going anywhere."

"Why not? You've made her feel about as welcome as ants at a picnic." Bella's tart voice startled Lise.

Her sister-in-law was busy glaring in equal measure at her husband and her brother, while she gently patted her baby's back.

Jake grimaced and then came around the table toward Lise. He pulled her into a bearlike hug. It was a little awkward because he'd never been very demonstrative, but he held her tight for a long time.

"I didn't mean half what I said. You know I've got a hot temper and I'm sorry I took it out on you. The idea of some creep stalking you scares the crap out of me and I don't like knowing you've been facing it all on your own, but that doesn't mean I want you to leave now."

She hugged her brother back. "I just didn't want you to worry."

He pulled away from her. "Do you really think I haven't been worrying about you living alone in a city a couple hundred times the size of Canyon Rock?"

"I—"

"Don't apologize again. Joshua is right—you've got nothing to be sorry for. I love you, Lise. You're my little sister. I'll always worry."

She couldn't remember the last time Jake had told her he loved her and she could feel the tears tightening her throat. "I love you, too."

She didn't know what else to say, but Bella came to her rescue. "Why don't you gentlemen clean off the table and make up while Lise and I put the baby to bed. We can have dessert in the living room after you've both got your civilized manners back."

Lise was shocked when her brother agreed. Marriage to Bella had certainly mellowed him some.

Half an hour later, Lise found herself sitting on the sofa with Joshua while Jake and Bella shared the smaller loveseat.

She still wasn't sure what had stopped her from taking one of the armchairs. When she'd come into the living room after helping Bella put the baby to bed, Joshua had been sitting on one end of the couch. And he'd looked at her in such a way that she'd found herself approaching him without conscious volition.

She very nearly sat right down beside him, and only a last-minute spark of sanity had directed her to sit on the far end of the sofa. To cover her confusion at her own actions, she spent some time smoothing her skirt over her knees before looking up to survey the other occupants of the room.

Judging by the way Joshua and her brother were eyeing each other, she wasn't sure how much making up had gone on during kitchen detail. Jake she understood. He was feeling helpless and that was bound to come out in bad temper, but she could not comprehend what had Joshua so annoyed.

Maybe he didn't like the way her brother's anger had upset Bella. He should know by now that Jake would do just about anything to make his wife happy. He'd never hurt Bella's feelings on purpose.

"So what are you going to do about Lise's stalker?" Bella asked Joshua without preamble.

"Your brother doesn't have to do anything," Jake slotted in. "Lise can move back to the ranch. I'll hire a private investigator and light a fire under the tail of that no-account sheriff."

Lise had known that would be Jake's answer. "*I'm not moving in with you.*"

"She's moving in with *me*."

She gasped and stared at Joshua. "What are you talking about?"

"Like hell she is," Jake thundered.

"Want to bet?" Joshua asked, his voice smooth as silk.

Lise shivered even if her brother looked unaffected.

"If I leave Seattle, how are we going to track Nemesis?"

His dark eyes spoke a message she didn't quite understand. "I guess I should have said I'm moving in with you."

"That is not going to happen," Jake said from the other side of the room, looking ready to get up and take Joshua outside to *discuss* it.

There were times her brother reminded her of his prize bull. All testosterone and dominant male behavior.

She dismissed him with a frown and turned to Joshua.

"You're moving in with me?" she asked, her voice a much higher pitch than she was used to.

"That's right. Until we find out who the stalker is and deal with him, I'm your faithful sidekick."

She couldn't imagine him as anyone's mere sidekick. "When you said you were going to help me, I didn't for a minute think that meant you were going to move in with me."

"How else am I supposed to protect you?"

"I thought that was what the new security measures Hotwire and Nitro are installing at my apartment were for."

"They're backup."

"You are not moving in with my sister."

Joshua finally deigned to acknowledge her brother's blustering. "I'm not threatening to seduce her. I don't do sex while I'm on the job."

Lise spluttered while Bella stared in shock at her brother. "*You're charging her for your help?*"

"No." She and Joshua said at the same time.

Bella sighed with relief. "Then it's not only a job—it's personal."

Lise didn't like the speculative gleam in Joshua's eyes, or the smug expression on Bella's face. The one time she and Joshua had gotten personal, she'd been completely overwhelmed. She didn't need that kind of reaction to a man clouding her life. Not now. Not ever.

"It's not personal!"

"It would be a damn sight easier for you to catch your stalker in Canyon Rock than in Seattle where no one knows you," Jake asserted.

"It's not simply a matter of catching him." She had to make him understand. This was important. "I thought about it a lot on the plane ride here and I'm through running. He's not going to get the satisfaction of thinking he's dictating my life anymore."

Joshua's look of approval was in direct contrast to the ugly word that came out of her brother's mouth.

Bella just looked thoughtful.

"Your determination to fight back might very well get you hurt, little sis."

"So could crossing the street during rush hour, but I'm not going to hide in my apartment because of it."

"It's not the same thing!"

"No, it's not," Joshua said before she could answer, "but staying in Seattle makes sense right now. Nemesis has escalated since the move. It's only when he acts that we have a hope of tracing who he is."

"And how are you going to do that?"

"By using counterintelligence techniques. Nemesis definitely has sound devices—and maybe even visual ones—planted in Lise's apartment. That's a damn good lead."

"You think he has visual?" Her skin crawled with images of some slimy guy in a dark room watching her go about her business. "Where?"

"I'm not sure he does, but we know what he can't see. The entryway, hall, or your bedroom. If he could, he would not have thought I left when you shut the door."

She hoped Joshua was wrong about Nemesis having any kind of visual, but she was sure now that her stalker had been listening to her every move and conversation in the apartment. She recoiled at the idea of some shadowy figure listening to her live her life.

"Our best chance of catching Nemesis is to use his own equipment against him."

"And if that gets my sister killed, or raped?"

"That's not going to happen." Joshua's extreme confidence soothed the jangling nerves inside her, even if it didn't calm her brother down appreciably. "And there's no reason to believe this is a sexual fixation. In fact, as we've discussed, the crime seems more vengeance-related."

"Which does not mean she's not at risk."

"I agree."

"Please. There's no reason to believe I'm in *any* physical danger."

"Have you forgotten being shoved into traffic?" Joshua asked.

She'd deliberately left that out and she didn't appreciate Joshua revealing it.

She gave him a look that told him so. "If he'd wanted to hurt me, he would have pushed me into traffic when a car was coming. I wasn't in any real danger."

"What the hell are you talking about?" Jake was back to looking furious.

She felt ready to explode herself. Joshua's view of what her brother needed to know and hers were about as far apart as the north and south ends of the ranch.

She pressed her lips together, remaining stubbornly mute.

If he wanted Jake to know every little detail so bad, Joshua could tell him.

He did.

"And the Seattle police didn't do anything about it?" Bella asked with outrage.

"No one saw me get pushed," Lise felt compelled to explain. "The sergeant who filed my report thought I'd been jostled by the crowd."

Joshua's dark brown gaze was filled with purpose. "I can get the police to take her seriously. We can even bring the FBI in because Nemesis crossed state lines to stalk Lise, but there's only so much *they* can do. We're better off handling this on our own."

"Why?" Lise asked, having liked the sound of making that annoying police sergeant listen to her.

"The authorities are hampered by rules and procedures." He paused so his next words had maximum impact. "We aren't."

She shivered at the menace in his voice.

"Which does not mean you have to move in with my sister," Jake asserted before Lise could say anything else.

Joshua crossed his arms over his chest and stretched his long legs out in front of him. "What exactly is your problem with me being Lise's bodyguard?"

"You want her."

"No, he doesn't—"

Joshua shocked her by interrupting her hasty denial. "If I do, what's it to you? She's well past the age of consent, not to mention having been married before."

"You said you don't do sex on a job," she reminded Joshua, her heart thumping in her chest at an alarming rate.

Before Joshua could answer, Jake was saying, "Damn it, you can't deny it. I've seen the way you look at her—it's like a hungry wolf ready to devour its next meal."

Lise had felt like that meal once, and it was not a memory she was comfortable with. "Joshua and I are not involved."

"And if they get involved it won't be any of your business, Jake Barton." Bella's tone left no doubt she thought her husband was being unreasonable.

"She's my little sister. How can you say that?"

"She's also a twenty-eight-year-old woman. Get a grip."

"This is ridiculous." Lise couldn't believe how off-target the conversation had gotten. "Joshua is helping me, not threatening me with bodily mayhem. I'm grateful and you should be, too, Jake, because if Joshua hadn't offered to help, I would have disappeared rather than put you and your family at risk."

The next afternoon, Joshua went looking for Lise.

She'd disappeared after lunch and he didn't like the idea of her being alone, even on the ranch.

She'd been quiet all morning, even playing with Genevieve in a subdued way. She'd avoided *him* as much as possible and he wanted to know why.

He found her standing on the edge of the small pond, her stillness so complete, she seemed a part of the land.

He stopped a few feet behind her.

"I used to come here when I was a little girl and life seemed unfair."

Her awareness of his presence startled him. His quiet approach had surprised trained soldiers.

He shifted to stand beside her. "Did it help?"

"Sometimes."

"You've been avoiding me all morning." He looked sideways at her, but could read nothing in her still profile.

"Jake thinks you want me."

"I do."

She turned toward him and the deeply troubled expression in her eyes tugged at him, but he could not reassure her to the contrary.

"I'm not interested in a relationship, Joshua."

"You made that clear the night of Genevieve's christening."

He hadn't been thinking about a relationship then, either. He'd been thinking about sex—hot and consuming, but temporary.

"I thought I did." She chewed on her bottom lip. "Why did you come to my apartment in Seattle?"

"Because Bella wanted you here for Thanksgiving."

"I see." Lise's tense stance relaxed a little. "She asked you to come and fetch me."

"No, Bella didn't ask me to come."

Lise was back to looking worried.

"I thought you were trying to avoid me because of what happened between us last year. I came to apologize and bring you to Texas with me."

"You were going to apologize?" She sounded shocked by the possibility.

"Yes."

She crossed her arms around her waist, hugging herself. "You don't have anything to say you're sorry for. You didn't force me to do anything I didn't want to."

He hadn't forced her, but he had frightened her. "Hell, Lise, you ran off without saying good night to anyone else and didn't come back to the ranch in the three days before I left."

"I got busy." She was a lousy liar.

"*Right.*"

He'd made a huge tactical error in letting Bella talk him into coming early for his niece's christening. He hadn't had enough downtime to get his more primitive reactions under control after the last job. Coupled with the fact that he hadn't had sex in way too long, he'd been an explosion waiting to happen.

His desire for Lise Barton had tipped him over the edge.

"I got too intense, too fast, and it scared you. I'm sorry."

"You didn't scare me." She put up her hand when he would have accused her of lying again. "You didn't. The kiss was incredible. Your passion overwhelmed me, but it didn't frighten me." She sighed, looking both emotionally defenseless and a little disgruntled. "My reaction to it did."

He hadn't expected that response. At all. He'd spent months feeling guilty because he'd sent her running and she was telling him her own reaction had done that. "Why?"

"A woman could lose herself in feelings as strong as the ones you brought out in me."

"And you're afraid of losing yourself?"

"Yes." Clear hazel eyes hid nothing.

"Is that what happened in your marriage?"

"Not totally, but I lost enough of myself that when our mutual identity disintegrated, figuring out who I was on my own took a lot longer than I wanted it to."

"You think going to bed with me could do that to you?"

"I think the emotions that would accompany making love to you could destroy me."

Such honesty from a woman stunned him. However, he didn't agree. "Sex does not have to be soul-destroying."

Only the emotion of love could do that, and she didn't have a thing to worry about on that score. No way was she going to fall in love with a badass mercenary, and she didn't have to worry about him getting moon-faced. He'd learned a long time ago that he didn't do that love thing.

She turned back to face the pond as if he'd never spoken. Pulling her light jacket close around her, she stood silent for so long, he thought she wasn't going to say anything else. Then she started to talk.

"I married my best friend when I was eighteen years old. I would have done anything to get out of my father's house, and when Mike asked me to marry him the night of our senior prom, I jumped at the chance."

"What happened?"

"Life." She laughed, but it was a hollow sound. "We didn't have a passionate marriage. I guess you could say we just weren't compatible in bed, but he was still my best friend and I trusted him completely. He encouraged me to pursue my writing, believed in me when I lost faith in myself, but friendship wasn't enough. Or at least it wasn't for him."

"He wanted the passion." What she was saying shocked him because Lise had been like living fire in his arms the one time they'd kissed.

"Yes, and when he found it with someone else, he asked for a divorce."

"He had an affair?"

"No. Mike is too honest for that, but he fell in love. We loved each other, but this was different, or so he told me."

"You still loved him."

"Yes, and I trusted him. When my marriage ended, I didn't

just lose my husband. I lost my closest friend, the one person in the world I'd let myself totally rely on."

Did she still love the other man, the man too honest to have an affair but untrustworthy enough to fall in love with another woman? Were leftover feelings from her dead marriage why she was so bothered by her reaction to Joshua?

"You feel passion with me."

"It's too intense. I don't want to feel anything that deeply again."

He understood. Too well. Emotion could mess up your life, but he thought she was confusing desire with love and they weren't the same thing. He didn't know if he could convince her of that fact, but he was pretty sure he was going to have to try.

He wanted Lise Barton and no way could he promise he would never act on that desire, no matter how good his intentions were.

Nemesis paced his one-room efficiency apartment.

Where was she?

Rain beat against the dingy windows, the gray skies making his home dark even though it was still daylight outside.

He didn't like this wet climate, or the cold that his small baseboard heaters didn't completely dissipate. His physical discomfort was something else to blame Lise Barton for. She'd ruined his life in every way that mattered.

She'd been gone for three days now, and he'd been unable to find credit card charges for Joshua O. Watt.

The satisfaction Nemesis had felt in discovering that Joshua's last name was different from his sister's had faded to nothingness in the face of his quarry's continued absence.

The man must have used cash to pay for their hotel room, so Nemesis had no way of knowing where it was. He consoled himself with the thought that even if he'd driven her out of state to Oregon or something, they wouldn't have gone far.

No way would she have run . . . not without her precious computer and the book she was working on. He'd hacked in to make sure it was still there and he'd found the book she'd been working on for the last month.

In his fury at her deviation from the plan, he had deleted it.

He didn't regret the rash action. It would show her she could not play with him. He had a project launch schedule he was not about to let her impede.

He had to see his goal realized.

It would vindicate him and all the other men she had wronged with her meddling in affairs that were no concern of hers.

He'd reverse planned everything down to the time of day for his initial contact with her. But his plan had not taken into account this disappearance. She wasn't supposed to leave her apartment. It did not fit her profile—he had spent a great deal of time compiling the necessary statistics on her.

He had nothing better to do with his time.

Not now.

Up until three days ago, she had behaved exactly as he had anticipated. She had waited to go to the sheriff until he broke into her apartment. It was a sign of how right his ultimate goal was that the sheriff had dismissed her complaints as unimportant.

And as Nemesis had expected, even then she had avoided going to family for help. He had encouraged her separation from her family by subtly implying he had designs on her sister-in-law and niece. Which he didn't.

If Lise were as smart as she thought she was, she would have realized that. The innocent should not pay with the guilty.

The man, Joshua Watt, was no longer innocent.

Nemesis's efforts had borne fruit, however, precipitating Lise's flight to Seattle. While he had expected her to run, it had been a surprise when she'd opted to relocate to such a wet and cold climate, but he had followed her regardless. He had a mission and could not allow slight personal discomfort to sidetrack him.

Fury made him shake as he realized that she had already messed up his plans for Thanksgiving. He'd planned for them to spend it together, but she had thwarted him.

No, not her . . . the man. Joshua Watt.

No mere woman could hinder him—even the home-wrecking bitch. None of her efforts would have done any good if his wife had not found help from misguided men.

Despair surged through him as the memory of what he had lost tormented his agitated mind.

He must not focus on what he had lost, but on the justice he would mete out to the woman who wreaked such havoc with her horrible book.

He would see justice done on the Day of Judgment *he* had assigned.

Chapter 4

Lise sat on the porch swing, a throw around her shoulders to ward off the chill. Her white flannel nightgown wasn't warm enough for the winter weather, but she had needed to be outside. She'd spent so much time hiding in her apartment the last few months that the outdoors had called to her like the irresistible sirens of old.

The stars that were invisible in Seattle's light-polluted night sky glittered overhead and the fragrance of fresh air teased her nostrils. At three o'clock in the morning, the ranch yard was deserted. Even the dogs were sleeping. And she was thoroughly enjoying the solitude.

No stalker could see or hear her. Nemesis did not know where she was, and that would change tomorrow. So, for tonight she was determined to enjoy every nuance of the freedom she would not have again until her stalker was caught.

Being drawn to the swing could be attributed to having spent so many evenings of her childhood curled up on it, telling stories in her head and avoiding the coldness of the ranch house. Only she wasn't remembering her childhood, or telling herself a story in her mind, or even plotting her next book.

Instead she was reliving the volatile feelings she'd had in Joshua's arms last year on this very swing before she'd come to her senses and rejected him. Those feelings had been so different from anything she'd experienced with Mike, she'd been terrified. And she'd run.

Just as Joshua had accused her of doing, but tonight she could not run from the memory. She didn't know why . . . perhaps because she'd realized today that Joshua still wanted her and while that desire frightened her, it also exhilarated her.

His wanting her confirmed her femininity in a way she was beginning to see she needed very badly, even if she didn't want to explore the ramifications of it.

But knowing he wanted her impacted her senses almost as much as the kiss had and she was filled with unwanted sexual excitement. If she closed her eyes, she could almost taste his lips again.

Remembering the moment when his mouth had laid claim to her own made her nipples pebble with a stinging sensation against her nightgown. Had she ever wanted Mike this way? She didn't remember it if she had. Pressing against her swollen breasts with the palms of her hands, she tried to alleviate the growing ache. It didn't do any good. Between her legs throbbed and she clamped her thighs together, moaning softly.

This was awful.

She was not an overly sexual being. The coupling of male and female flesh did very little for her. It was a pleasant way to connect on an emotional level, but that was all.

This consuming ache was not pleasant, nor did it feel particularly emotional.

She was a physical animal, in touch with primitive needs she'd been certain she didn't have.

In a reflexive move, her hands squeezed her breasts and she cried out softly, unbearably excited by the simple stimulation.

A harsh sound to her left caught her attention.

Her eyes flew open.

"Joshua . . ."

He stood a few feet away, sexual energy that matched her own vibrating off of him in physical waves that buffeted her already overstimulated body. He was just as he'd been on the night of the christening. Only this time he remained where he was, staring at her instead of joining her on the swing.

His face was cast in grim lines, his naked chest heaving with each breath of air he sucked in. The black curling hair on it tapered to the unbuttoned waistband on his jeans. The shadowy opening hinted at his maleness.

She wanted to lean forward and lower the zipper so she could see it all, which would be incredibly stupid.

Only right that very second, she could not quite remember why, not with her fingertips tingling with the need to act.

She watched in mesmerized fascination as a bulge grew in the front of his jeans. A large bulge.

"Lise . . ."

She looked up.

A gaze so hot it burned to her soul flamed her. They remained like that for several seconds of hushed silence, their eyes speaking intense messages of need while their lips remained silent.

The past ceased to exist.

The present consumed her.

Her reasons for caution melted away as her fear turned to a firestorm of desire. His presence devoured everything around them, leaving nothing but male and female communicating on the most basic level.

He took the steps that brought him within an inch of the swing. If she moved it, she would bump his legs.

She shivered at the thought of even that slight touch.

Dropping to his knees with a grace that spoke of leashed power, he knelt in front of her so they were eye level.

Neither of them spoke.

She couldn't.

He reached out and put his hands over hers where they pressed against now throbbing, turgid peaks. The heat of his skin seeped into hers, making her burn with unnamable longing.

When his head lowered to let their lips meet, she met him halfway. She wanted his kiss, desperately.

She concentrated on each individual sensation of his lips slanting over hers, his beard stubble prickly against her chin, his taste . . . like the most irresistible nectar, the heat of his mouth, the warmth of his breath fanning her face. She had never known the intense pleasure she found in his mouth, the conflagration of her senses she experienced when they touched.

Part of her was still cognizant enough to know she should stop him for the sake of her own sanity, but it was a tiny voice lost in a hurricane of physical sensations.

Joshua felt like he was going to explode in his jeans and he hadn't even touched her naked breasts, but he was going to.

Oh, yes . . . he was going to.

He began undoing the long row of buttons on her night-gown, until he could spread the opening wide, gently brushing her hands away from herself in the process. She would never know what it had done to him to come outside to check on her and find her sitting in the swing, moaning and touching herself.

If she'd had her hand between her legs, he would probably be buried there himself right now.

A man only had so much control and when he was around Lise, his was pushed to the limit.

He broke the kiss to dip his head so he could see the pale beauty of her perfectly formed breasts in the moonlight.

The nipples were swollen and turgid, their color dark with the blood that had rushed into them in her arousal. And she *was* aroused. He could smell the tantalizing fragrance of her humidity along with the sweet scent of her skin.

Tomorrow, he would fly her back to Seattle and the job would begin, but tonight, she was his.

He leaned down and kissed each dark nipple softly, then began to lave one with his tongue, reveling in the taste of her skin as much as its petal-softness.

She groaned and pressed herself against his mouth.

It was an invitation too sweetly given to ignore. He took her nipple between his teeth and teased it with the tip of his tongue in the heat of his mouth.

Whimpering, her breathing grew increasingly erratic and he gently nipped her.

"Oh, yesssss . . ."

He pulled her nipple and the surrounding aureole completely into his mouth and started suckling her.

"Oh, my gosh . . . Joshua, *that feels so good.*"

He loved the breathy quality of her voice.

Concentrating all his expertise on pleasuring her breasts, he moved from one to the other, savoring each until she was writhing against his mouth. Her hands were buried in his hair, trying to tug him closer. Something primitive held him back from touching her more intimately just yet.

He wanted the mystery of her breasts. Wanted to give her the ultimate in pleasure from touching them alone this first time. And he knew he could. She was so responsive, incredibly beautiful in her passion.

She writhed on the bench, alternately pulling his hair and pushing his head against her curves.

"Joshua. Please. It's too much. You have to stop."

A pirate's laugh rumbled in his chest and he suckled harder.

"No." Agonized groan. "*Yes.*" She sighed and then cried out. "*Don't stop.* Oh, *harder*, please, Joshua, just a *little harder.*"

He gave her what she wanted and when her body bowed in rigid pleasure, he once again carefully bit down on the nipple in his mouth.

She cried out and came with one body-racking shudder after another while he kept stimulating her breasts until she went totally limp.

He ached to take her completely, but he held himself in check. Barely.

They were outside where someone might come to explore the strange noises and discover two people making love instead. She would be horrified to be caught in such a way. Even more important—at least to him—once he'd had her, he wouldn't be able to live with her without having her again.

Sex and his kind of work did not mix.

Lise deserved the best and he couldn't give it if he was walking around in a sexual daze all of the time.

That didn't mean he didn't want her, though. Damn it to hell and back. He did. It took several seconds of measured breathing before he could lift his head and look at the effect his ministrations had wrought. When he did, his self-control came as close to disintegrating as it ever had in his life.

She lay back against the swing, her body utterly relaxed and her eyes half-closed. Moonlight revealed the flush of sexual completion and her rock-like nipples still glistened temptingly. "That was amazing."

Her words were at odds with the moisture filling her passion-dark eyes.

What the hell?

The tears spilled over and tracked down her cheeks in a slow, steady pattern.

"Why are you crying?" He hadn't hurt her; he would know if he had.

She shrugged, making no effort to cover the pale pink nakedness he was battling not to touch again.

"I lost myself for a while, just like I knew I would."

She didn't sound happy about it, but she didn't sound angry, either. Her tone was more resigned than anything, and he liked that even less than the tears.

She sighed and rubbed at the wetness on her face with the backs of her hands. "Do you want to come to my room?"

If she'd asked with the passion that had filled her voice earlier, he would have found it impossible to say no despite knowing how stupid giving in to his desire for her right now would be, but she didn't. Her tone still held a resignation at odds with her sexual satiation. It was as if she were admitting she could not resist him, but even the pleasure he'd given her did not make up for what she felt that cost her.

Anger simmered through him. He hadn't done a damn thing she didn't want.

He also had not touched her in some power play designed to make her helpless to deny her own desire. "I didn't touch you to seduce you."

He didn't want anything that wasn't freely given.

"Then why?"

"I couldn't help myself." And that was the appalling truth.

One he didn't like facing any more than he liked her emotional reaction to her climax.

So, he stood up and swung her small body into his arms, its contours all too soft against him. She let her head fall against his shoulder, her silky hair doing things to his skin he didn't even want to think about, her breasts moving enticingly with every step he took.

He should have buttoned her back into her nightgown before picking her up, or better yet, let her walk on her own.

Manfully ignoring the provocation of her flesh, he carried her up to her room and dropped her on the bed and turned to go.

Her hand came out to grab his arm and he swung around with the lightning-quick reflexes he'd honed over sixteen years of soldiering.

"Aren't you staying?"

"No."

"Why not?"

"First, because it's a bad idea for us to get physically involved at this point, and second, because you don't really want me to."

Her mouth twisted wryly. "You're wrong about that."

"Your body wants it, but your mind thinks it would be a mistake and I agree."

"I see."

He doubted it, but he'd pushed his self-control as far as he could that night. If he stayed one second longer, he was going to join her on the bed and to hell with both of their reasons for saying no.

Lise watched Joshua walk out of her bedroom without saying another word and it was all she could do not to call him back. Which said what about her intelligence?

Good night and granny's garters, *why had she let him touch her?* Was she a brick shy of a full load, or just plain stupid?

She'd known any level of intimacy with him would be devastating and she'd been right. She'd never gotten as lost to herself when making love with her ex-husband as she had when Joshua touched her. His expert caresses had decimated her solid reasons for avoiding a sexual relationship, and it had not simply been the reality of his hands on her body.

The mere memory of the one kiss they'd shared had been enough to destroy her good intentions.

She'd been primed and ready when he showed up on the porch and found her trying to assuage a need more intense than any she'd ever known. He'd taken immediate advantage and she'd let him. Had, in fact, reveled in his touch to the point of experiencing a glorious explosion of pleasure at his hands.

He'd liked it, too. The bulge in the front of his pants had been unmistakable.

So why had he refused her invitation to share her bed?

He'd said it was because she didn't *really* want him, but he had to have known she would have let him make love to her completely, despite her misgivings. She couldn't have stopped herself. Because she did want him. A lot.

He'd been right about one thing, though. She *wasn't* happy being at the mercy of a physical desire that put her emotions at risk again.

Had that really mattered to him?

A mercenary, Joshua was a man who in all likelihood used sex as a tension reliever. She had a hard time seeing him as so fastidious about why sex was offered that he would turn down a woman he wanted as much as he wanted her. Such sensitivity did not fit with her image of him, but neither did his refusal to let her pay him.

He was a puzzle she could not afford to get caught up in.

He had said before that he didn't do sex on the job and maybe that rule explained his coming to his senses before they did the deed.

Regardless of his reasons, she should be grateful for his withdrawal, not feeling this aching void in the core of her being and a terrible temptation to go find his bed since he'd refused to share hers.

Dusk shrouded the landing strip in shadows as Joshua landed his plane at the small municipal airport outside of Seattle.

Although the touchdown was smooth, Lise's stomach sank with the final decrease in altitude. She'd eaten a small breakfast and nonexistent lunch. Fatigue always affected her appetite, but this time it was more than lack of sleep that left her feeling blechy. It was the knowledge that they were at the end of their journey.

The jet engines cut off, surrounding them in absolute silence. She and Joshua hadn't talked for pretty much the entire trip, although he had invited her to sit in the cockpit with
him. It had been interesting, but each mile closer to Seattle
had increased her sense of oppression.

"Traffic is going to be terrible getting back into Seattle this
time of night," she said, so she wouldn't have to focus on
what was really bothering her.

Returning to her stalker's orbit.

Joshua shrugged as he pushed open the plane's door, then
lowered the stairway. "We can have dinner before going back
into the city. If the traffic is still ugly, we'll survive it."

"Do we have to go back to the apartment tonight?" she
asked.

One more night away wouldn't make a huge difference,
would it? She cringed inside at the spineless thought.

"Let's talk to Nitro and Hotwire and hear what they
found out before we make any major decisions."

Knowing Joshua realized she didn't want to go home made
her determined not to give in to her emotional weakness.

Besides, she had a book to finish. The delivery deadline
she'd told Bella about had been real, just not unexpected.
However, because her concentration had been off, Lise was
behind her writing schedule and knew it would take a lot of
work to get the book done on time.

"I should get back to work."

He didn't say anything, but put his hand out to help her
down the steps.

A man with blond hair and blue eyes, but looking every bit
as intimidating as Joshua ever did, waited on the tarmac at
the bottom of the stairs. Hotwire. She remembered from the
brief meeting before her and Joshua's flight to Texas.

He stuck his hand out to grab one of the bags from
Joshua. "Hello, Miz Barton. It's a pleasure to see you again."

Hot Georgia honey rolled off his tongue, and she couldn't

help smiling at him as she let him guide her down the last couple of steps.

"Where's Nitro?" Joshua asked as he took her arm, putting his body between her and Hotwire.

The look he was giving his friend was pure possessive male and totally confusing after his rejection the night before. He was acting like a stallion protecting his mare from a rival.

How ridiculous was that? Not only did Joshua have no claim on her, but there wasn't so much as a tiny test tube of sexual chemistry between her and the fair man. Unlike the explosion of combustible chemicals that erupted between her and Joshua whenever they got within three feet of each other.

Hotwire waited to answer Joshua until they'd closed up the plane and started walking across the tarmac toward the parked cars. "Nitro's keeping the apartment under surveillance. We're hoping to lure the perp into showing himself while Miz Barton here is still gone."

"Why would he do that?" Lise asked, momentarily distracted from Joshua's perplexing behavior.

They'd reached the rental car and Hotwire pressed the remote unlock button. "We sent a few false signals on his bug, indicators that the electronics were breaking down. Then we cut the transmission completely this morning."

"You think he'll believe it's broken and try to break into my apartment to fix it?"

"That's what we're hoping."

It couldn't be that simple, could it? Lise thought what it would mean to her to identify the stalker and felt chills go up and down her arms at the prospect.

Joshua opened the back door on the passenger side, indicating she should get inside. She did, but had to suck in air when he leaned across her to lock the safety belt in place.

He stopped when his face was directly in front of hers. "Comfortable?"

"Um . . . yes."

He nodded and stepped back, allowing her to breathe normally again.

"So, what did you find in the apartment?" he asked Hotwire as the two men got in the front seat.

Hotwire whistled softly and started the car. "This guy knows his electronics, but he's not using high-end stuff. My guess is he doesn't have the financial resources for professional equipment. He's made modifications to amateur spy tech items that indicate he's got a pretty good understanding of what he's doing."

"What kind of spy stuff?" Lise asked from the back seat.

Hotwire met her eyes in the rearview mirror, his expression as dark as Joshua's eyes. "He had a transmitter inside your desktop computer. One of the pens in your pen cup had a transmitter as well, but the battery was dead, so we don't know how long it has been there. One of your stereo speakers has a minicam transmitter—"

"*He could see me?*" she interrupted, even more freaked by the reality than she had been when Joshua had mentioned it was a possibility in Texas.

"Yes, but only when you were in certain parts of the living room."

Thinking about the direction her speakers faced, she knew exactly which parts. Her maple rocker was one of them, the place she spent most of her relax time. A knot formed in her stomach and squeezed.

"What else?" Joshua asked, as if what Hotwire had said hadn't been enough.

Hotwire flicked a glance at Joshua before looking back at the road. "Her car has a sound and position transmitter in the antennae. It isn't satellite connected, but he can follow her within a two-mile radius and she would never know it."

The whole trip from Texas to Seattle, Nemesis had been following her.

He'd known exactly where she was at all times.

Thinking of some of the small hotels she'd stayed at, the long stretches of deserted highways she'd driven, and the falseness of her sense of security in her anonymity made her stomach churn around the painful knot.

Bile came up in her throat and she forced it back down. "Hotwire, could you please stop the car?"

They came to a sudden but smooth halt beside the road. She unbuckled her seat belt, shoved the door open and jumped from the car. She sucked in air and tried not to give in to the sick sensation, but image after disturbing image flashed through her mind, making it almost impossible not to throw up.

Suddenly Joshua was there, wrapping his big arms around her, pulling her into the heat of his body. "It's going to be okay, Lise. Relax."

"He followed me . . . the whole time I thought I was safe, by myself. He was there, tracking me, knowing where I was every second of every day."

Joshua turned her body and she buried her face in his chest, inhaling his scent and letting the strength of his body infuse her own.

"I know . . . shh . . . I know . . ."

She believed him. Even though she could not imagine Joshua Watt afraid of anything, she believed that he understood her fear and empathized with it.

The nausea finally passed, but she nestled against Joshua, unwilling to give up the haven of his arms.

"Is she all right?" Hotwire asked.

Joshua pulled away and looked down at her questioningly.

"I'll be fine."

"You sure?"

She nodded. She turned to Hotwire. "Sorry about that. I shouldn't let it get to me."

The blond man looked at her like he was measuring her mettle and then his mouth creased into a smile. "You'll do."

For some reason that made Joshua frown, but he kept his

arm around her as he led her back to the car. Hotwire pulled out onto the road before Joshua spoke again.

"So, you didn't find anything that couldn't have been planted when he broke into her apartment in Houston?"

"Right."

"I haven't noticed anything out of place." She had assumed that had meant Nemesis had not broken into her current home, but now she wasn't willing to make such naïve speculations. "You don't think he's been in my current apartment?"

"No, ma'am, I don't."

She didn't know why that made her feel so much better, but it did. "Call me Lise."

"All right, Lise." He drawled her name, making it sound like it had six syllables.

She giggled at his Southern silliness.

"Was anything traceable?" Joshua asked shortly.

"No." Hotwire turned the car into a restaurant parking lot. "The perp bought the kind of stuff they sell on dot-com sites for spyware. There's too much of it out there to trace an individual purchase."

"What was the range on the audio transmitters?"

"Two miles. He stuck with the same family of gadgets."

Joshua frowned, making no move to get out of the car. "Too bad."

"Why?" Lise asked.

"His base could be anywhere within a two-mile radius of your apartment."

"And there are a lot of apartment complexes and neighborhoods around your building," the blond man added. "He could be living pretty much anywhere."

Joshua unbuckled his seat belt and turned in toward her. "One good thing is that with all the domiciles around you, it would be really hard for the perp to use an ear-dish."

"What on earth is that?"

"It looks like a mini-satellite dish, but it's used to detect sound. Some have a range of more than one mile. However, in an area like your neighborhood, it is virtually impossible for the perp to lock in on your apartment without getting a lot closer."

"And people would notice someone in the street pointing a satellite dish," she surmised.

"In most cases, yes, but if he has a van that he's made up to look like a technician's vehicle, maybe not. We'd notice, though."

She presumed he meant Hotwire, Nitro, and himself.

She sighed, realizing they were discussing the type of equipment that often made it into her books. "I don't know why I didn't think of that."

"No reason you should have."

"I write adventure fiction. While my heroines are more familiar with an AK-47 than a listening device, it still should have occurred to me."

Joshua just shook his head.

Hotwire smiled and she figured he had women following him around like puppies after bacon with the kind of charm he exuded. Even if he *was* intimidating and dangerous in turn.

"You're a good writer."

She felt her eyes widen with surprise that he'd read her work. "Thank you. Did you read my books when you were at the apartment?"

"No, ma'am . . . I mean, Lise, we were too busy doing the bug sweep before you got back."

"Then how . . ."

"Both me and Nitro read your books when Wolf is done with them."

"Who's Wolf?"

"I am," Joshua growled.

Chapter 5

She had no problem imagining how Joshua had gotten such a nickname. The man was pure predator at times.

"You read my books . . . all of them?"

His jaw went taut and she could tell he didn't like having that fact revealed. "Anything recent."

She didn't know how to take that. She wouldn't think there'd be a lot of time to read in his line of work, but maybe she was wrong. "I guess you enjoyed them?"

"Yes. I liked them a lot."

His praise warmed places left cold by Hotwire's revelations and she smiled. "Thank you."

He shrugged. "It's the truth. So, you haven't totally cleared the apartment?" he asked Hotwire, effectively changing the subject.

"No. We left her car transmitter intact. The sound transmitter in her computer is now broken and we've rigged the video transmitter to send a constant picture of her empty apartment. Nitro and I made sure no one could be aware that we've been inside her apartment."

Joshua inclined his head in acknowledgement. "We'll have to take the jury-rig off once she's home."

"You're going to leave the minicam in?" she asked.

"If it conveniently breaks, too, there's a good chance he'll figure out you've got professional help and he'll become a lot more cautious."

She hated the idea of the stalker seeing her, even in brief glimpses when she was in the line of the camera, but she was willing to put up with it if it meant catching him.

"So, you don't think he'll break in while I'm gone right now?" she asked Joshua.

He shook his head. "Too risky. He doesn't know when you're coming back and you left your car behind, so he has no way of tracking your arrival. Everything about his behavior so far indicates that he plans his actions carefully."

She had to agree, but it was still very disappointing.

"If he doesn't try today," Hotwire said, his tone encouraging, "we'll keep your apartment under surveillance when you go grocery shopping and do other things that take you out of the building."

"He'll know where I am," she said, thinking of the transmitter they'd left on her car.

"Which is all the better because he'll be confident you aren't anywhere near home."

She nodded.

Hotwire eyed Joshua. "Right . . . if you're hanging around, Wolf, ain't no way he's coming near."

"I'm not leaving Lise alone."

"Didn't think you would, buddy, but you're going to have to be covert when she leaves the apartment and you have to stay out of the line of sight of the minicam at all times."

Joshua just stared and Hotwire smiled, though it didn't quite reach his eyes. "Guess I don't have to tell you that."

"Are you and Nitro going home, then?" she asked.

Hotwire shook his head. "We rented an apartment in your building."

"Did you check the other vacancies?"

"No sign of unauthorized use."

"And the other tenants?"

"Only three have taken apartments since Lise moved in and none of them fit our perp's parameters."

Joshua dropped Lise off at her apartment, walking her inside but leaving when she got on the elevator. Although she knew he would come to her apartment later, an immediate sense of isolation overwhelmed her with the shutting of the elevator doors.

A dark, silent shadow separated from the wall when she let herself in and she could only be grateful Hotwire had told her Nitro would be there. Otherwise her heart would have climbed right up her throat.

However, not being surprised by his presence was a far cry from being prepared to meet the man again . . . particularly on her own.

He was taller than both Joshua and Hotwire, and had the classic bone structure, long black hair, and unreadable expression of an ancient Apache warrior.

She shivered even as she stuck her hand out toward him. "Hi, Nitro. Joshua said you would be here."

He didn't smile and she got the distinct impression he didn't do it very often, but he did shake her hand.

"Thank you for helping me," she said, her voice a lot lower than she'd intended.

"Wolf asked." He released her hand and stepped back. "I'll switch the camera back to live feed." He turned without another word and left her standing in the hall, feeling a little disoriented.

For the next hour, he silently worked at her computer out of the line of vision of the minicam in her stereo speaker.

She puttered around, made a cup of tea, and then took it into the living room. Flipping on the television, she curled up in her rocker, trying very hard not to show the discomfort she felt knowing that her seat could be seen via her stalker's minicam transmitter.

An hour later, Joshua arrived and she wanted to jump up and greet him, but she was supposed to be alone. She'd actually missed his presence, which was both foolish and pathetic. She could almost be grateful that she was being watched so she didn't reveal her idiocy.

She continued watching her show while Joshua and Nitro had a low-decibel consultation by her computer. The show ended five minutes later and she picked up her tea things to take into the kitchen. Walking to the sink, relief that she was no longer on candid camera released tension in her muscles she hadn't even realized was there.

"Nitro said you did a good job of pretending to be alone."

She turned from dropping the cup in the sink to face Joshua and had to suck in air from the impact. He was gorgeous, everything a man should be. It would be easier on her if there was some sort of flaw she could latch onto, but even the small scar near his temple was sexy.

"It wasn't hard," she forced herself to answer without giving away the longing that grew with each moment in his presence and no amount of self-protective lectures could diminish. "He's not exactly sociable, is he?"

Joshua opened the fridge and pulled out a bottle of beer that hadn't been there before she left.

He twisted off the cap and took a swig. "He just came off assignment."

"So?"

Was it just her, or had he come closer? She could smell the beer and a spicy scent she'd only known when she was around him. All male. All Joshua.

Eyes the color of burnished walnut pinned her in place as his body moved, shrinking the distance between them. "It takes a while to start reacting like a normal person and not a battle-ready soldier."

She leaned back against the sink, trying to create a sense of space and failing dismally. "Do you mean to say this is your *normal person* mode?"

"Uh-huh."

She mentally strained at the bond linking them so effectively. "Hotwire is a lot friendlier than either you or Nitro. Why is that?"

Joshua's eyes narrowed. "Don't let that sweet Georgia accent fool you. He's every bit as deadly as me or Nitro."

"I didn't doubt it for a minute, but he's also about as charming as a new preacher at Sunday dinner."

The bottle landed with a thud on the countertop behind her and Joshua's hands settled on either side of her. "Would you rather go to bed with a man who can charm you than a man who turns you inside out with passion?"

She swallowed and then licked her lips. "I wasn't talking about going to bed with anyone."

"Keep it that way."

"Excuse me?"

"Don't start thinking about Hotwire as a potential bed partner."

Her hands came up to push against a solid chest that seemed to be pressing into her. "I can think of anyone I like."

"No." He kissed her. It was short, but powerful to the point of leaving her weak-kneed. "You can't."

Her fingers tingled from the heat of him. "Why can't I?"

"Because you want me and when this job is done, I'm going to show you how much."

"Conceited toad."

His smile about finished the job his kiss had started. She was pretty sure she would have slid right down the cupboard if he hadn't been so close and practically holding her up with his body.

"Conceit isn't justified. Confidence is, and I'm confident the attraction is mutual."

"Is it?" she asked, remembering his rejection the night before.

He pressed his pelvis into her and the hard length against her stomach answered her question before his sexy, "Oh, yeah," did.

He kissed her again and she hung, suspended by the connection of their two lips, until he stepped back.

"It's late. You need to get to bed."

She nodded, mute from the kiss and sensual threat of his words.

"You can have the bathroom first."

"Thanks," she croaked out.

The shower helped relax her, but no amount of hot water or scrubbing could rid her mind of the image of her and Joshua together on a bed. After drying off, she pulled on a cranberry red t-shirt that had almost faded to pink, she'd had it so long, and a pair of white flannel pajama bottoms covered with miniature rosebuds.

She considered her image in the mirror ruefully. Sexy she was not. She looked about ten years old. She grimaced and stepped out of the bathroom.

Joshua was leaning against the wall.

He looked her up and down and the expression in his eyes made her feel like she was wearing a black silk negligee. So much for looking like a child.

"It's free," she said inanely.

He said nothing, but walked past her, allowing his arm to brush hers, the contact burning to the core of her.

She stood outside the closed bathroom door for several minutes as unwanted fantasies of his naked body occupying the same space she had just vacated teased her brain. The shower shut off and she realized she was going to be caught mooning like a love-struck calf if she didn't get her tail in gear.

Five minutes later, she stood, stymied, on the verge of the living room with extra bedding and one of her pillows for him to sleep with. If she made up the couch as a bed for either herself or Joshua, Nemesis was bound to realize someone else was in the apartment because part of the couch could be seen through the surveillance camera.

A sound behind her alerted her that Joshua had come out of the bathroom and she turned. The question she was going to ask about sleeping arrangements flew right out of her head. He was wearing a pair of charcoal gray knit boxers and nothing else.

His body could have graced the cover of a body builder's magazine . . . or *Playgirl.*

Not that she'd ever bought one, but if the magazine ever had a series of naked pictures of Joshua, she might.

He nodded toward the bedding in her arms. "Is that for me?"

"Ye . . ." She had to clear her throat. "Yes."

"Thanks." He took a step toward her, his hand extended to take the blankets.

"Where are you going to sleep?" she squeaked out.

"In your bedroom."

"Oh." It made sense. He was a big man and needed the big bed more than she did.

"Where should I sleep?" she asked, as if it were his apartment rather than hers, which irritated her.

She was not a simpering, shy innocent, even if she did have hot flashes from the sight of Joshua in his skivvies.

"In your bed."

Her mouth fell open. She hadn't considered sharing a bedroom with Joshua.

"*I'm not sleeping with you.*"

His brows rose in mockery. "Oh, you will, but not tonight. I'll take the floor."

"But . . ."

He didn't wait for her to finish, but turned and went into her bedroom.

She followed, not the least calmed by his assurance he'd be sleeping on the floor. "You won't be comfortable on the floor."

"Your plush carpet is a vast improvement over many of the places I've slept in the last sixteen years." He bent over and started making up a pallet.

She'd never, ever stared at a man's butt before, but she couldn't tear her eyes away from the sight of Joshua's.

Had Mike even had a butt? She certainly had never noticed it with a surge of lust like the one gripping her insides at the moment. An experience that made his assertion she would sleep with him one day sound entirely too plausible.

"Is that how long you've been a mercenary?" she asked, trying to ignore the furious pounding of her heart as well as the direction of her thoughts.

"No. I was an Army Ranger for six years."

"You must have been really young when you entered the army."

He shrugged, straightening. "Eighteen."

She'd been the same age when she'd gotten married, but his career as a soldier had lasted longer than her marriage. She sighed and looked at the bed and then back at him.

It was king size. She'd bought it because she'd fallen in love with the headboard, which had been hand-carved to resemble a plethora of roses. Above and beyond the beauty of the piece was an inner rebellion at the idea of sleeping in a small bed simply because she was no longer married.

"I would be a lot more comfortable sleeping on the floor than you would be."

"No."

He had a pretty deep streak of White Knight in him, no matter what he thought.

"Be reasonable, Joshua. You're a lot bigger than I am."

"We could just as easily share the bed. It's big enough, especially considering how tiny you are."

Her heart started trying to pound out of her chest again. "I don't think that would be a good idea."

Remembering the types of dreams that had plagued her since their incendiary kiss at the baby's christening, *appalled* didn't begin to describe how she felt at the prospect of sleeping in the same physical space as Joshua.

Something must have shown on her face because his frown was hot enough to singe her.

Lise's horrified refusal pissed Joshua off, even though he agreed with it in principle.

No matter how big the bed was, he wasn't going to get a wink of sleep sharing it with her, but it aggravated him that she was so obviously appalled by the prospect.

He was the one who had walked away the night before. She should realize she had nothing to fear from him.

"Why not?" he demanded. "Do you think I'll sneak onto your side of the bed, or something?"

Her cheeks turned an interesting shade of pink. "No."

"I would never try to coerce you."

Her blush intensified. "I'm aware of that."

"Then what's the problem?"

Why was he arguing this? It was a bad idea, damn it. He needed someone to sew his lips shut.

She took a deep breath, pressing her breasts against her thin cotton t-shirt. "I dream about you."

"You dream about me?" Now *that* was interesting.

"Yes, since that time last year."

"Naughty dreams?" He asked it to rile her, and the way she impaled him with her eyes told him he'd succeeded. "I don't see the problem. They're just dreams," he said, to push her just a little more.

"After last night, they'll probably only get worse," she gritted out.

"So?" He liked the idea of her having the feminine equivalent of wet dreams about him.

She glared at him. "Cryin' out loud, can't you just accept that it bothers me to dream about you?"

"No, I don't think so."

She tucked the multi-toned blond strands of her hair behind her ears, her hazel eyes green with temper. "I wake up hugging my pillow."

He raised one brow.

Her small hands fisted at her sides. "I'd be embarrassed to death if I woke up hugging you instead."

"I wouldn't mind."

She looked ready to explode. "I would."

"You didn't mind me holding you next to the car tonight."

"That was different."

"You didn't mind me holding you last night."

She paled.

He sighed. Enough teasing. "You're not going to wake up with me between your legs if you hug me in your sleep instead of your pillow."

He was about to add that he had no intention of sharing her bed when she spun away, wrapping her arms around herself protectively. "That's not what I'm worried about."

He remained silent, waiting to hear what was making her feel so vulnerable.

She turned back to face him, looking harassed. "What if I touch you like I do in my dreams?"

Just the thought was enough to send his sex throbbing and into full mast.

Her eyes widened, telling him where she'd been looking. "*Good night.*"

"I don't have any plans to do anything about it."

"That's good." She didn't sound convinced, but he couldn't tell if she was uncertain of his intentions or her own.

Her rapid breathing and obvious fascination with the tenting in his boxers was making it hard for him to remember that she could be certain of *his* control, if not her own. He was the professional with a rule about no sex on the job.

His sister's insidious voice saying it was more than a job, that it was personal, filtered through his mind.

Hell. "I'm glad you dream about me."

"You are?"

"Yes." At least the torment was mutual.

"Why?"

"Because I dream about you, too."

"Then you understand why I should sleep on the floor."

"No." He was already in pain from unsatisfied desire—what was sleeping on the floor in comparison?

She frowned at him. "You're really stubborn, you know that?"

"I'm thirty-four. That's not going to change anytime soon."

"I guess not."

"Go to bed, Lise."

"I will when I'm ready."

"You will right now if you want to sleep alone." His control was slipping and if she didn't hear it in his voice, it was because she was deaf.

He would have laughed at how fast she scurried over to the bed, but he hurt too much.

Nemesis had been right.

Lise Barton had returned to her apartment.

She hadn't been able to stay away from her computer—her writing that was so important to her. Her vehicle for filling other women's heads with lies and immoral beliefs. She destroyed other people's lives and she had to pay.

He would administer the retribution. It was his destiny. She would learn to regret her desire to lead other women astray.

His head itched and he scratched it. His hair felt greasy and his body smelled. He needed a shower, but he couldn't take a break from monitoring her. The bitch was too inconsistent.

What if she went somewhere again and he wasn't ready to follow her?

It bothered him that he still did not know where she had spent the last few days. There was no record of her flying out of either SeaTac or PDX. He'd even hacked into airline records for flights that originated as far away as Idaho and Northern California. Nothing.

No record of Lise Barton flying anywhere.

She couldn't have gone incognito, either. Not with today's security-conscious travel identification requirements.

Knowing he had prevented her from spending Thanksgiving with her family mitigated his fury a little at being deprived of his original plans for the holiday. She didn't deserve to spend the day with her people when she had made it impossible for him to spend it with his family.

Though he knew where she *hadn't* been—Texas—he didn't know where she *had* been. He couldn't even be sure she'd spent the time away from Seattle with Joshua Watt. The man had dropped her off at her apartment, but had not stayed, which told Nemesis exactly nothing.

And that was precisely what he'd been able to find out about Joshua Watt. *Nothing.* His family was from the East Coast, but Nemesis had been unable to find out exactly what Joshua did for a living or where he lived.

He didn't like that.

That sort of hole in key information was exactly what could mess up a launch schedule. Although Watt had gone away, Nemesis would not make the mistake of assuming he wasn't coming back this time. He'd been fooled once. He would not be again.

Therefore he needed more information about the man.

Damn the broken audio transmitter. He had only limited visual on his video transmitter. Unlike in her apartment in Texas, where the speaker had given him a view of all the common living areas and the entry to her bedroom, he now could only see parts of her living room.

It had been enough to verify her arrival home and that she'd stayed there, but he wanted to hear what was happening in the rest of the apartment. He needed to replace the transmitter somehow. He was tempted to install another video unit at the same time, but it would be safer to try to put an external tap on her phone line than to try to replace the bug.

However, he did not have a plan in place for such an eventuality.

Which infuriated him.

Agitated, he jumped up from his chair in front of the video monitor. His schedule was slipping. Even after spending all of yesterday restructuring it. There were activities he would have to remove from his plans in order to be ready for the final launch when his sign came.

He'd spent fifteen years as a project manager and he knew how to finesse a schedule, but there were some things that simply could not be taken into account. Things that could throw a plan completely off.

Joshua Watt's interference was one of those things, but Nemesis refused to allow the other man to get in the way of meting out justice to Lise Barton.

Soon, she would pay the ultimate price for her home-wrecking ways.

Then, maybe he would be able to sleep at night and the loss that haunted him would not hurt so much.

* * *

Lise woke up, her entire body throbbing from what she'd been doing with Joshua in her dream. She could feel wetness between her legs. She reached down, sliding her hand over her stomach to the dewy curls at the apex of her thighs. Just the light touch made her shudder and she gasped. Then she slipped a finger between the folds of her labia and touched herself.

Her flesh was slick, like silk, wet and swollen.

She pressed downward and her body gave an involuntary jerk. She yanked her hand out of her pajama bottoms and stared up at the darkly shadowed ceiling, panting. She could just barely hear Joshua's quiet, even breathing from the floor beside the bed. She would die if she made noise climaxing from touching herself.

She was not a sexual person. Or so she had always thought. Intimacy with Mike had been more emotionally fulfilling than physically stimulating. She'd never really bothered with the whole self-pleasure thing because climaxes weren't all that exciting. A lot of work for a short burst of muted pleasure.

So, what was with her total preoccupation with her sensuality?

She didn't want Joshua to wake up and find her in an embarrassing situation, but temptation to wake him up in order to create a situation of another type entirely rode her like a cowboy breaking a new horse.

The only thing stopping her was the absolute knowledge that making love with Joshua would be a *huge* mistake. She was already connecting to him on a dangerous emotional level.

If they made love, how would she deal with the aftermath when he moved on? And he *would* move on. Joshua wanted sex from her, not a commitment. Not even a relationship.

But as her body lay there, throbbing with a need she could not deny, she had to wonder if she would have the strength to resist her own yearnings.

Chapter 6

Joshua stretched. Low-level illumination from the street-lights outside filtered through the bottom edge of the curtains on Lise's bedroom window, verifying that it was still dark outside.

Hard and aching, Joshua had to wonder how intelligent his choice had been to stay in the apartment, much less sleep in the same room as Lise. Her even breathing indicated sleep, but he knew she'd had a restless night just like he had. He'd heard her tossing and turning and he was positive it wasn't because she'd been thinking about her stalker.

At one point she'd even uttered one of those little moans that sent his hormones through the stratosphere. It had taken reciting the entire Army Ranger creed in his mind to keep from responding to the sexy sound.

He flicked the Night Glow function on his watch. Four-thirty A.M. was a little too early to be waking Lise, but he could get up and start working.

He stood up and headed for the door. When he opened it, light filtered in from the hallway and an impossible-to-ignore compulsion had him turning back to see Lise in her bed.

Dark blond hair spread across the burgundy pillow, she looked small and fragile in the middle of the huge bed. He almost laughed at the thought. Small, maybe, but the tough little Texan was anything but fragile. She'd withstood the mental stress of being stalked by a nutcase and hadn't even fallen apart after he'd shoved her into traffic.

Sure, she'd been terrified when Joshua showed up at her door, but even then she'd been intent on keeping the people she loved from finding out the truth and being put at risk themselves. She was an amazing woman.

And an exciting one.

He wanted to join her on the bed and peel away the too-thin fabric of her top so he could get to the silky skin beneath. He'd had fantasies all night long about her breasts, what he wanted to do with them for both her pleasure and his. If he didn't move soon, he was going to do something she said she didn't want.

Her eyes opened without warning and her lips curved in a sleepy, soft smile. "Joshua."

His hands clenched at his sides. "It's not really morning yet—go back to sleep."

She pushed herself into a sitting position, the covers falling to her waist. It didn't reveal anything, so why was he salivating like she was wearing a peekaboo nightie?

"Why are you up?" she asked, her husky voice traveling along his nerve centers like the most pervasive agent in chemical warfare.

"I couldn't sleep. I wanted to get started on the investigation," he said, giving her part of the truth.

She pushed back the covers and scooted to the edge of the bed. "I'll help you."

"You don't have to. It can wait until later."

She stood up and crossed the room to her dresser, where she pulled out a pair of slouchy socks and tugged them on her bare pink feet. "I won't go back to sleep, so we might as well get started."

He was too busy watching the way her unfettered breasts

swayed under the cotton of her top to answer her coherently, but she didn't seem to notice. She stopped when she reached him, though. He was blocking the door.

"Joshua?"

"Uh-huh?"

"It would probably be easier to work in the kitchen at the table."

"Unless you get something on over that scandalous excuse for a shirt, the only thing we're going to be working on is how fast I can get your nipples red and swollen like they were the other night."

She gasped and covered her breasts with her arms, then stepped back as if he'd made a move toward her. "My shirt is not scandalous."

"It's thin. I can see every damn line of your body."

She looked down at herself. "It is not. It's loose. It doesn't show anything."

"Honey, I'm not sure a trench coat would be enough covering for you, but we could try it." Then a vivid image entered his head of her in a trench coat and nothing else. His sex pulsed and he shook his head at his own idiocy. "Maybe not."

She stared at him like he'd lost his last brain cell in a bad bet.

He sighed and rubbed his hand over his face. "Just put some clothes on, okay?"

"Fine, but you have to dress, too."

He looked down and realized he wasn't wearing anything but his skivvies. They were soft cotton boxers that clung to his thighs and did nothing to hide the condition of his body. "Don't worry, I'll get dressed."

They met in the kitchen ten minutes later and she set about making coffee while he flipped open his notebook and started going through his notes. "We need to discuss a few things."

"Like what?" She wasn't looking at him, and he figured she was trying to forget what had happened in the doorway of her room.

He wished her luck.

"Compiling a list of suspects, for one. There's no reason to wait for Nemesis to act again to start narrowing down the possibilities."

"Sounds good." She stood, watching the coffeepot percolate, and he didn't tease her about it.

They both needed space. A few hundred miles might just work to calm his libido . . . or not. He'd wanted her while fighting through the humid jungle to reach a small boy being held captive by a group of fanatics who thought more of ransom money than human life.

He shook off his thoughts and focused on his list. "What about your ex?"

She turned abruptly to face him, her expression shocked. "Mike?"

"You said he fell in love and married another woman."

"Yes."

"How is that going, do you know?"

"He's happy. They've got a little girl and I think she's expecting again. He would have no reason to stalk me—besides, he's not the type."

He didn't like hearing her defend the man she'd once loved enough to marry, but he wasn't about to ask himself why. "Criminals don't run around with a big C stamped on their foreheads, Lise."

She rolled her eyes. "I know that. It's just that he's so honest, so upfront about things. If he was mad at me for something, and I honestly can't imagine what, he'd come right out and tell me."

"Does this Dudley Do-Right live in Canyon Rock?"

"Yes."

"It should be easy enough to check if he's taken any extended vacations lately."

Lise shook her head. "You're really barking up the wrong tree on this one."

"I don't bark at trees."

"You're cranky this morning."

"I'm horny. There's a difference."

"Not from where I'm standing," she said with asperity and a blush that made him want to kiss her senseless.

"Okay, let's move on."

"Gladly."

"What about other lovers?"

"There aren't any."

"At all?"

"At all. I got married when I was eighteen and divorced when I was twenty-six. I've spent the last two years focused on my career."

"What about sex?" If he sounded appalled, that was because he was. *Two years without sex?*

"We're not all sexual time bombs ready to go off with little to no provocation." Her look said that was exactly what she thought he was.

"A t-shirt thin enough to show you weren't wearing a bra is not small provocation."

"Oh, please. Let's not go there again."

"So, no other lovers?" He just had to be sure.

"None."

"Any wannabes?" A thwarted man could be a dangerous man.

"I didn't date."

"At all?"

"No!"

He put his hands up to ward off any more explosions. "All right. I just find it hard to believe no one asked you out in two years."

"I'm a writer. I keep to myself and I wasn't interested. Men can tell these things."

"You didn't act uninterested with me."

"I liked you."

"You say that in the past tense. Don't you like me any-more?" He was pushing her again, but he loved watching this woman everyone else thought was so shy and quiet spark like a lit roman candle.

She could explode over him anytime.

"I don't like you right now," she said with enough bite to make him laugh.

"Sorry. I didn't mean to upset you," he lied without com-punction.

She didn't believe him anyway, and her little harrumph let him know it.

"Okay, what about disgruntled readers?"

"I don't get a lot of negative mail on my books. Once in a while someone offended by the aggressive personalities of my heroines writes and accuses me of promoting lesbianism or far-left feminism, but for the most part, people who read what I write like it."

"I want to see those letters."

"No problem. I keep a weird letter file."

He made a note of that.

"Anything else?"

"Do *you* have any ideas at all?"

She shook her head. "I really don't. If my dad were alive, I'd almost think he could have hired someone to torment me, but I don't have any enemies that I know of."

"Bella said he was a cold son of a bitch, but would he re-ally have done something like that?"

She looked at him and what he saw in her eyes kicked him straight in the gut. "Probably not, but he made no pretense of caring for me."

"Why?"

She shrugged. "My mom died from complications after my birth. He accused me more than once of killing her."

"That's insane."

"Yes, it is. He was a man with a very twisted view of life."

"You don't share it. Neither does Jake."

"Maybe the fact he ignored us so much was a good thing." She turned to pour two mugs of steaming coffee. "There were other people in our lives. Our grandparents on Mom's side were alive until I was ten. Dad's parents were out of the picture before I was born. If he was anything to go by, they weren't a great loss."

"My stepfather never distinguished between me and my sisters in affection. He cared about us all. It's the kind of father I'd want to be if I had kids."

"He's a wonderful man."

"Yes, but your dad wasn't."

"No, and growing up was harder because of it, but I didn't grow up in the African desert where babies starve to death every day, or in a home where drugs are more important than food. Life could have been a lot worse."

Joshua agreed, but he had a hard time understanding any father who wouldn't love a daughter as incredible as the woman standing in front of him.

"That son of a bitch. He deleted my book."

The sound of Lise swearing was enough to command Joshua's full attention, not to mention the fury in her tone.

He got up from the table where he'd been going over the file of "weird" letters Lise had gotten from readers over the years and went in to stand behind her at the computer. "What do you mean?"

She turned her body, her face flushed with bad temper. "He deleted the book I'm working on."

"Shit." She'd told him she was fighting to make deadline as it was. "Do you have backup?"

"Of course, but it really makes me mad that he was inside my computer. I feel violated." She shook her head, a cynical expression twisting her beautiful features. "But then, what's new about that? He's been violating my life for months."

She grabbed a memory fob and plugged into the front USB port on her computer, then clicked her mouse.

Joshua flipped open his cell phone and speed-dialed Hotwire's phone.

His buddy was letting himself into the apartment a minute later.

"What's this about the perp playing on your computer? I did a thorough scan of your system when we were checking the apartment for bugs and didn't find any footprints."

Lise looked up, her eyes snapping. "I don't know about footprints, but that jerk-off deleted my book."

"Do you mind if I take a look?"

Lise got up. "Go right ahead. I'm going to write on my Dana." She grabbed what looked like a black keyboard with a small display screen at the top. "I'm not going to let him stop me from making my deadline."

Joshua smiled at her. "Go get 'em, tiger."

She stopped, startled, and stared at him as if he'd sprouted a halo or something.

Joshua winked at her and turned, whistling "We Will Rock You" by Queen on his way back into the kitchen.

Lise watched Joshua walk away with a sense of unreality and a silly grin twitching at the corners of her mouth.

"He likes you," Hotwire said.

She shifted her gaze to the blond man. "I think maybe you're right, and here I was believing it was all just unbridled lust for my body."

Hotwire grinned. "That, too."

"I—"

"Hey, it's obvious. He's been pissing a circle around you since you got off the plane. Nitro and I are laughing our as— tails off because of it."

She couldn't help smiling at Hotwire's imagery. It was pretty apt for the way Joshua had been acting, justified or not.

"Is he like this a lot?"

"Nah. He wasn't even this territorial with Melody."

"Who's Melody?"

"Wolf'll tell you sometime, maybe."

She realized her curiosity was showing again and sighed. "Sorry. I didn't mean to pry. It's a bad habit I have."

"I don't think Wolf would mind if you asked him about it."

"I think you're confusing his feelings of protectiveness because he's helping me with something else."

"Nah. He's got a savior complex that goes bone deep, but it doesn't extend to sexual possessiveness."

She hadn't meant that; she'd been talking about Hotwire's belief that Joshua wouldn't mind her prying, but why bother correcting him? For some reason he believed Joshua's feelings for her involved more than lust.

If she argued about it with him, she might foolishly allow him to convince her.

She hugged her Dana to her chest, intrigued by Hotwire's other comment. "What do you mean, *a savior complex*?"

"Joshua figures he's got to save the world. He's risked his life for other people so many times, I think he sees it as a way of life."

"But he's not proud of what he does."

"No. He figures that since he gets paid for it, that negates the good he does."

"But he doesn't get paid for all of it, does he?" she guessed.

Hotwire shook his head. "No, he sure don't, but don't go thinking that counts any with him. It doesn't."

"What about you—does it count with you?"

The charming Georgia boy transformed into an emotionless mercenary before her very eyes. "We've all got our reasons for doing what we do."

She didn't let the transformation faze her. She just grinned wider. "I guess you do, but I'm willing to bet that Joshua isn't the only man around here with a savior complex."

She emulated Joshua's wink and turned away before Hotwire could answer.

She heard nothing but silence behind her for several seconds and then the sound of furious typing on the desktop's keyboard reached her ears.

Joshua laid aside his notes. He had a few letters written by potential suspects from the manila folder Lise called her "weird" letter file.

While Lise had not saved envelopes, she had noted on each letter what city and state or country it had been written from. She'd also jotted down if the letter came from a penal institution and which one. That was something, but finding the people who had written the letters wasn't going to be completely straightforward.

He stood up and stretched before going to the edge of the living room. Lise defiantly sat in the maple rocker that was in direct line to the hidden camera and typed away on her small black keyboard.

"Ready for a break?"

She didn't respond and he waited until her fingers stopped their rapid clicking on the small keyboard, and then he asked the question again. Hotwire got like that sometimes and Joshua had learned to wait for the opportune moment to break his concentration.

She looked up, her expression dazed. "A break?"

"Yeah."

"I . . ." She looked down at the keyboard in her lap and started reading out loud to herself, then said, "Maybe in a little while," before going back to reading the words aloud.

"Okay."

Soon she was typing again. From her zombie-like tone, he figured *a little while* was going to take longer than a few minutes.

He walked over to where Hotwire was working on her computer and dropped the stack of letters beside him. "See what you can find out about these people."

His buddy nodded. "You got it."

"I'm going for a run—you okay to stick around here for an hour or so?"

"Sure." Hotwire grabbed the letters and started shuffling through them. "Could take that long to get preliminary locations for these."

"Thanks."

"No problem, Wolf. She's unique, your Lise."

"She's not mine." Even if he got her into his bed, she wouldn't be his.

Not permanently.

She inhabited a fairy tale world of heroes and White Knights. In her world, princesses gave their hearts to princes, not the soldiers who served them.

But he was going to possess her body sexually, so long and so well, she'd never forget him, no matter how many Dudley Do-Rights came and went in her life.

Lise looked up from her Dana when she heard the outside door close. Had Hotwire left?

Her gaze traveled to the clock on the wall. Three o'clock already? Her stomach growled, letting her know it had been a long time since breakfast. She stood up and did almost a complete backbend, cracking her back and stretching muscles in the process.

Writing for such long stretches left her muscles cramped and her mind wasted, but they were worth it when she had so much to show for her time at the keyboard.

Straightening, she found herself looking into Joshua's eyes. They burned through her with such intense focus her mouth went dry.

He stood right outside of the camera's range, his dark hair damp, wearing a fresh t-shirt and smelling soap-clean like he'd just stepped out of the shower.

She opened her mouth to speak, but he jerked his head toward the speaker with the minicam and she turned it into a yawn instead.

It wasn't hard. Her writing jag had exhausted her.

She grabbed her word processor and barely suppressed the urge to thumb her nose at the camera. She had no idea how many pages she'd written, but the file she'd saved was sixty kilobytes in size. On a Dana, that was a lot of pages.

She allowed herself a triumphant grin at the room in general and walked out of the line of vision of the minicam.

"You ready for that break now?" he asked.

She yawned for real this time. "Yes. I could eat something, too."

"You left your lunch sitting on the table."

"Lunch?"

"I made you a sandwich. Nothing big. I told you about it. You said, *all right*, but kept typing."

She felt heat steal up her neck. "I get like that sometimes. You can talk to me and I'll respond, but I don't remember the conversation at all. Jake gets no end of amusement out of it."

Joshua's smile could only be classified as pure, one-hundred-percent sex appeal, and it did bad things to her heart rate.

"I've got a snack made for you if you want it."

She headed toward the kitchen. "You don't have to tell me twice. I'm starved."

She noticed her computer chair was empty when she passed it. "I heard the door shut."

His expression turned wry. "The last time was about the fifth time it opened and closed today. Nitro's been and gone.

I went running and came back and Hotwire left a second ago."

"No wonder you look like you just took a shower."

"I went running five hours ago."

She grimaced. "Oh . . ."

He chuckled. "We had a meeting and then I worked out on the floor of your bedroom while you were writing."

"I could use a workout. My muscles ache from sitting in one position for so long." She stopped beside the table and did some side stretches.

Joshua watched her with distracting interest and she bumped the table sliding into her chair.

She took a long drink of the juice he'd poured her and then a bite of her sandwich. It was Heavenly, and she didn't talk again until she'd eaten most of it.

"I take it you got a lot done on your book?"

"Yep."

"Hotwire installed an invisible firewall on your system that should trap anyone trying to get in and give us a lead to their computer."

"Nemesis didn't leave a trail when he deleted my file."

"No. He did a better sweep job than a soldier in the field during war games."

"That makes sense. When I used my firewall software to try to trace his e-mails, I came up with nothing."

Joshua spun a chair around and straddled it, his arms over the back. He liked watching Lise eat. She was dainty, even if she wouldn't appreciate him saying so.

"Hotwire got a little further with the e-mails, but he's still working on it."

"So, am I supposed to use my computer now?"

"It's up to you. Stick with the Dana if that makes you feel better, but download to the computer every night so he doesn't track the fact we're on to him. Just keep a current backup of your file."

"I always do."

"Good."

"Thanks for working on that."

"Thank Hotwire. He did it. Computers are not my specialty."

"What is your specialty?"

"Tactics and warfare."

She didn't flinch as he'd expected, but watched him with eyes he swore saw into his soul. "You said you'd done a lot of things you wouldn't want put in your memoirs."

"Yes." He'd lived as a mercenary for ten years and his six years in the Army Rangers had been only marginally better.

"Everyone has things in their past they aren't proud of."

"Would everyone do them again?" Because he would.

He'd made a lot of tough calls in his life, but the few regrets weren't about the warfare he'd waged on behalf of the people who had needed his help. That didn't mean things didn't weigh on his conscience. It didn't matter how many times a man had to kill, he never learned to take it in stride.

At least he hadn't.

"Few people have lived lives so full of heroism that they'd want to."

"I'm no hero."

She waved her hand, dismissing his words. "Tell me about what y'all discussed while I was writing."

He didn't feel like arguing with her to disillusion her, so he went with the change of subject. "I read through the letters you keep in your 'weird letter' file."

"I did that, too, right after the stalking started, but I couldn't see a correlation between any of the letters and what was happening to me."

"You can't limit yourself to linking like events. Five of those messages were written from prison, four of them by men who have since been let out."

"Some of the letters were really disgusting." She shivered. "Have you looked into the men's whereabouts?"

"One is doing parole in the Midwest and from all accounts hasn't left town since getting out. Another is doing time again, but in a county jail, and the other two skipped parole and no one knows where they are."

"Do you think one of them is my stalker?"

"I don't know," he replied honestly, wishing it could be that easy, suspecting it wouldn't be. "One of the men was in for sexual assault."

Her face blanched and he reached out to touch her before thinking better of it.

"No one is getting near you."

"Thanks." She licked a crumb from the corner of her mouth and he wanted to follow her retreating tongue with his own.

He forced his thoughts away from that dangerous path. "There were a few more letters I thought we should investigate."

"Which ones?"

"You've had two letters from a right-wing conservative group that claims to have discovered the new way to salvation. They've got major issues with women, especially assertive and strong ones."

"You think I'm being stalked by a cult?" She sounded incredulous.

"No, but one of the cult's followers might have fixated on you. It's something we're going to have to look into."

"This isn't going to be straightforward, is it?"

There was no sense lying to her. She was too smart to believe him, anyway. "No."

The apartment intercom buzzed.

"Are you expecting anyone?"

"No."

He followed her into the hall and she pressed the black button on her intercom. "Yes?"

"Miss Barton, this is the security desk. A package was delivered for you today that wouldn't fit in your mailbox."

"I'll be down shortly to collect it." She snagged her keys from the hook. "Be right back."

Joshua put his hand on the door, preventing her from opening it. "How often do you get packages?"

"Quite a lot, actually." She patted his arm as if trying to reassure him.

It was a strange sensation. No one but his mother and sisters believed he needed that kind of thing.

"This is nothing new, Joshua. My publisher sends me manuscripts for proofing, author copies of my books, and I order a lot of books online, too."

"That doesn't mean this package is innocent." His gut was telling him things were escalating. There was no overt proof of it, but he knew it all the same.

"You can't go with me." She hugged herself in a way he'd learned meant she was feeling threatened. "For all we know, Nemesis is one of the apartment building's security guards."

He liked the way her posture put her breasts into prominence, but he didn't think he'd mention that.

"That wouldn't surprise me," he said instead. "Security here is pretty damn lax."

"The Realtor who helped me find my apartment said the security here was very tight."

"I got in without any problem."

"It may have escaped your notice, but most burglars aren't former mercenaries." A smile twitched on her lips and he got the distinct impression she was laughing at him.

Another new experience for him.

"I'm not a former anything." He was still a soldier for hire and neither one of them had better forget that fact.

"I know, but my point is," she said with exaggerated care,

"there are only a handful of people in the world with your skill set. If Nemesis was one of them, we wouldn't have any concrete information on him at all."

On that point, Joshua had to agree, but he didn't agree with her going to the lobby alone. "I'll call Nitro and have him in the lobby when you come down. He'll follow you to the elevator since his and Hotwire's temporary apartment is only one floor below.

She didn't argue and he hadn't expected her to.

Chapter 7

Lise was too nervous to chat with the security guard like she normally did when picking up a package.

But that was going to get her nowhere, which was where running away to Seattle had gotten her, so she didn't do it.

Taking the box, which felt light for its size, she thanked the female security agent and then headed straight for the elevator. Nitro came along beside her, but did not betray by a flicker of an eyelash that he knew her.

Once they were on the elevator, he kept his eyes straight ahead and she examined the package. Wrapped in brown paper, it was about the right size for a book delivery, but too light, unless there were only a couple of books and a lot of weightless packing. The return address was smudged beyond recognition and the postmark was from Seattle's city center post office.

While Amazon.com was Seattle-based, deliveries from the bookstore had the company name emblazoned on the boxes themselves and she couldn't remember making a recent order. Though that didn't mean a great deal. She'd often surprised herself with book orders when they got delivered.

Talking wasn't the only thing she did with her mind fully engaged in her book.

The elevator stopped on Nitro's floor and he stepped out,

stopping just on the other side of the open doors, but not turning around to look at her. "Don't open it until I'm up there."

He didn't wait for her agreement before leaving and the doors slid shut almost immediately after.

Both Joshua and Nitro's attitudes weren't doing much for her nerves. She'd thought she had mentally prepared herself to live under the siege mentality that being stalked induced, but she realized she'd been trying to hide from reality again. Yesterday, she'd used her work to do it, typing away while Joshua and his friends discussed her plight.

She should have been in on that, taken an active interest in their plans, but she'd lost herself in the fictional world she'd created. A world where the heroine always triumphed and the bad guys got theirs. It wasn't a new defense mechanism. She'd used the stories in her head to hide from her father's rejection and her focus on her writing had effectively masked the cracks in her marriage until Mike's request for a divorce had plunged her into painful reality.

Here she was, trying to hide again. She didn't *want* to believe the package was from her stalker, so she kept trying to come up with an alternative. She hated knowing that everything coming into her life was suspect now. However, not wanting to face reality was a far cry from being able to get rid of the prickly feeling she got every time she looked down at the nondescript box in her hands.

Joshua waited impatiently for Lise to return.

He didn't like that walk down the hall by herself, even if he knew Nitro would not have left the elevator if there had been anyone else on it with Lise when it stopped at his floor. Knowing his friend's competence didn't stop Joshua from picking up his mobile to call and see if Nitro had returned to his own apartment, but as he went to dial, the door opened and Lise walked in.

She put a plain brown box down on the hall table and hung up her keys, her expression troubled.

He flipped his phone shut again and attached it to the clip on his belt. "What's the problem?"

Biting her lower lip, her eyes skittered to the package and then to him. "I can't read the return address and the post-mark is from the post office here in Seattle." She glared at nothing in particular. "I hate feeling like this."

"Like what?"

"Besieged."

Joshua knew what she meant. Thus far, all of her actions in regard to her stalker had been defensive. You couldn't live large behind a defensive shield. It was a simple reality of combat. Taking the offensive could be a huge risk, but it also freed a person to act instead of react.

"Has he sent you anything before?" She hadn't mentioned it, but he had not interrogated her on all the events leading up to her current situation.

It shamed him to acknowledge it, but he'd been too busy fighting the ungovernable desire that plagued him whenever he was with her. Sixteen years as a professional soldier and a tiny woman laid waste his defenses. It was damn embarrassing and not something he would ever willingly admit to.

"No." She looked at him with troubled eyes as turbulent as a war-torn country. "But prior to pushing me into the street, he'd never done anything to put me in danger, either." Her small fingers curled and uncurled at her sides, the knuckles turning white. "Maybe the sergeant was right. Maybe that wasn't my stalker at all."

He squeezed her shoulders, pulling her infinitesimally closer to him. "Don't start doubting yourself now."

She looked at his hands on her shoulders and then back at his face. "You do that a lot."

"What?" Her mind definitely went places he had trouble following.

"Touch me."

"And that surprises you?"

"Yes."

"Why?"

"You said no sex on the job."

He brushed the delicate column of her neck with both his thumbs, entranced by the rapidity of the pulse he found there. "I'm not touching you sexually." Much.

"It's just a *friendly* touch," she mocked.

"Yeah." A real friendly connection.

"And you caress all your *friends* this way, right?"

His lips quirked. He liked the way she made him smile even when she was stressed. "Not Hotwire and Nitro."

Her hazel eyes filled with humor. "I can't imagine."

Neither could he, but what she didn't know and he had no intention of telling her was that he couldn't imagine touching another woman in this casual way, either. Even when he was having sex, he tended to keep the fondling to what was necessary to achieve his partner's climax. With Lise, he wanted his hands on her all the time, even when he wasn't aching with desires he couldn't do anything about right now.

Her small hand settled against his heart and her pixie face took on a very serious cast. "I'm glad you're here, Joshua. Thank you for helping me."

For several seconds, he couldn't say anything and he had to force himself to let her go and step back. "No problem." He picked up the box. "Let me get Nitro in here before we open this."

"He said he'd be up, but why does he have to be here to open it?"

"He's an explosives expert."

"*You think it might be a bomb?*"

"Your stalker's behavior so far hasn't indicated that level of violent intent, but caution never hurts."

She glared at him, her eyes promising mayhem and retribution. "My heart missed several beats there. Maybe you need to be a little more circumspect about your precautions."

He liked her sass, but he didn't agree. "It's no use hiding from the possibilities."

She straightened as if driving herself up and mentally soldiering on. "I know you're right. I have a bad habit of hoping if I ignore something, it will go away."

"Like a stalker?"

"Yeah, among other things."

Lise watched the dark, silent man use a swab chemical detector like the ones security employed in airports.

They'd brought the box into the kitchen and he was working at the table.

Joshua had suggested she go down to his friends' apartment while Nitro did the scan, but she'd wanted to watch. Her professional curiosity had been aroused. Besides, she'd argued, if Joshua had really believed it was dangerous, he wouldn't have allowed her to bring the package up from the security desk in the first place.

He'd admitted she was right with a real lack of grace and allowed her to stay, grumbling about independent, stubborn females. However, he'd made her promise to leave if Nitro found anything doubtful.

So far, Nemesis had been very careful to avoid giving any sort of concrete evidence for her to take to the police. She didn't think they'd find anything dangerous or traceable in the package. Unless he wanted to kill her, and nothing so far indicated he wanted to do anything more than terrorize her, there was little chance the package was any danger to anything but her mental well-being.

Nitro's efforts were no doubt overkill, but they were fascinating to watch.

"What does that do?" she asked Nitro as he scanned the package with a handheld wand.

"It detects electromagnetic emissions."

She looked at Joshua for a clarification.

"If there is an electric timer or trigger for a bomb, the wand will pick it up."

"It's clean." Nitro flipped open a knife that seemed to appear out of nowhere.

He sliced the packing tape holding the brown paper to the box and then pulled back the flaps. It was filled with packing peanuts and Nitro carefully removed them after doing an additional scan with his wand thing.

He pulled a tissue-wrapped bundle from the box and looked at her. "Do you mind if I unwrap it?"

She shook her head. "Go ahead."

He peeled away the generic white tissue to reveal two pieces of a broken crystal heart on a pedestal. A groom was still attached to the base, but the bride had been crushed, the tiny shards of colored crystal that had comprised her still in the tissue.

Both Nitro and Joshua looked at her as if asking what it was.

"That's a wedding cake topper. It's a lot like the one I had when I married Mike." Uncannily like it, actually.

Joshua took the tissue bundle from Nitro and examined it. "How much like it?"

She leaned back against the counter, not wanting the men to know that her limbs seemed to have stopped working. She hated being weak. "Almost identical. It's like he's seen my wedding photos, or something."

"Maybe he did."

Bile rose in her throat, but she swallowed it back down. She was not going to be a wimp about this.

"He could have seen it one of the times he broke into my apartment in Canyon Rock." She'd kept her wedding album with her other pictures in a cabinet.

Joshua set the tissue bundle down on the counter and started rifling through the box. "You kept your wedding photos?"

He sounded surprised. She supposed a professional mercenary didn't make it a habit of saving mementos.

"Yes." It was part of her past, just like her awful picture missing her two front teeth in first grade and the photos that saved for posterity her pimple-faced adolescence.

Joshua looked at Nitro. "No note."

She couldn't say she was sorry. The implied message was upsetting enough—she didn't need a vitriolic note to add to the effect.

That night, it wasn't an erotic dream that woke Lise. It was the sound of a ringing telephone.

She rolled across the huge bed and scrabbled for the cordless phone on the table beside it. She encountered a hard, hairy wrist instead.

"Joshua?" she asked groggily.

"Yes. Here's the phone." He put it in her hand. "If it's Nemesis, try to keep him talking for a trace."

"You put a tracer on my phone?" she asked, shock waking her more effectively than the sound of the phone.

"Don't worry about that now. Just answer it."

She pressed the Call button as Joshua came down to sit beside her on the bed.

"Hello?"

"Hello, Lise." The digitized voice made her hand clench tightly around the phone. "Your boyfriend appears to have abandoned you."

"He's not my boyfriend."

Digitized but obviously scornful laughter met her denial.

Joshua's warm hand settled over her thigh as if he was making a statement.

She wasn't alone.

Not at all sure which was messing more with her nerves—the call, or Joshua's nearness—she asked, "Who is this?"

How many times had she asked that same question? At least once in each of his phone calls. It irritated her that she hadn't stopped asking it because he sure as certain wasn't answering it.

"*Nemesis*. Are you pretending you don't know?"

"Nemesis isn't your real name."

"It is now. That is what I've become, what you've made me." Even through the voice distortion, she could hear the passionate anger in his voice, the accusation.

"How did I make you that? I don't even know you."

"Are you sure about that, Lise Barton?" Again the awful, almost mechanical laughter.

No, she wasn't, and that bothered her. A lot. Nevertheless, she said, "I'm positive. None of the people I know would do what you're doing."

"They don't have the guts."

"It doesn't take guts to stalk a woman, it takes insanity."

Joshua squeezed her thigh in warning and she remembered she was trying to keep the lunatic talking, not make him mad enough to hang up.

"You deserve what you get. You lead other women astray."

What in the world was he talking about? She didn't even belong to a local writer's organization, much less a women's group of some kind. "What do you mean?"

"Don't pretend ignorance. You know!" Fury vibrated in each word.

"But I don't."

"Don't lie to me! You know! You destroy families." His voice lowered to almost a whisper through the digitizer. "Maybe your family needs to be destroyed—then you would understand how heinous your crime really is."

Sick fear curled through her insides.

"My family hasn't done anything."

"That's true. They're innocent and the innocent should not pay with the guilty, but they love you. To love you they must share your distorted view of the world. I have to think about this . . ." His voice trailed off like he was talking to himself.

"No. Leave my family alone. Please."

"I don't know." He sounded unsure, almost confused, and terror ripped through her at the thought of him hurting anyone she loved.

"*They're innocent*," she stressed.

"But you're not!" His voice boomed across the phone lines, condemnation vibrating in every syllable.

"Please tell me what I've done."

"Your husband divorced you. He found out you weren't worth loving, didn't he? He married a woman who gave him children, a woman worthy of marriage. You aren't, Lise Barton."

She knew the man speaking had to be crazy to do what he did, but his words hurt anyway because they tapped into an old fear. One she'd tried so hard to leave behind in her less-than-pleasant childhood, the fear that she wasn't worthy of love.

"You're wrong."

"You're defective. You couldn't even give him children. God punished you with infertility and now I will punish you, too."

His words shocked her into silence.

"You want to destroy other women's marriages. All because you couldn't keep your own."

She had to keep her head about her, not give in to the palpable insanity blasting her through the phone. "I don't want to destroy anyone's marriage. What are you talking about? I have a right to know what I'm accused of!"

"You have no rights. You've already been tried and convicted."

"By *you?*"

"Your own actions have convicted you and you will be punished."

The words were still echoing in her ear when the click that signaled he'd hung up crossed the line. She pressed the Disconnect button with a trembling hand and then fumbled the phone back to the nightstand.

"What did he say?"

"He said I destroyed other people's marriages. That's why he's become my Nemesis." She tried vainly to make eye contact in the darkness. "I don't understand, Joshua. I've never even told a girlfriend she should leave her husband. Not that I wouldn't . . . if I thought she was at risk, or something, but the issue has never come up."

Joshua's cell phone buzzed. He picked it up. "Yeah?"

She could hear the echo of a voice from the mobile phone's headpiece.

"Hell."

"Who is it?" she asked, not caring that it was rude to interrupt a phone conversation.

"Nitro—he says the call was made from a pay phone across town." His attention went back to the phone. "He said *what?*" Joshua demanded.

More talking at the other end indicated that Nitro was recounting the horrific conversation verbatim. They must have put a wiretap on the phone as well as a tracer. She was grateful.

She didn't want to forget anything that had been said, especially the threat to her family.

They had to do something.

"My guess is he's hacked into her medical records," Joshua said and then paused.

She could hear Nitro's voice, but not what he was saying over the mobile phone.

"Hold on a sec," Joshua said.

He turned the bedside lamp on and then faced her, his expression serious. "We need to know where he got the information about your infertility. My guess is your medical file, but is it something you told other people?"

She snorted, anger replacing the feeling of fear and helplessness the awful phone call had instilled in her again. "I'm not infertile. I have an odd monthly cycle, that's all. The doctor said it *might* take a while to get pregnant, but Mike and I never even tried. Not only is Nemesis insane, he's also an idiot."

And she wished, just at that moment, that her tormenter could hear her opinion of him.

"Is this women's cycle thing common knowledge?"

"No." She hadn't even told Mike because it had never become an issue in their marriage. "It's not a big deal."

Joshua nodded and returned to the phone. His expression turned feral and he said a really ugly word. "Like hell he is going to hurt them."

Good—Nitro had shared that part as well.

"Will you fly down and move them?" Joshua asked, then said, "Tomorrow would be good." A pause. "Your house. Right. It's as much of a fortress as mine." He smiled. "We'll have to ask Bella what she thinks after she's seen both of them."

Lise listened to him making plans to move her brother's family to safety with a growing sense of guilt and self-condemnation. Something she had done had put her family at risk. Jake was going to be furious about having to leave the ranch. Thank God it was winter and not roundup, or he'd insist on staying while sending his wife and daughter to safety.

But *she'd* done this, messed up everyone's lives.

A tiny voice of reason tried to tell her it wasn't her fault, but it was no match for the emotions roiling inside her.

Joshua shifted to put his free arm across her thighs, boxing her in, surrounding her with his presence. So obviously lend-ing her his strength that she about choked on another wave of emotion.

She couldn't handle it. She'd spent the last two years proving to herself she could make it on her own and that concept of herself was being blasted to heck and gone by her anonymous enemy.

Somehow she'd made all this happen and there was nothing she could do to make it right. She had to rely on Joshua and his skills. A new kind of helplessness filled her, a sense that she could never make up to her family for what the problems in her life were costing them.

She needed space. Joshua was too close. Everything was too close. Her skin felt too tight for her body, like she was going to explode out of it. Nemesis's words rang in her head and Joshua's conversation with Nitro jumbled over them.

She had to get away.

She tried to move Joshua's arm, but he wouldn't cooperate.

"Joshua . . ." She pushed at his wrist, but she might as well have been trying to move a tree.

His gaze fixed on her as he spoke to Nitro.

She glared at him. "Let me go."

His eyes narrowed and he looked down to where she was trying to drag his arm away from her.

He shook his head, just once; then, instead of moving away, he scooted her closer to him so her thighs were touching his beneath the blankets.

He said, "Relax," before he went back to discussing possible ways for Nemesis to have gotten into her medical files.

Tangible pressure pushed against her, the stress of her circumstances like a vise, slowly squeezing the life out of her.

She hated this.

He put his finger over the mouthpiece. "Just to be clear— no one but you and your doctor know about this female problem?"

It wasn't a problem, except in Nemesis's warped mind, but she wasn't going to argue the point. If she opened her mouth, stuff would come out that she had to keep inside. Fear. Frustration. Anger—and this carrion guilt that was sucking her soul dry.

So she nodded her head.

"You didn't tell your brother?"

She actually laughed at the thought, the sound as mechanical as Nemesis's voice, and found she could speak after all. "No."

If Bella talked about her menses with her brother, they had a much different relationship than she had with Jake and somehow she just couldn't see it.

Joshua's eyes narrowed with concern and he studied her face as if reading sign. Jake had taught her to track when she was eight, but somehow she thought Joshua was probably better at it than she was.

Suddenly, he dipped his head and before she could protest, he kissed her full on the mouth. It lasted only a second, but the contact went all the way to her anxious soul.

"It's okay, honey." He spoke against her lips and then brushed his mouth against her temple before speaking into the phone again. "It has to be the medical records. Find out if they're online, or if he broke into the clinic to get them."

Nitro said something and Joshua agreed.

Lise tried to get up again. She couldn't give in to the need to lean on Joshua.

In one of his powerful, swift moves that were forever taking her by surprise, he pulled her right into his lap. Wrapping his free arm tightly around her, he continued the conversation with Nitro. Joshua's body language was clearer than a billboard. Stay put.

She didn't want to.

She struggled, but if his gentle cage had been difficult to get out of, this intimate hold was impossible to break.

Joshua finished his conversation and then flipped the phone shut before tossing it on the nightstand beside her cordless phone. He wrapped his other arm around her and rubbed her back with his big hand for a long time, saying nothing.

"I don't know what he means by me leading other women astray," she finally said when the silence had stretched beyond what she could stand.

"Shh . . . we'll talk about it in the morning."

"But—"

"We can't do anything about it tonight."

"What if—"

"Let it be." His tone was firm.

"I don't like you telling me to shut up."

Incredibly, a chuckle rumbled in his chest against her ear. "Heaven forbid, but do you really want to dissect it tonight, Lise?"

"Yes. I'm too wound up to sleep."

"Okay, what do *you* think he meant?"

She thought about it, but her train of thought derailed as Joshua's caresses strayed lower on each downward sweep until he was smoothing his hand over the upper curve of her bottom.

The more intimate stroking made her acutely aware of her physical surroundings.

Joshua wasn't wearing a shirt and her cheek was nestled against the silky curls on his chest. He smelled good, warm and musky, and she couldn't help nuzzling him just the tiniest bit to inhale more of his scent. His heartbeat was steady, but increasing, and the corded muscles of his thighs weren't the only hard things under her bottom.

Her muscles contracted in an involuntary Kegel and she grew warm and wet where the apex of her thighs fit over his growing erection.

Good night! How could she be so upset one minute and so turned on the next? *Was she depraved?* Her family was in danger and here she sat, wanting to devour the man under her. She could see herself doing it, kissing and nipping at his body in a way she'd never even fantasized doing with another man.

Remnants of the emotional storm buffeting her fought with the sensual images and she grasped at them to stop herself from doing something stupid. Like attacking him in a passionate frenzy.

"I did it," she whispered against his chest, not wanting to meet his eyes. "I put my family at risk. What am I going to do, Joshua?"

Chapter 8

Joshua tipped her chin up and forced her eyes to meet his stormy brown gaze. "You're going to trust me to protect them and you're going to stop believing that bullshit about it being your fault."

The anger in his voice startled her as much as his glare; his jaw looked hewn from granite.

"But it is. If it weren't for me, they wouldn't be forced into vacating their home. Jake's going to hate that. He's really attached to the ranch."

"He's more attached to my sister and niece."

"I know, but he's still going to be upset."

"This image you have of your brother as some emotional wimp really doesn't jive with the man he is, Lise."

She grimaced. "This is not about his ability to deal with the tough stuff that comes his way. It's about me being the conduit it comes by."

Joshua squeezed her, the comforting gesture at odds with the fury still glittering in his eyes. "*You're* not the one forcing him to go. That would be the lowlife scum stalking you."

"But that's the whole point." *Didn't he get it?* "He's stalking *me*!" Her lip quivered and she bit it.

Joshua pressed his forefinger against her bottom lip, gently disengaging it from her teeth. "He's crazy. You're not. Your supposed *sin* is all in his head. Look at the twisted way he views the breakup of your marriage. Your husband falls in love with another woman and ditches you and this Nemesis creep tries to make it out to be your fault. Whatever he's got against you is going to be just as distorted and removed from reality."

Her rational mind said she should believe him, but her heart was struggling with a debilitating fear that her family was going to be hurt. "What if something happens to Jake, or Bella, or *the baby?*" The last came out as an uncontrollable wail of distress.

She had to protect her niece.

"I won't let it." He cupped her face in both hands when she jerked her head in a negative. "*I won't.*" His fingers were warm against her shock-chilled skin, their bodies so close she could feel his heartbeat against her shoulder.

"You are not responsible for the actions of a madman." He spaced each word out as if it were its own sentence, driving the point with the intensity of his expression.

She opened her mouth to speak, but he shook his head and his lips pressed the words back into her throat. The intimate connection electrified her and excitement roared through her, destroying everything in its path.

Every inhibition was gone.

Every argument against making love to Joshua ceased to exist in her mind.

Nothing was left but a need to bond on the most intimate level possible with this man.

Joshua was done talking.

He stoked the fires he could feel ignite in Lise with all the expertise thirty-six years had given him.

He hated the way Lise was trying to take responsibility for being the victim of a piece of vermin like Nemesis. He was going to erase those thoughts from her mind if it took all night to do it.

His cock twitched under her thigh.

Okay, so his motives weren't totally altruistic, but she needed what he could give her, as much or more than she needed his protection. He might not be anyone's idea of a knight in shining armor, but he could do things for her that her Dudley Do-Right ex-husband hadn't been able to.

He was going to make her scream.

His name.

When she came.

He cupped her cheek, the skin soft like silk, and pulled his mouth from hers. "You're so beautiful."

Her eyes fluttered shut as a look of total sensual abandon came over her features. "Joshua . . ."

He had to taste her lips. Really taste them, not just kiss them. He closed the slight distance he'd created between their mouths. She parted her lips on a soft sigh and he licked them, tracing the pretty pink contours before slipping his tongue inside her mouth and savoring the sweetness waiting for him there.

He explored the silky, warm depths, teasing her with advance and retreat forays until her tongue followed his back into his mouth. He sucked on it and she moaned, an earthy sound that went straight to his dick. Her fingers dug into the muscles on his chest, her body tense with sexual energy.

He continued to throb under her bottom, but made no move to alleviate the torturous need.

He wanted to feel her hands on him, was aching for the release he knew she could give him. But even more than that, he wanted to touch and taste every square centimeter of her luscious body, saturating his senses with the very essence of her. He wanted to experience her as he had never experienced another woman.

Completely.

The way she was kissing him back told him she wanted to do the same thing, and the knowledge was about to send him over the edge of his control. Sliding his hand down her rib cage, he teased himself with the seductive warmth of her skin through the thin cotton. When he reached the hem, he let his hand rest there, testing his ability to wait to touch bare skin.

She groaned and wiggled and he felt the t-shirt slipping upward as she tugged at it. He could not deny the invitation, allowing his fingers to glide upward, this time under the loose shirt. Her lips and tongue went wild under his, devouring him with a passion that seared his insides with raw fire.

The petal-soft mound was tipped with a turgid, swollen peak and he teased it with his palm. Then, cupping her completely, he got drunk on the taste of her mouth and the perfect sensual weight filling his hand.

An animal-like sound vibrated through her mouth to his lips and he pulled away to look at her passion-contorted face. "You like this, don't you?"

"Oh, yes." Her lips were swollen and glistening from his kiss. "Can't you tell?" And she pressed her breast against the hand cupping her.

He squeezed, gently fondling her, his body trembling in a way he'd never admit to as she offered her ripe flesh so generously to him. "You're one amazing, sexy woman, Lise."

"Oh . . ." Emotion he wasn't ready for welled in her eyes.

He kissed her again, blocking it out with a deluge of desire stinging their bodies with each driving drop.

He played with her, clasping her nipple between his thumb and forefinger, rolling it, pinching it and then soothing it to almost softness before starting all over again. Her fingers locked in his hair, and she kissed him with the ferocity of a she-wolf claiming her mate.

The sounds she was making drove him crazy, but not as insane as the feel of her bottom squirming against his hard length. He wanted to be inside her. Only the minute he got sheathed in her tight wetness, he knew it would be over and he wasn't ready to give in to the all-out drive for fulfillment.

He switched his attention to her other breast, giving it the same teasing torture until she broke her mouth away from his and screamed, not in release, but with a surfeit of tension and pleasure. He felt pre-cum wet the tip of his penis in reaction.

"I want you!" She glared at him, her expression as primitive as he felt. "You're teasing me."

"I'm pleasuring you."

She turned in his lap, drawing a long groan from deep inside him, and straddled his legs. With ferocity he would never have thought she was capable of, she shoved him backward and followed him down, licking and kissing his chest, his neck, his shoulders, his face, inhaling against his skin.

His she-wolf imprinted her senses with him.

She sucked his male nipples, making him buck under her. "Take off your clothes, Lise."

She smiled, all teeth and no humor. "Why?"

He couldn't believe she'd asked that. "I need to be in you, you little witch."

"Maybe I want to play for a little while."

He flipped her under him with a move he'd learned in the Rangers and whipped her shirt off over her head to expose curves flushed with desire and swollen from his ministrations.

She covered them with her hands, hiding them from his view, an unmistakable look of challenge glinting gold in her hazel eyes.

"Uncover them," he growled.

"Make me," she taunted.

He did. Grabbing both her small hands in one of his and stretching them above her head. "There."

"What are you going to do now, look at them?" The

taunting quality of her voice demanded mastery, but his mind told him this woman would never be mastered.

"*Yes*," he hissed.

And he did. Stretching her arms lifted her curves so that the dark, engorged nipples were prominent and tantalizing. Her breasts rose and fell with each panting breath she took and she watched him watching her, her expression as mesmerized as he knew his was. Her nipples puckered more tightly and the scent of her arousal surrounded them both.

His nostrils flared, inhaling it as his cock grew even harder in his shorts.

He straddled her and rubbed it against her mound.

She arched under him. "Do it again!"

He did, but then he stopped moving.

She looked up at him, anticipation shimmering in her eyes. "Aren't you going to touch me?"

"When I'm ready." This mating dance was more exciting than anything he'd ever known.

"Be ready now," she practically yelled at him.

He shook his head, smiling. "I'm still looking."

"Are you afraid you can't do it right?" she goaded.

He sucked in air, spellbound by the passionate creature she'd become. She arched her back, the demand in her posture leaving no doubt what she wanted.

And he wanted to give it to her.

Reaching out, he lightly brushed the underside of each beautifully curved mound. She quivered.

He looked up at her face. "Is that what you wanted?"

Her eyelids had fallen to half mast, her mouth open slightly as she sucked in shallow breaths close together. "More."

Just one word and not even a demand, but he acceded. They both knew he would. He began to draw circle after circle on each soft mound, purposefully keeping his fingers away from her extremely tight, blood-engorged nipples.

"Joshua . . ." It was a breath of need and the primitive male animal in him rejoiced in the sound.

"What do you want?"

"You *know*."

"Say it."

She glared. "Do you think I won't?"

He just waited. How far would they push this sexual game before they both exploded?

"Touch my nipples. Suck them, Joshua. Please."

The *please* destroyed his control and he released her hands to close his over both proud breasts. He kneaded her flesh, drawing her nipples between his fingertips. Rolling them between his thumb and forefinger over and over again, he grew iron-hard and her succulent points became more and more engorged with blood until they were about twice their normal size.

She grabbed his head and pulled his mouth downward. He opened it over one hard peak and then sucked it inside. When he started to suckle, she lifted them both off the bed with the power of her response. They fought the sensual battle, him pleasuring her, her body demanding more and pleasuring him with each movement until he could barely breathe, his chest was so tight.

He reared back and yanked her flannel pants off, exposing the smooth flesh of her thighs and the golden curls of her mound. He buried his face in it, taking another deep breath of her scent, his body shuddering in reaction to it. He had to taste her.

Without warning, Joshua's tongue parted her nether lips and caressed her wet and throbbing clitoris. Every nerve ending in Lise's body went on red alert and she pushed herself against that marauding tongue, needing more. Always more.

He pushed her thighs wide, exposing her to him in a way

that made her totally vulnerable to his mouth . . . to his desires. But she didn't feel vulnerable. She felt powerful.

This was not the safe, accommodating sex she'd known in her marriage. This was wild, primal, and intense.

She exercised her power, closing her thighs, taunting him again with her refusal to be dominated. At the same time, she arched her pelvis upward, inviting him to try.

"Do you want my mouth on you?" he demanded in a guttural roar.

She gyrated her bottom, brushing his lips with the hair on her mound and then retreating. "What do you think?"

His answer was to slide his hands between her legs and push her thighs apart just as if she wasn't trying to hold them together as hard as she could. Exerting pressure until her muscles were stretched just this side of pain, he relentlessly opened her body completely to his questing mouth.

"Yes, Joshua, yes!" She loved the game, reveling in the ferocity of their lovemaking.

"Do you want to come, sweetheart?"

He didn't wait for the answer he had to know already, but started licking all over the sensitized heart of her again. She couldn't form a coherent thought after that, but she did make a lot of noise. Just none of it could be recognized as words.

He thrashed her swollen, slick flesh with his tongue until she was straining against his hold on her thighs and her fingers were buried in his hair, pulling and pushing from one second to another. Then he took her clitoris between his teeth and sucked.

She shattered into a million bitty pieces, her scream echoing in the room around them. More heated wetness gushed from the core of her and he lapped it up like it was irresistible nectar.

Bucking against the tongue that would not still, mini tremors shook her, keeping every muscle in her body tense. She began to sob. The pleasure was just too much.

"Joshua, please!"

He lifted his mouth and she collapsed back onto the bed. Her body trembled from head to foot. He kissed the inside of both of her thighs and then her damp curls. "Beautiful."

Her head went from side to side on the bed, no words making it past a throat raw from screaming. All of a sudden and without him touching her in any new way, her body bowed off the bed again, her muscles going into momentary rigor before she fell back in a heap of quivering limbs. Small, involuntary jerks shook her again and again.

"*What's happening to me?*" She'd never experienced anything like this.

"Aftershocks." He pressed another kiss to her thighs.

Moving upward, gentling the volcanic vibrations of her body with his mouth and the press of his body, he let her calm down until her breathing was almost back to normal and then he started it all over again. Touching her, kissing her, making her come. He brought her to two more climaxes in quick succession using both his fingers and his mouth.

The aftershocks went on and on until she lay, emotionally spent, physically exhausted, and unable to so much as lift her hand from where it again rested on his head.

Silent tears tracked down her cheeks. Her body did not visibly shudder with the earthquake going on inside her, but she'd cracked open a lost part of herself. She'd known this would happen and had been afraid of it, but she could not regret giving in to her need.

Joshua had given her something in return for her loss: knowledge of the wildly passionate woman living inside her. She was not a dud at sex, nor was this tumult of experience something she would ever diminish again as not worth pursuing.

He carefully disentangled her fingers from his hair and got up, stepping away from the bed. She was so sated, she couldn't work up any interest in where he'd gone, but when he came back, he was wearing a condom.

He slid a pillow under her hips and then rolled on top of her, lining his penis up with her very wet, very swollen womanhood. She locked her hands behind his neck and twisted her legs around his, opening herself to him as completely as it was possible for her to do. No more subterfuge, no more she-wolf games pretending she wanted to hold anything back from him.

He hooked her knees over his forearms so that she was spread even wider, ready to receive him.

"Lise?" She saw the question in his eyes and she gave him the only answer possible at that moment.

"Yes, please, yes."

He slowly pushed inside. Despite her slick wetness, her body had trouble stretching to accommodate him. Rocking her hips and thrusting his pelvis in rhythm, he eventually achieved total penetration.

When his pelvis met hers, she felt stretched almost beyond capacity, pushed to the limits of her endurance, and she could only be grateful she was so slick with her own arousal. No way would it have worked otherwise.

"You're big."

He laughed. "Is that a problem?"

"I don't think so."

Lise didn't sound too sure of herself, and Joshua wanted to laugh again. She'd gone from fierce to uncertain in the space of a heartbeat.

He pulled out of her clinging heat and thrust into her, causing her to gasp and her eyes to fly wide. She felt so damn good, better than he'd fantasized, and that should have been impossible.

He smiled a predator's smile and met her eyes. "We fit."

She licked her lips. "Yes, we do."

She turned her face into his chest and bit him, not hard, but his precious she-wolf was leaving her mark.

His jaw locked and he kissed her. Hard. She kissed him back and he could feel the sexual tension building in her again.

Amazing.

He started moving in an age-old rhythm he made uniquely theirs. She thrust up against him, her inner heat clasping him so tight; each tiny movement made his head feel like it was coming off. He felt himself losing control, her renewed arousal sending him straight into oblivion, and he pistoned against her, not even sure if he could hold back until she came again.

He felt his body going rigid, the pressure building at the base of his erection, and then he was exploding with nuclear proportions, and incredibly she was crying out with him, straining her body toward his. She bit him again, right above his left nipple, and it was a lot harder than the first time.

He reveled in the primitive mating act and felt himself spurt again inside her. His climax lasted longer than any he'd ever known, but they both collapsed at the same time.

He kissed her, savoring the sweet softness of her lips. "Damn, Lise, you're good."

"I'd say we're good together." She turned her face into his neck, but he could feel the smile on her lips. "I didn't get to touch you, though."

She said it like a question and he grinned as well, feeling way too good for a hardened mercenary. "I only had one condom."

"Oh."

He could tell she still didn't understand.

"If you'd touched me, I would have lost control too soon. I wanted it to last."

"I guess we'd better invest in a big supply then, because next time, *I want to touch*." She gave a huge yawn. "I'm sleepy."

"I'd better move before I crush you." Or got excited again.

"But this feels good."

It did. Too good, but they couldn't make love again and if he stayed on top of her, that's what he'd want to do. Besides, he had to take care of the condom.

He forced himself to get up, go to the bathroom, and clean up before he climbed back into bed. He didn't have to pull her into him. She sought out the warmth of his body the second he was horizontal.

He hugged her.

"That was incredible," she whispered against his chest and then kissed where she'd bitten him. "I hurt you—I'm sorry."

"It didn't hurt, little she-wolf. I liked it."

"I did, too."

Lise woke up throbbing from another erotic dream and rolled onto her back . . . or tried to, but there was a big, warm body that was where hers was trying to go.

It all came back.

The phone call from Nemesis in the middle of the night. Joshua and her making love.

The feeling of both losing and gaining something in herself.

Her body tingled from remembered pleasure, which was not to say that waking up beside one-hundred-and-ninety pounds of masculine perfection wasn't pretty pleasant in itself. It was—oh my, yes, it was.

"Morning, Lise." His voice rumbled in her ear.

She hugged the intimacy of waking up beside him tightly to her heart. "How'd you know I was awake?" She hadn't moved the tiniest bit since trying to turn onto her back.

"You're breathing like a woman who woke up remembering what we did last night."

Heat started at her toes and worked its way up her body. "I did."

That husky voice, sounding all sexy and sated, was *hers*. Incredible.

She'd never once in all her life sounded so much like a sex-pot. She liked it. She liked knowing she could match Joshua's primitive passion as well. Another man would have made her feel awkward about the way she'd behaved the night before, but not Joshua. Of course, another man would not have engendered that response.

Only this one. "Last night was unbelievable."

He moved beside her, letting her body settle back, and he leaned above her on his elbow. "Yes, it was."

His dark brown eyes shimmered with unnamable emotion as he leaned over to kiss her, his mouth making promises she tried very hard to remember were nothing more than physical. No matter how it felt.

He started nuzzling his way down her neck, his kisses making her shiver. "I've never had it so good."

That shouldn't be possible. She knew he'd had a lot more women than she'd had men. His oodles to her two weren't even sporting odds, but she believed him. Because what had happened between the two of them had been something very special.

"I guess you know I haven't, either."

His eyes questioned her. "Never?"

"I told you my marriage wasn't passionate."

"Were you married to a eunuch? Lady, you are hotter than an erupting volcano when you make love."

She laughed, feeling free and full of life. "No, just a man who made a better friend than a husband. It's too bad neither of us realized that when we were eighteen."

"None of us make the best decisions when we're that young."

She remembered him saying he'd entered the army when he was eighteen. Did he regret it? "Why did you go in the army so early?"

"I wanted to be a soldier. My dad was an Army Ranger. He died on assignment when I was four, but I can still remember him. He was a big man, strong and quiet. As much as Lee always treated me like his own, a part of me knew I wasn't."

"So you followed in your real dad's footsteps?"

"Joining the Rangers made me feel like I had part of him to carry on. Wherever he was, I wanted him to be proud of me."

"I bet both your mom and your stepdad already were."

"Yeah, they were great parents, but there was something about me that didn't fit. I always figured it was whatever I got from my dad."

She didn't doubt it. Joshua was a born warrior and there weren't too many of those around. If his dad had been Special Forces, chances were he'd have been one of the few, too.

"I'm not so sure Mom and Lee are all that proud now. I operate in a murky world."

She didn't believe his family could be disappointed in him and told him so. Murky world or not, he was a man of absolute integrity, if a law unto himself.

He just shook his head. "Don't romanticize me, Lise. You'll end up getting hurt."

He was probably right, at least about her ending up hurt, but she didn't think she was romanticizing him. He was the material modern-day heroes were made of, even if he never wanted to admit it.

He pressed the lower part of his body against her hip and she felt his morning erection . . . or was it from waking next to her? She chose to believe the latter.

She teased him, "I thought you said no sex on the job."

"That doesn't apply."

"Because I'm not paying you?" Was Bella's take on their relationship the reason Joshua had let his sexual hunger slip its leash?

"Because it's more than sex, and living with you and not making love to you ceased to be an option when you responded to my kiss last night." Then he kissed her again.

Her heart constricted in her chest and she tried not to read more into that statement than he'd meant, but it went clear to her toes, making them curl. He wasn't promising her a future, but he was giving her more than his body. Which she had a hunch was a lot more than he'd given another woman in a very long time.

It was enough.

She reached down and touched his thigh, wondering if she were bold enough to touch his penis. The she-wolf of the night before was lurking below her happy, morning-after exterior. But they couldn't make love and she didn't know if he would let her do what she wanted to do.

Heck, she didn't know if she could do it well enough for him to get anything out of it. She'd never tried it before, had never wanted to, but she'd read things.

Joshua stopped kissing her when she touched him and he seemed to be holding his breath. She explored the muscular contours of his thighs, venturing very close to his masculine arousal, but not quite touching it.

"Put your hand on it. *Please.*"

Her head came up at the guttural sound of his voice.

He looked like he was in pain. "Touch it, Lise."

She obeyed the need in his voice, letting her fingers trespass onto his swollen flesh. It bobbed in her hand, a pulsing beat pounding against her fingers.

She squeezed experimentally.

He groaned, loud. "You're killing me."

"No, I'm not. I'm pleasuring you," she said, using his answer of the night before when she'd complained about him teasing her.

"Yes, you are." His pelvis tilted up, to push more of him against her hand. "Your touch is pure pleasure."

The velvety hardness slid against her fingers, growing more steel-like with each caress. Panting, he put his hand over hers, increasing the pressure and the pace. She was happy to oblige his silent demand for more, and there was something very sensual about letting him show her what he needed.

It was so honest. So real. No hidden fumbling in the dark.

But the rest of his body beckoned and she hoped he would indulge her. "I want to make you come, but first I want to touch all of you."

His erection throbbed in response to her words.

"Will you let me?"

"Yes," he ground out from between teeth in a face clenched with desire.

Dropping his hand away, he settled on his back, leaving himself completely open to her desire. His eyes invited her with dark warmth and she liked it. Unlike the night before, when making love had been a battle between a wolf and his mate, one in which they were both ultimate winners, this morning he was removing boundaries and letting her lay claim to whatever territory she wanted.

She got up on her knees and pulled the sheet back so she could just look.

And what a body to stare at.

Every single one of his muscles was perfectly sculpted and defined. He had scars, too, and the lurking she-wolf, or maybe it was just the primal woman in her . . . liked the marks that showed he was a warrior. Although she wished he'd never had to experience the pain that would have accompanied each mark on his gorgeous body, they were infinitely exciting to her.

She slid down to his feet, intent on truly touching him everywhere. Pleasure coursed from her fingertips to all sorts of interesting places in her own body as she explored each nook and crevice of bronzed skin over sculpted muscle.

He moaned and moved and encouraged her with a litany of praise that excited her as much as touching him did.

She purposefully left his hard length for last because she didn't want just to touch . . . she wanted to taste like he had.

When she reached his face, she traced it with her eyes closed, memorizing his features with her fingertips, and then she kissed him.

He growled something low in his throat when her lips touched his, and suddenly she found herself flat on her back with almost two hundred pounds of vibrating male animal above her.

Chapter 9

His mouth devoured hers as his body caressed her from chest to ankle. Her breasts rubbed against the hair on his chest, and nipples tenderized from a night of lovemaking sat up and took notice. It felt so good she squirmed against him to increase the stimulation. Their legs tangled, his hairy thighs rubbing against smooth flesh that prickled with sensation.

Then he started his own exploration and it felt so good, she almost forgot what she'd wanted to do.

Almost, but not quite.

This morning, she was determined to give, not just take.

Not that he'd complained last night, but he'd given her more pleasure than any body should be able to handle and she was determined to give it back. In spades.

"Joshua . . ."

He looked up from kissing her, his eyes wild. "What?"

"You said *I* could taste *you*."

The feral quality that came over his expression shook her even as it provoked an untamed hunger for him deep inside her.

"You did taste me."

"I meant here." She pushed up with her pelvis to caress the hardness against her.

"Are you sure you want to?" he asked in a rasping voice while his body vibrated above her.

"Yes."

"Not all women like it."

"I will." With him. "Are you afraid I won't do it right?" She wasn't too sure herself. "I can't do that thing I've read about where women take men all the way into their mouths. Even if I could, I don't think it would be possible with you."

He laughed, the sound harsh and amused at the same time. "The mere idea of your tongue even touching my cock has me ready to come. *I guarantee you do not need to deep throat me to satisfy me.*"

Deep throat. It sounded like some kind of porn term, but it described exactly what she was talking about, what she'd heard men liked. "Mike—"

"Is not in this bed with us and never will be," Joshua said fiercely. "I don't care what good old Dudley liked—we're talking about me, and I get turned on by anything my little she-wolf is willing to do."

She had been going to say that Mike had never asked for it and she'd never offered, so it would be her first time, but she realized Joshua really didn't want to hear about her sexual past. He was wholly consumed with the present.

"I want to taste you."

He shuddered, the well-defined muscles of his body going rigid. "I would kill to feel your mouth on me."

He did that flip thing he'd done the night before, only this time she ended up on top. She landed against him with a thud and air rushed out of both of them with an *oomph.*

"You don't have to do any killing. Just lay back and let me touch you," she said when she got her breath back.

"Yes."

She crawled off of him and knelt beside him again, her own body throbbing at the prospect of what she was going to do.

His erection jerked as she looked at it, a small drop of pearly moisture forming on the tip.

He really did want her to taste him.

She smiled, reached out, and ran her hand up and down the satin-like hardness. "Your skin is smooth here, soft to the touch, but about as yielding as a tire iron."

Lambent sensuality looked back at her. "Whereas you're soft all over."

The peaks of her breasts were puckered and tight in her excitement. "Maybe not *everywhere*."

His gaze slid down the column of her throat to her chest with tactile intensity and her skin goose-bumped just as if he'd touched her.

An expression of satisfaction crossed his features. "Maybe not those beautiful little raspberries, but even they're softer than my dick right now."

Her gaze settled on his hard-on. Veins visibly throbbed beneath skin that had gone dark plum from the blood pulsing through it. *Good night!* She figured even her bones were softer than that particular part of his anatomy at the moment.

Her nipples throbbed in response to his arousal and an image formed in her head worthy of a wolf's mate, but would he like it? She'd bet her overdue advance check he *would*.

Her wolf had no inhibitions she could discern.

Licking suddenly dry lips, she tried to swallow moisture into a parched throat. "I'm going to touch you."

"I thought you wanted to taste me."

"I do, but first I want to touch you."

"You already have."

"I mean with my breasts." Her voice choked off and she nodded toward his erection. "There," she whispered past an excitement-clenched throat.

"Are you trying to kill me?" he asked in an all-too-serious tone. "Because I'm in mortal danger of exploding from excitement."

"Is it too much for the big, bad wolf?" Cryin' out loud. She'd never been the taunting, teasing type, but she couldn't seem to help herself with him. "You're going to explode, all right, but I promise you'll like it."

His laughter sounded more strangled than amused. "It damn well might be too much. If you make me come before you get me in your mouth, don't blame me."

Feminine power thrummed through her. "You're a big boy. You can handle it." She arranged herself in a straddle position over his legs.

"Don't be so sure about that, honey. What you want to do plays heavily in one of my favorite wet dreams about you."

"You don't have wet dreams about me." Okay, so he'd said he dreamt about her, but she couldn't believe he came in his sleep like a horny teenager.

His dark brows rose and he reached around her to caress her bottom with his callused hands. "I don't?"

She stilled above him, holding onto his upper thighs to keep her balance. "You're thirty-six years old and sexually active. You don't have wet dreams."

"I'll admit they come few and far between for me any-more." He grimaced. "At least they did until this past year."

"But . . ."

"I haven't had a woman since we kissed at the baby's christening, and I'd been on a job for several months before that. Those dreams and my fist have given me my only sexual relief for longer than I care to think about."

For a man like Joshua, that was a lifetime. "I don't believe you."

His eyes challenged her to change her mind and she did.

"Why?" she demanded.

"I didn't want anyone else."

"But I told you I wasn't interested in a relationship."

"A man's libido is not controlled by logic, honey, or haven't you figured that out yet? Besides, I had hopes I could convince you that mind-blowing sex isn't exactly a relationship and get around that particular issue."

He was right—sex wasn't a relationship, and she'd be a smart woman to remember that. But all she wanted to remember right now was the smell, the taste, and the texture of his skin.

His thighs flexed and she clamped hers against them. "I wish I could ride you right now."

His eyes shot sensual sparks at her. "I do, too, but as combustible as we are . . ." He paused while one hand curved around to settle over her womb, his thumb brushing the sensitive hair at the top of her mound. "I'd make you pregnant for sure."

She wondered if he had any idea how profound it felt, not to mention sexy, to have his hand against the part of her created to cradle life.

His eyes were touching her as intimately as his hand. "Too bad mercs make such poor fathers."

She didn't say anything to that—she couldn't.

Was he saying he was tempted by the prospect?

She didn't want to read too much into casually uttered words during loveplay, but she had a blindingly sweet image of herself holding Joshua's baby. It shouldn't fit with the wild feelings of sexual excitement coursing through her, but it did. And it made her entire body tighten with another level of stimulation.

Unable to wait any longer, she leaned forward and rubbed one taut peak up and down the length of his turgid and pulsing flesh.

It felt so good, she moaned.

So did he, only his sounded more like a growl.

Then she did the same thing with her other puckered nipple, feeling the contact sting through her in a direct line from the tip of her breast to the inner core of her.

"I like this," she said on a heavy sigh.

"I love it."

She smiled and did it again. It felt even better than the first time, but she wanted more control. She wanted to surround him. She pressed her breasts together on either side of his stiff and throbbing shaft.

He surged upward, saying something that both shocked and excited her unbearably.

"Is it really called that?" she asked, just before opening her mouth to kiss the tip of his broad head on her next downward stroke.

"Yessss . . ." he hissed. "Oh, hell, baby, do it again!"

She did, this time letting her tongue swirl around his tip. His taste was unlike any other taste she'd known. Salty like tears, but sweet, too. His fingers clamped onto her nipples, fondling them as she stroked him with the tunnel she'd made with her breasts; she couldn't help rubbing herself against his thighs where she straddled him.

Each time his head came into contact with her mouth, she increased the length of time she spent licking him and he moaned, moving his body with increasing urgency.

She wanted to satisfy that need.

She kissed him, her slightly parted lips lingering on the blunt tip of his manhood before she released her breasts and gently brushed his hands away so she could sit up. His fingers were reluctant to release her and made the letting-go another rousing caress.

She trembled and closed both hands around his big sex. Then she put her mouth over his head, stretching her lips wide to accommodate him. She savored him with her hungry mouth, stopping in startled delight when more salty sweetness touched her tongue.

"Don't stop. Lise!"

She delighted in the unique flavors filling her mouth and the sense of having control over such a masculine man. For at that moment the predator wolf was completely at the mercy of the carnal woman in her.

She gently squeezed his shaft and licked all around his broad head.

"Suck it, *Lise!*"

She teased him with a couple more swirls of her tongue before moving her mouth as far down on him as she could go, then sucking. He surged up toward her, gagging her when he hit the back of her throat, but instead of bothering her, she feasted on the proof of her ability to drive him out of control. She pulled back a little and he cried out hoarsely.

She experimented with going down again and then pulling back. He loved it, going wild beneath her, almost dislodging her with his excited movements. She moved her hands in a sort of tandem with her head's up-and-down motion.

She wasn't too smooth at it, being all too new to this sort of thing, but he didn't seem to mind.

His fingers dug into her hair. "I'm going to come."

He tried to pull her head away, but she wanted it all. He'd called her his she-wolf and she was, for that moment in time, his sexual mate, determined to match him in every way. She increased the movement of her mouth and hands, resisting the tug of his fingers in her hair.

"*I mean it.*"

She wondered at the desperation in his voice. Didn't he understand this was exactly what she wanted? What she needed?

She sucked harder, hollowing her cheeks around his throbbing erection.

He gave a loud shout and flooded her with himself.

Deep emotion welled inside her, eclipsing her physical and mental enjoyment in his climax even as she continued to pleasure him with her mouth, though gently now. Feelings that were a hot, deep crimson expression of the cool, pale pink love she'd had for her ex-husband surged through her.

She physically shook with the enormity of her discovery.
She loved him.
Desperately.
Passionately.
And irrevocably.

He would not thank her for saying so. He'd done nothing, said nothing, to indicate he saw their relationship as anything more than transient and physical. In fact, he'd implied it wasn't a relationship at all.

It was fantastic sex.

Yet acknowledging the vibrancy of an emotion she'd thought never to feel again gave her a deep need to express it.

And there was only one way open to her.

The physical, through the very sex he said he wanted from her. She could love him with her body.

Following the example he'd set the night before, she continued to stimulate him with her mouth.

He jerked and bowed under her, grunting and shouting in turn until he stopped surging upward into her mouth and pulled her head away from him. She looked up at him, hoping her newfound love did not glow in her eyes, but helpless to stop herself from wallowing in the sight of him in the aftermath of his pleasure.

He tugged her up beside him, his hands insistent until she was full against his body. He panted, his body still rigid even after his release, and his hold on her was unmistakably possessive.

His breathing slowly went back to normal, and then he leaned above her, his dark gaze devouring her. "Thank you."

Such tame words for her wolf, especially when the look in his eyes was more carnal than grateful.

"You're welcome." She stretched her jaw.

He rubbed her cheeks with his thumbs. "Sore?"

"You're awfully big," she said bluntly.

"I'm sorry." Despite the massage he tenderly gave her

jaw, he didn't sound all that sorry. "I didn't want to hurt you."

That sounded sincere.

She smiled. "You didn't." Nuzzling into him, she pressed her body as close as she could get. "I could have stopped if I'd wanted to."

"Are you sure about that?"

Remembering how he'd tried to stop from coming in her mouth, she nodded.

He'd been wild, but he would never force her to do anything she didn't want to. She began to understand the rejection he'd given her that night in Texas. He really didn't want anything that wasn't freely given.

He was too much a man to settle for grudging acceptance of his flesh.

His hand slid down to her mound and his fingers trespassed on the slick, swollen folds of her feminine core.

She vibrated with the power of her reaction to his touch.

"Your turn," he growled.

Two fingers slid inside her at the same time his mouth covered one taut, aching peak. He sucked and she cried out in pleasure as he began to make love to her with his hand in a way that emulated the rhythm of full intercourse.

In seconds, she was squirming, straining, begging for him to finish it, and he did. Starbursts went off inside her with audible force, and she had to bite her lips shut to stop from crying out her newly discovered love.

Lise spent the morning, or what was left of it after she and Joshua showered together, writing on the cushy, overstuffed sofa. The rocking chair was too hard. She ached in places she hadn't even felt in two years that she could never remember exercising to the point of soreness.

This time when Joshua called her to lunch, she put her Dana down and went.

Gingerly sliding into one of the hard kitchen chairs, she looked around. "Where's Hotwire? I thought I heard him earlier."

Joshua put a bowl of steaming soup in front of her and a plate of crackers with cheese in the center of the table. "He was. He left a couple of minutes ago."

Spreading her napkin over her lap, she asked, "Why didn't he stay for lunch?"

"He had stuff to do."

"Oh." She shifted in her chair, looking for a comfortable position to sit on the wooden seat. "Any news?"

"Nitro landed in Austin thirty minutes ago and headed straight for the ranch with a rental car."

Which meant they'd be hearing from Jake shortly. He wasn't going to take leaving the ranch with equanimity. If nothing else, he'd be even more convinced Lise needed to get out of Seattle.

She took a bite of soup and realized immediately it wasn't canned. "This is homemade."

Joshua shrugged. "I don't like prepackaged foods. It's a leftover attitude from all those packages of instant soup I was forced to consume on field marches in the army."

She smiled, shifting slightly again. "Makes sense."

"Lise, are you sore?"

She reached for a piece of cheese and cracker. "What makes you ask?"

"You look like you're sitting on an unhappy porcupine."

She felt her cheeks heat. "Oh."

She hadn't meant to be obvious, and she was sure his other sexual partners didn't get incapacitated like this after a single night and morning of lovemaking.

"So, are you?"

Examining her soup for recognizable ingredients suddenly became a very important pastime. "Maybe."

She wasn't looking at him, but she heard him get up and leave the kitchen. Where had he gone?

It was really silly to be so bothered about telling him she was sore. After all, he had a big part of the responsibility. *Big* being the operative word, but it wasn't just his size. It was submitting her muscles to an athletic workout they'd never seen equaled, even in her earliest days of marriage.

When he walked back into the kitchen she was totally unprepared when he picked her right up out of her chair. "*What are you doing?*"

He dropped a fluffy throw pillow from her bed on the wooden chair and then gently set her back down. "Making you more comfortable."

"I would have been fine," she protested.

His expression said, *Yeah, whatever,* and she subsided. It was a lot more comfortable on the pillow.

She forced herself to say, "Thank you."

Sitting back down, he shrugged.

They ate in silence for several minutes while her mind played over why she'd gotten sore, how much she'd like to do it again, and how incredibly exciting she'd found it to taste him. Images of him lying on his back, stretched out for her pleasure, inundated her mind and made her thigh muscles quiver.

Not a good direction for her thoughts to go.

"Did Hotwire find anything out?" Joshua had told her the other man would be researching likely suspects via the computer.

"A couple of things."

"That's great. What are they?"

"One, he was able to back-trace the e-mails." Joshua didn't sound all that excited by that piece of luck.

"Isn't that good news?" she asked as she carefully stacked a piece of cheese on a cracker and then popped it into her mouth, all the while managing to avoid Joshua's gaze.

Maybe if she didn't look at him, her imagination would behave.

"They're all written from different Internet access computers in libraries within an hour's drive of Seattle."

"Don't people have to sign in with their library cards to use the Internet computers?"

"Yes, but he used other people's names and their library card numbers."

"Are you sure?"

"Yes. One of them was an eighty-year-old woman, another a ten-year-old boy. We're fairly sure Nemesis is male and grown up."

She twisted her mouth at his gentle sarcasm. "How did he get them?"

"We're not sure. He could have hacked into a database, or done something as simple as wait for library patrons to leave their cards lying around while they looked for books or worked on the computer."

Lise sighed. "He's smart."

"But not smart enough." Joshua's voice promised retribution to Nemesis when they found him.

She believed that voice because as smart as Nemesis was, she was absolutely convinced he was no match for Joshua and his friends.

"Don't worry about it. We'll catch him."

"I'm not."

"I mean it, Lise. You aren't alone anymore."

Her head came up at that and she met his eyes, which had the effect she'd known it would, and she started melting in interesting places that had nothing to do with the conversation at hand. "I know that. I trust you to deal with this."

And he'd probably never know just how hard it had been to put that trust in him and relinquish control of her life in any way, but she didn't regret it.

Joshua made a sound of irritation, his eyes narrowed. "Then what's the problem?"

His dark gaze probed her features as if he were trying to see into her head, or maybe even as deep as her soul.

"Nothing is wrong."

"Are you embarrassed?"

"Not exactly." Although she realized that definitely was playing a part in her feelings at the moment.

She was amazed by the side of herself she'd discovered the night before and that morning, but self-conscious about it as well. The way she and Joshua had made love had gone against all the good-girl teaching she'd received in the small Texas town of her birth.

"What exactly are you?"

Hot and bothered. Sore. In love.

And that one was just downright scary.

"Out of my depth, I guess," she admitted ruefully, thinking a twenty-eight-year-old woman with a successful career should not be so bound by the conventional ideas of her youth. "I'm not used to the sex thing."

His lips tilted, but not in a full-blown smile. He was back in semimercenary mode. "The sex thing?"

"You know what I mean." And she hoped he realized she wasn't going to thank him if he tried to make her spell it out.

"Yeah, I do. You're really good at *the sex thing*. You have nothing to be embarrassed about."

Right, like that was the one thing she'd be worried about. If she'd done it right. Cryin' out loud, even she was savvy enough to figure out that a man shouting and going rigid as a fireman's pole when he came meant she'd done it right.

"That's not the problem."

"Then what is?"

"*It's* nothing."

"Something is making you reluctant to meet my eyes. I don't like that, so I want you to tell me what the issue is."

"I like sucking you," she admitted, revealing the thing that had surprised her the most, even if it was only a tiny portion of her behavior that so unsettled her. "A lot."

His face clenched and his body jerked. "Damn, sweetheart, you shouldn't say stuff like that if you want to get any work done today."

"I'm sorry."

He shook his head and laughed. "Don't apologize. I'm glad you like going down on me, but I don't understand why you're uncomfortable about that."

"I think maybe I like it too much." Remembering how she'd knelt in front of him in the shower and brought him to another climax with her mouth confirmed the niggling concern.

She'd loved it. And she would have done it again if he'd asked, even though her jaw had felt stretched afterward.

"That's not a problem for me."

The way he said it made her thighs clench.

"Does it make you feel better to know I like putting my mouth on you, too? I love the way you taste, especially after you climax."

She rolled her eyes. "Men are *supposed* to like sex."

He stared at her like she'd gone nuts. "So are women."

"I didn't before."

"You didn't like sex? At all?"

"It wasn't quite *that* bad, but I sure didn't understand what all the fuss was about. I feel things with you, sexual urges I've never had before." Like *wanting* to take him into her mouth, *wanting* to taste him come.

It probably had something to do with the intensity of her emotional feelings about him that outstripped anything she'd felt in that regard as well, but that wasn't an area she was going to explore with him right now. If ever.

She was vulnerable enough to this soldier of fortune who

lived his life job to job without a plan for the future that included her.

Predatory satisfaction gleamed back at her, but then, like the turning of a dimmer switch, his face lost all expression. "Are you bothered because you have those feelings with a man like me?"

"What do you mean, a man like you?"

"A mercenary."

Chapter 10

Were all men this dense, or was it just the really primitive ones? It didn't really matter how many other men might make such a mistake, but the fact that Joshua had done so offended her no end.

"Of course not. I can't believe you'd accuse me of something so shallow. Just what have I done to make you think I would ever react that way?"

He put his hands up, like he was surrendering, when she knew he didn't even have the word in his vocabulary.

"Don't bite my head off. It was a legitimate question." But his stoic expression softened the tiniest bit.

"Not in my book."

"Speaking of your book, how is it coming along?"

Which meant talk about her unexpected issues with her newfound sensuality was over. She hoped.

"I'm having a hard time getting focused today."

Which was another thing she was finding it difficult to adjust to. She was used to being able to tune out the world when she worked, but she found it almost impossible to tune him out completely—or the memories of their shared passion.

"I'm sorry about that. Nemesis has wreaked a lot of mischief in your life, hasn't he?"

"Now that you're here, dismissing him from my mind is pretty easy." She made herself another cracker snack. "I feel safe."

"Good, but it's obvious he's still impacting you."

"Wondering if I'm the original fallen woman is impacting me a whole lot more than thinking about some loser who gets his kicks out of terrorizing me."

"*You are not a fallen woman.* Hell, that's not even a condition women can aspire to anymore."

Trust Joshua to see it as an aspiration. She almost smiled. "The only other man I've ever made love with is my ex-husband."

"Does that bother you?"

"No. Not really. I don't know," she finally admitted.

"Is it having sex with a man you don't love or one you're not married to that bothers you?"

She did love him, but that wasn't the point. "I never expected to have an affair."

She'd never wanted to and she honestly didn't know how she felt about being involved in one now. Everything was such a jumble inside of her, but one truth emerged amidst the chaos.

"I don't want to stop making love with you. To be honest, I don't think I could."

"I'm glad, because I'd hate to have to try."

She did smile then, relieved and happy that the compulsion was mutual. "Do you think Bella likes doing that kind of thing to Jake?" she asked curiously. "You know, making love to him with her mouth?"

It would help if she had some close girlfriends she could ask this sort of thing, but she lived so much of her life inside her books; she had few outside friendships, none close enough for the type of discussion she was having with Joshua.

He actually blanched. "That is not something I want to contemplate about my baby sister."

"See?" She glared at him, feeling vulnerable all over again. "Even *you* think it's depraved behavior."

"*Even me?*"

"You know what I mean. No one could accuse you of being inhibited."

"I wouldn't have accused you of it last night, either."

That did not make her feel any better and she said so.

He sighed with exasperation. "There's nothing depraved about you liking taking me in your mouth, but a man does not want to think of his sister kissing with her tongue, much less having sex with her husband, *in any way.*"

"Oh." Duh. She'd been thinking in the abstract, or she never would have asked the question to begin with.

She didn't really want to know that kind of stuff about Jake, either.

"But if it will make you feel better, I'd say it's a safe bet Jake and Bella enjoy a complete and varied sex life."

"You think so?"

"Yeah, I think so." He shook his head. "I can't believe we're having this conversation. You do realize it is the twenty-first century don't you?"

"Yes, and my high school sex education teacher in Canyon Rock, Texas, called a penis a *manhood* and a woman's vagina her *womanhood*. As far as she was concerned, a woman's clitoris didn't even exist."

"You are ten years out of high school, Lise."

"Well, yes, but this is the first time since then that I've been in a position to question my own sexual attitudes." Sex with Mike had never been even borderline adventurous.

Joshua reached out and ran his fingertip along the V-neckline of the light cotton sweater she'd thrown on after their shower earlier. "You've got damn fine sexual instincts, I'd say."

Her skin tingled from his touch, and she could hear her own heartbeat in her ears.

She'd been talking about attitudes, not instincts, but his

words of praise made her feel proud all the same. Despite her misgivings, she liked knowing he was so pleased with her sexuality. After her divorce, there had been times she'd wondered if she wasn't something of a sexual amoeba.

She didn't feel that way now.

Embarrassed or not, wholly comfortable with the situation or not, she felt fully alive and functioning and she liked it.

His fingertip dipped into the valley between her breasts, under her sweater. "You're a perfect sexual partner for me and that's all that really matters, isn't it?"

A laugh burst out of her and she pulled back from that disturbing caress with a smile. "Has anyone ever told you that you can be awfully arrogant?"

"No."

It took her a second, but she realized he was serious.

She just stared at him for something like five full seconds. "Cryin' out loud, Joshua, are the people around you blind?"

"No. They've seen what I can do. So have you." And from the look in his eyes, he was definitely referring to the sex thing.

She shook her head at his blatant confidence.

"I suppose they've never mentioned that you're as bossy as a rooster in the henhouse, either?" she asked, thinking how naturally he'd taken the details of her life over.

"I've never had anyone compare me to a rooster before— now, a *cock* is a different matter." He winked at her.

She picked up one of the crackers and tossed it at him.

He caught it midair and popped it in his mouth, an expression on his face that made her want to fly across the table and jump his bones.

She forced herself to take a spoonful of soup instead. The pillow under her bottom notwithstanding, she was too achy to contemplate anything like that at the moment.

"So, did Hotwire get a chance to research any of the suspects?"

"Yeah, but there's another list I need from you."

"Who? My Sunday School class in third grade?" He'd asked about pretty much everyone else the day before.

"The people you've interviewed for your books."

That made sense, though she couldn't imagine any of them stalking her. Of course, a year ago she wouldn't have been able to imagine anyone stalking her at all. "Okay. I'll put it together after lunch."

"I'm giving you a massage after lunch, then you are taking a nap. You can put it together after you're rested."

"Bossy rooster," she accused while wondering what sort of massage he meant.

He just laughed and winked. "You bring it out in me."

She rolled her eyes. "I'm so not buying that."

Joshua shrugged.

"So what *did* Hotwire find?"

"One of the men who skipped parole has no computer experience in his background and the other has been picked up. He was in Louisiana peddling crack in the District in New Orleans."

"The other guy could have studied computers in prison."

"He didn't—not formally, anyway."

She didn't ask how he was so sure about that. She got the distinct impression that Hotwire knew how to access files denied to most people. "Maybe he played with computers in his spare time. Prisons have a lot of options like that for inmates nowadays."

Joshua looked supremely unconvinced. "It would take a lot more than a casual acquaintance with computers to do the things Nemesis has done."

"You mean the hacking?"

"And the modifications to his espionage equipment. That

could only be done by someone with a strong understanding of electronics."

She sighed. "So, what you're saying is that he's not my stalker?"

"That's my gut feeling."

"What about the other possible prospects?"

"Strikeouts. Every one of them lives too far away from both Texas and Seattle to have done the things Nemesis has done without taking some significant time off from their jobs."

"And none of them have."

"Right."

She stood up and started clearing the table for something to do. "Where do we go from here?"

"We keep digging."

"What can I do?"

"Make that list of people you've interviewed and I'd like to have a look at the rest of your reader letters, too."

She stopped halfway to the sink. "But why? They're from people who *like* my books."

"Lise, you're not very social. Even back in Canyon Rock you spent most of your time either with Jake and Bella or alone in your apartment."

She had a few friends, but for the most part, he was right. "And?"

"Nemesis accused you of leading other women astray."

"He's nuts."

"Absolutely, but the point is, he has to have a reason, no matter how obscure, for believing that. The only possible source Hotwire, Nitro, and I can come up with is your books."

It made sense and was a conclusion she'd come to as well. "I still don't understand how reading my fan mail is going to help find someone who hates me enough to stalk me."

Joshua shrugged. "It's worth a try."

"Okay. Do you need me to get them for you?"

"They're in the same file drawer as the other folder was?"

"Yes."

"Then I'll find them."

She opened her mouth to agree when the phone rang. Her heart skipped a beat, but when she picked the receiver up, her brother was on the other end. She'd been expecting the call, but not his pronouncement that he wanted to come to Seattle and help find the stalker. She was glad Joshua was there to help her convince Jake that Lise's best chance of catching her stalker was to stay in Seattle for the moment and that Bella needed Jake's protection more than Lise did.

Joshua's massage turned out to be total sensual pleasure as well as torment. Not only did it hurt to have sore muscles rubbed into submission, but once the pain was gone, having his fingers so close to her sexual center made her damp with desire.

He noticed, and by the time he finished the deeply intimate massage, both she and Joshua were straining from the effort of not doing anything about the feelings arcing between them.

He announced she needed a hot bath before her nap to relax her, but refused to join her, completely serious about the need for her muscles and feminine flesh to recuperate from the exercise she and Joshua had given them. When she started to nod off, her body as boneless as it had been after climaxing, she had to admit that soaking in the steaming, softly scented water had been a good idea.

Joshua caught her dozing and insisted on drying her off, then carrying her to bed and tucking her in.

When she woke up, dusk had fallen and Joshua was quietly conversing with Nitro in the kitchen. Lise joined them, not too proud to sit on the pillow Joshua had left on the kitchen chair. She felt infinitely better, but she wasn't going to risk being too sore to enjoy Joshua in her bed that night.

She hoped he'd gotten some condoms. She had no idea how much time they had together, but she was determined to maximize the moments of intimacy with her mercenary bodyguard. "Hi, guys."

Joshua came away from where he'd been leaning against the counter and dropped a soft, quick kiss on her mouth.

She darted a glance at Nitro to see how he'd taken Joshua's claim-staking gesture. The other man's face was impassive as usual, but his eyes were smiling, surprising her.

Maybe he was warming up to her.

She turned back to Joshua. "I thought I'd make that list for you now."

"First, you need to eat something."

"You've got a real thing about feeding me."

"I like to cook."

"He made some homemade sorbet. It's good." Nitro's words stunned her.

Mostly because he'd spoken at all, but also because she had a very hard time picturing her soldier of fortune puttering around in the kitchen. When she tasted the tangy lemon sorbet, she thought *puttering* was definitely not the right word.

She ate it while making the list and then got up to put the bowl in the sink.

"Can I go out?" she asked.

Joshua had picked up her list. "Out where?"

"Anywhere. I hate being cooped up inside—I feel like I've been living in a prison cell since the Seahawks game. The only time I left my apartment was when you took me to Texas." She rinsed her dish and put it in the small apartment dishwasher. "I hate being inside all the time."

"You're a writer," Joshua said, sounding disbelieving.

"Yes, and I bought a laptop with one of my first advance checks and a Dana later. I like being mobile. When I was back home, I spent hours writing in secluded spots on the ranch. I feel like Nemesis has stolen my life from me."

"It's going to get better."

"He's threatened my family, Joshua." Which made her feel doubly helpless and that made her angry.

Joshua came over and started rubbing her shoulders, proving intimate massage wasn't the only one he was good at. "He's not getting near them. We're going to get your life back and you'll get out of this apartment, but right now, we want Nemesis to think you're running scared. We want him overconfident."

"And frustrated," Nitro added.

"What do you mean?"

Joshua kept up his soothing ministrations. "He can't hear you right now and that's going to really piss him off. He wants control and he hasn't got it. When he does finally see you leave, we want him primed to act."

"Which means you want me to stay holed up in my apartment." She stifled the urge to argue. He was right, after all, and it wasn't Joshua's fault she felt so stifled.

"For the time being."

She looked at Nitro and read a surprising understanding in his eyes.

"Couldn't you guys sneak *me* out?" She couldn't help asking, tilting her head to get more solid eye contact with Joshua. "You go running every day and aren't worried about Nemesis seeing you."

"I go disguised and I leave the apartment building by a route he's unlikely to watch."

"Then take me out the same way." She'd only been back in her apartment for a couple of days, but she was already feeling stir-crazy. "I'll wear a disguise, too. Nemesis isn't as allseeing as he'd like me to believe he is."

Joshua's lips curved just slightly. "No, he's not. And he's not as smart as he thinks he is, either, but we don't know what he is watching outside your apartment. For all we know, he's tapped into the security cameras in the apartment building."

"If he has, then he's seen you, Nitro, and Hotwire enter and leave my apartment." There was a camera at the end of her hall.

"No one has seen us. We feed prerecorded footage of an empty hall to the camera when we come and go," Nitro said, surprising Lise again, this time with the sheer thoroughness of the mercenary's covert behavior.

They'd gone to a lot of trouble to protect her and be there for her. It wasn't fair for her to repay them with a bunch of whining. "Please forget I said anything. I'll be fine."

She forced a smile to prove she wasn't the stressed-out basketcase she seemed to be.

She was writing when the phone rang again.

She finished the sentence she was typing before leaning over to grab the cordless headset off the table next to the sofa. "Hello?"

"Are you having fun retyping your book?"

Unexpected and all-consuming rage filled her at the inhuman sound of Nemesis's digitized voice. "I don't know what you're talking about."

"Are you saying you didn't notice the disappearance of your book? I don't believe you, Lise Barton."

"And you think I care?" The sarcastic words slipped out, born of her fury that he would threaten her family, besides all the other grievances she could lay at his door.

"You should. You should care very much what I think. I hold your fate in my hands."

"You hold a phone in your hands, not my fate."

An ugly laugh was her only answer.

"How did you know about my book being deleted?" she asked, playing dumb, trying to control the anger roiling through her.

"How do you think? I did it."

Hearing him say it in such a triumphant voice made her even madder than she'd been when she discovered what he'd done.

Nemesis added, "Don't leave town again, Lise Barton. It made me angry."

"Right, so you hacked into my system and deleted my book," she mocked, infusing her voice with the very real derision she felt for the kind of coward that terrorized a woman and hid behind anonymity to do it. "More likely a sector went bad on my hard drive."

"If I hadn't been the one to do it, how would I have known about it?" His outrage was palpable.

He didn't like being questioned.

Good. She didn't like being stalked.

"I don't know, but if I had to take a guess, I'd figure you must have gotten a friend to hack into my system. If *you* were smart enough to do it, you would also be sufficiently computer savvy to realize I back up my files."

"You bitch! I know more about computers than you ever will."

"You sound like a three-year-old fighting over playground turf. If you did do the hacking, I bet it was luck." She wanted to push him, needed to push him.

She could not forget the sound of her brother's voice on the phone earlier, pleading with her to come into hiding with him, demanding that she allow him to come and help her find her stalker. This bastard had upset her family's lives as well as her own.

"A four-year degree and twenty-five years in the industry is not luck." Even the digitizer could not mask the near hysterical volume of his voice.

"Oh, I'm so convinced," she jeered.

"Don't mock me."

"What are you going to do to stop me? Call me again?" She laughed and hung up the phone, dropping it in its cradle with an obvious look of contempt on her face which she purposefully turned toward the video camera in her speaker.

Then she picked up her Dana and started typing again. It was all gibberish, but he didn't know that, the bastard. If he was watching her, and she was sure he was, he would be livid at how little importance she was attaching to his phone call.

"What the hell did you think you were doing?" Joshua demanded from several feet away, his voice vibrating with wrath that had far more impact on her than Nemesis's anger. "You didn't even try to keep him on the line long enough for a trace."

She didn't look up, not wanting the dweeb stalker to realize she had company.

She grabbed the stylus and tapped her lip before speaking as she often did before reading a paragraph aloud. "What difference does it make? He called last time from a pay phone across town and that piece of information netted us nothing."

"So, that made you decide to taunt him?"

"He threatened my family, Joshua. I think the guy's a jerk and I'm going to tell him so."

"Forget it."

"I can't." The next time she got a call, she was going to tell Nemesis what a lowlife she thought he was in very explicit terms even an idiot could understand.

"We don't know how he'll respond to that, damn it. Things could escalate rapidly."

She moved so only her legs and busily typing fingers were in range of the camera. Hotwire had very meticulously outlined the area of the living room that could be seen by the camera transmitter.

She didn't want Nemesis seeing her doing so much talking. He might think she was more upset and talking to herself, and she refused to give him the satisfaction. "So, they escalate. Our only chance of catching him is to force him into acting anyway."

"Not by making him murderously angry." Joshua was the one that sounded furious enough to spit nails.

She looked up, meeting a dark brown gaze filled with a lot more worry than anger. "I'm sorry, Joshua." She'd done it again. Put her emotions first, rather than acting with logic and self-control. "Truly. I don't want to mess with the plan, no matter what I've said today, but I really couldn't make nice to him. I just couldn't."

She hoped he understood, but he probably didn't. The only time she'd seen him lose his control was when they were making love. She was usually a lot more self-controlled, too, but her emotions were too close to the surface right now. If she attempted to explain it was because of making love to him, he'd probably go back to his *no sex on the job* rule.

And then if Nemesis didn't drive her round the bend, unrequited lust would.

"I never said you had to," Joshua said, "but antagonizing a stalker is dangerous. You're giving him more ammunition for his vengeance delusion, possibly sending him over the edge."

"You're right. I'll be better next time." She couldn't help the emotional catch to her voice. "Are you mad at me?"

She hated what her life had become, but she loved this man. That love was so new that the thought of sending him away from her because of her inability to control her growing rage was enough to tear a strip right out of her heart.

Joshua looked like he wanted to come to her. "I'm not angry with you, sweetheart. Just don't be so antagonistic next time."

She wished more than anything that he *could* come into

the living room and hold her, but if he did, he'd have to cross a section of space in range of the camera.

"Do I have to answer the phone again?" As difficult as it was to admit to herself and to him, she wasn't sure of her emotional control.

She needed a chance to get a grip on herself before she had to face Nemesis's inhuman voice over the phone again.

"No. I think he'd see you ignoring him as in character."

"Thank you," she said softly.

Joshua's face twisted, but he didn't say anything else and he turned to leave.

The phone rang a few minutes later and she ignored it. The answering machine picked up and the caller hung up. Afterward, she reached for the phone and turned the ringer off before going back to her book.

"She dedicated one of her books to victims of domestic violence?" Hotwire asked as Joshua laid the letters that had led him to the book in question on the table.

"Yes."

"We didn't read that one, did we?"

"No, it was actually her first book. I tried to buy it before, but it had a low print run and was hard to find. I've got a book dealer looking for me right now. Hell, he may have found it, but I haven't been home for over a month."

Nitro picked up one of the letters and read it. "She put nationwide hotline numbers and Web sites for abuse victims in the dedication?"

"More than that, she encouraged women to get help if they were in fear for their safety."

Hotwire whistled. "And you think her stalker is a disgruntled husband?"

"It fits."

"It does," Nitro agreed. "This creep has been deprived of

his victim and it makes sense he would turn his attention to the person he blames. Wolf's woman." Hotwire said.

"Yes." Joshua didn't deny possession of Lise.

She might not be his permanently, but she belonged to him right now and it made him angry enough to maim to see her as distraught as she'd been earlier. She'd fricken apologized for losing her cool, and he'd felt guilty because she wasn't the perpetrator, damn it.

She also wasn't a soldier, and no matter how self-contained she appeared on the surface, she was a woman with a woman's emotions. It wasn't just Nemesis pushing her to her limit; it was him, too. He was treating her like she was a seasoned warrior who could go into battle-ready mode and shut off her feelings as easily as he could. She wasn't.

"So, are there any live ones in these letters?" Hotwire asked.

"There are actually six letters from women who claim to have gotten help because they read the book."

"I'll start looking into it." Hotwire scooped up all the letters.

"There's no reason to assume his wife wrote a letter of thanks to Lise," Nitro said.

Joshua knew that all too well. "It's a place to start."

Chapter 11

"You think my stalker is a pissed-off husband?" Lise demanded, her expression disbelieving.

"Yes."

She plopped down on the side of the bed to watch him do floor stretches. He'd been working out in her bedroom again while she wrote. Her stare wasn't exactly disinterested, and he played to her obvious fascination.

"I guess it makes sense, but that book came out years ago, in the very beginning of my career. Why am I being stalked *now?*"

"It's only been five years." He stood up and did a couple of side-stretches, smiling to himself when her mouth parted and a small sound escaped. "Besides, she could have read it and acted on the dedication message within the last year or so."

"It had such a small print run." Her gaze snagged on his pecs as he flexed them shamelessly for her benefit.

She took a deep breath and seemed to gather herself, though her gaze remained glued to his body. "It's hard to believe anyone found a copy to read recently, but I suppose she could have picked it up used somewhere."

"That's what I'm guessing."

"What?" Her eyes had gone unfocused and he was having

a hard time himself sticking to the topic at hand. Her scent teased him, the sweet and feminine fragrance a reminder of how incredibly womanly the little she-wolf really was.

"Oh, um . . . and you figured this out from the letters in my file?" She perked up. "Does that mean you've got a lead on the stalker?"

He grabbed a small towel and started wiping the sweat from his skin. "The timing's not right for the letters you'd gotten from grateful wives. They were all written the first year after the book came out. So, I'm not sure we're any closer to identifying the perp."

It was damn frustrating. They went one step forward and then slid back again. Usually, he had infinite patience with this sort of thing, but Lise's safety was compromised and he didn't have his usual professional detachment.

She cocked her head to one side. "Sure we are."

"How?"

"We know he's a computer genius who has a four-year degree and twenty-five years of experience in the industry, which gives us an approximate age, and if your theory is correct, we also know he beat his wife. From what he's said, I think she left him and I have to wonder if he didn't lose his job, too. How else could he follow me across country?"

"That still doesn't give us a lot to go on."

"He's bound to do something big soon." Her eyes flashed with intent and temper. "I made him mad today and now that I understand his mind a little better, I'm positive that will spur him to action."

"You understand his mind better?"

"Yes."

"Why?"

"Because he's an abuser who doesn't take responsibility for his own actions, or he wouldn't be blaming me. That's a well-documented personality type."

"You seem to know a lot about it."

"I had my reasons for finding out."

"Did your father beat you?" Joshua thought she'd had a rough enough childhood as it was, but he had to ask.

"No, but he ignored the fact that one of our foremen slapped his wife around. I was a little girl—six or seven, maybe—when I saw it happen the first time and I went running to my dad. He told me to mind my own business. *That a man could not come between a husband and his wife.*"

He could sense from the vibrations coming off of her that there was more to the story. "What happened?"

"It went on for a couple years until she died in a car accident trying to run away from him after one of their fights. I remember going to her funeral. He cried by her grave and I wanted to scream at him that it was his fault."

"Why didn't you?" She was pretty feisty. He couldn't see her backing away from a fight, even as a child.

She sure didn't fit the first impression he'd had of her as a shy introvert.

"Daddy had let me know already that if I caused him any trouble he'd send me to boarding school."

Joshua couldn't believe he'd heard right. "He said what?"

"He got a call from the school when I mouthed back to one of my teachers. He told me if it happened again, I would spend my growing-up years in an all-girls boarding school."

Joshua's teeth ground.

"I got the foreman, though . . . at least as much as a child could."

He was intrigued. "How?"

"I caught a skunk. I have an affinity for animals, by the way, so don't make me mad when we're at the ranch." She smiled and winked and his dick stood up and saluted. "I let the skunk loose in his house. He had to stay in the bunkhouse for two weeks."

"Good for you."

"Daddy fired him when he caught him mistreating one of

the horses." She sounded thoroughly disgusted by her father's priorities.

Joshua knew he would have been, too. "So, you grew up and dedicated your first book to victims of domestic violence."

"I donated half my royalties to the prevention of it as well. I didn't need the money because I was living on the ranch."

He reached out and touched her, could not help himself from doing so. She was a real piece of work.

She accepted his touch with melting sensuality that went right to his groin. They ended up eating dinner close to bedtime, but neither of them cared.

Lise stopped by her computer and patted Hotwire on the shoulder. "Any luck?"

The blond man smiled even though he was shaking his head. "He hasn't tried to hack into your system again and there hasn't been another e-mail since you got back from Texas."

"He probably is afraid to leave his monitors in case I disappear again. He was seriously pissed when he couldn't find me last time." She didn't even bother to try to disguise the satisfaction that knowledge gave her.

"I keep hoping he'll cave and send a message from his personal computer, thinking he can hide its origins."

"That would be nice, but even if we can find the computer, will we find his location?"

"Not if he's using dial-up, but if he's got a dedicated line, that makes him more traceable."

"You know, I'm getting a lot of material for my writing."

"Yeah. When you think about it, this situation is a lot like one of your books."

"Only the heroines in my books are always more capable."

"To my way of thinking, you're doing pretty darn well,

Miz Lise. You're tough. You might not have the training, but you've got the guts."

She hadn't felt tough yesterday, but she was working on being more stoic today. "Thanks, but I think Joshua probably wonders when I'm going to flip out next."

"You're being too hard on yourself. Wolf is impressed with you. We all are."

Maybe he was right. A lot of things were distorted right now and it wouldn't surprise her if her perception was one of them.

A warm hand landed on her neck and she leaned back into Joshua without conscious thought. "Hi."

"Ready for a break?"

"I was taking one and chatting with Hotwire."

"I was thinking more along the lines of something that got you out of the apartment."

Hope unfurled inside her and she turned a brilliant smile on Joshua. "Do you mean it?"

"Yes."

He took her to Blake Island, the home of Tillicum Village. The small island was a one-hour cruise from Pier 55 in downtown Seattle, but it might as well have been a trip back in time to another culture. From the small cup of steamed clams they ate and then crushed the shells beneath their feet as thousands of visitors to the island had done before them, to the Native American dancing at the end of the evening, the trip took her mind into a totally different realm from the small confines of her apartment.

Joshua led her off by themselves after the dancing display, for a walk along the deserted beach. His hand rested lightly on her shoulder, but his warmth radiated along her side, even through the layers of clothing separating them.

"This is an amazing place."

"Hotwire found info on the Net about it. We figured you didn't want to spend your time away from the apartment in-

side a restaurant or museum, surrounded by a bunch of people."

She took a deep breath of the brisk, salt-laden air. "Y'all
were right. I miss the solitude I had back in Texas. Being
alone in an apartment and knowing you're amidst a couple
million people is not the same thing, but this feels so good."

The cruise had not been as crowded as it would have been
in the summer months, she was sure, and she was grateful.
"It's exactly what I needed."

He stopped, his feet bare inches from the incoming tide
line, and turned her body so they faced each other. She couldn't
see his expression because the only light around them was from
a star-filled sky she could not see in Seattle. However, warmth
and understanding reached out to curl around her in discern-
able waves.

"I'm glad you like it, honey."

The words *I love you* were on the tip of her tongue, but
she managed to hold them inside. She could not hold back a
kiss of passion and deep emotion that demanded expression,
however.

His face was cold, but his lips were warm and his arms
came around her with bruising force. Afterward, he turned
her around so they were both facing the glittering black
ocean, his arms locked around her midsection.

They stayed like that until it was time to go.

"You want me to go grocery shopping?" Lise asked.

The implication of Joshua's request hit her immediately. It
was time for the next step in their plan to catch her stalker.
While she was thrilled, she was also surprised.

Only three days had passed since Joshua had taken her to
the island, and somehow she'd gotten the impression they
were going to let more time go by before giving her the go-
ahead to leave the apartment on her own.

Perhaps the frequency of Nemesis's attempt at communication had swayed Joshua's timetable.

There had been several phone calls that showed up as *unknowns* on her caller I.D., but she hadn't answered any of them. Joshua had determined that cutting off her stalker's ability to contact Lise freely was the best way to force him to act. She also spent less time in the living room and more time writing at her computer, thus not giving Nemesis the option of watching her as much.

Hotwire had set the firewall up so that any attempt to breach it would create a pop-up message on her screen so she could call him to investigate it immediately. So far, Nemesis had not tried.

He *had* sent her another package. That very morning. This time the box had contained a pile of shredded pages from the book dedicated to victims of domestic violence, confirming Joshua's hypothesis that the book had been the spark for Nemesis's obsession.

Not that the confirmation had done them any good. So far, all the leads from that direction had ended up dead ends.

"We're hoping we've pushed Nemesis enough to risk breaking into your apartment while you're gone in order to fix his transmitter. He's got to be climbing the walls since you won't answer your phone and he's obviously decided it's too risky to send another e-mail."

"What if he decides to follow me instead?" she asked.

"All the better. Hotwire set up a receiver for me, so I can follow your car as easily as Nemesis. You won't see me, but I'll be right behind you."

She nodded. "Thank you."

"I need you to be aware of the risks involved here, sweetheart." Joshua put his hands on either side of her face, his eyes compelling her to listen. "My following you won't stop a bullet from penetrating your car window, or you from being rammed by another driver. I'll protect you as much as I can, but we don't know how escalated Nemesis's behavior is, and I want you to make an informed decision about doing this. Chances are, he will follow you, if for nothing else than to determine you haven't left Seattle again."

When he finished speaking, Joshua dropped his hands and stepped back as if saying with his body that the choice really was hers.

"If he was going to shoot me, wouldn't he have done it when I was sitting in my rocker, writing? There's a window right across from it." She hadn't considered that risk before, but then, the possibility that a madman might want to shoot her had never been high on her list of feasible alternatives to watching television on a weeknight.

"It's reinforced with a layer of bulletproof glass."

She couldn't have heard right. "What?"

"I had Nitro and Hotwire install it when you and I were in Texas. They'll remove the window and the casing when we've caught Nemesis."

She looked over her shoulder, into the living room and beyond to where sheer drapery panels blocked a direct view of the window glass. She couldn't see anything different, but she didn't doubt Joshua's words.

Shocked breathless by that level of protection, she could feel her mouth making guppylike motions. "Nemesis doesn't know the bulletproof glass is there any more than I did," she said finally, "but he still hasn't shot at me."

Joshua's taciturn expression did not lighten. "We can't assume that means he won't act with violent intent when you're on your own in your car."

He was right, but she didn't think that fact should prevent her from following through with the plan. She wanted her life back and if that meant taking some risks, she'd take them.

She told Joshua that and he smiled, both approval and concern for once easy to read in his dark brown eyes.

She was still thinking about that look later as she drove toward the grocery store. She'd been unable to catch a glimpse of Joshua in her rear-view mirror, but she knew he was there, just as he'd said he would be. Watching over her.

She squinted at a street sign as she passed it and realized she'd gone the wrong way for the grocery store. She was on a curving road that overlooked the Sound in West Seattle. Trying to remember if there was a convenient turnoff coming up, she debated between doing that or simply taking the scenic route around the point and doubling back.

When she tried to weigh the alternatives, she had to focus on remembering why it was a choice. A yawn surprised her and she raised her hand to cover her mouth instinctively, swerving a little toward the median. She quickly corrected for it.

Making love instead of sleeping might be more fun, but it was wreaking havoc with her energy level and thinking processes.

The road ahead of her started to blur slightly and she turned on the windshield wipers. They squeaked against the dry window and she fumbled to turn them off again. Maybe she needed the defrost on. She flipped the switch to High and blinked, trying to clear the fog from her eyes.

The car swerved toward the other side of the road.

Was something wrong with her power steering? She'd have to get that checked the next time she had her oil changed. Or did that kind of thing require a mechanic?

My, it was hard to breathe, like the air was too cold or something. She turned the heat on high, blasting her face with warm air, but it didn't make it any easier to get a breath.

An annoying beeping penetrated her thoughts about the

car. She pounded on the button for the radio, but all that did was elicit blaring noise. She fumbled to flip it off again, before she realized the beeping was her cell phone. She made it a habit not to talk on the phone when she was driving. Whoever was calling would have to leave a message.

But the beeping wouldn't stop. Had she turned off her voicemail, or was someone calling her over and over again?

The car weaved again as she grabbed the phone and flipped it open.

"Hello?" Her voice sounded slurred to her. Weird.

"Lise, pull over, *right now*."

"Joshua?" He sounded angry. "What's the matter?"

"Pull your fricken car to the side of the road. *Now, Lise*."

"You don't have to shout at me."

"Do it."

"Why?" A car honked at her as they came within inches of touching each other.

She glared at the other driver. "Stay on your own side of the road!"

"Stop your car!" He sounded frantic now, not just mad.

She couldn't think why, but maybe he needed her for something. Maybe they'd caught Nemesis. She turned on her blinker, somehow engaging the windshield wipers again.

What was she doing?

"Lise!"

Oh, yes, pulling over.

She dropped the phone, not liking the loud shouting so close to her ear. Then she guided her car to the side of the road, but misjudged the distance and her bumper grazed the guardrail as she came to a stop.

Oh no, she would have to have bodywork done. She was sure of it. She put the car in Park and then turned it off. No use wasting gas while she and Joshua talked, but why hadn't he just told her on the phone?

Told her what? She tried to remember.

Her head fell back against the seat before her extreme tiredness caught up to her.

Joshua's heart felt like it was going to pound out of his chest as he brought his car to a screeching halt behind Lise's Explorer.

She'd almost gone through the guardrail. Did she realize that? She'd been driving like she was drunk or high on something.

What in the hell had happened?

Lise hadn't gotten out of the Explorer and her head was resting against her seat at an angle. He slammed out of his car, his adrenaline pumping double-time, and sprinted to hers. He tried to yank the door open, but it was locked.

He pounded on the window, shouting at her to unlock the car, but she didn't respond.

He ran back to his car and popped the trunk, grabbing the kit he kept with him at all times. The slim-jim worked in seconds, but they felt like hours as prickles of cold sweat chilled his back and underarms and his gut clenched in genuine fear.

He couldn't remember the last time he'd been afraid.

It was an ugly feeling.

He yanked the door open, feeling like he was going to pull it from its hinges, and the faint odor of exhaust met him.

Shit.

He unbuckled her seat belt and lifted her out of the car.

She was breathing. Thank you, God!

He took her to his car and laid her on the hood. He couldn't administer mouth-to-mouth. The last thing she needed was his carbon dioxide in her lungs mixed with a little oxygen, and she was still breathing. Right, so no mouth-to-mouth, but he hated the feeling of helplessness that overwhelmed him.

He could administer an I.V., cauterize a wound, and even dig a bullet out with a sharp knife and do little additional damage, but he didn't carry oxygen in his kit. Damn it.

He started chafing her hands. "Come on, sweetheart, wake up. Let me see those pretty hazel eyes open."

But she continued to lie there as if asleep. Only it was a sleep he was terrified she would not wake up from. Then her body bowed and she heaved in air, doing a good measure toward clearing her lungs of the carbon monoxide.

"That's right, baby. Breathe."

She sucked in another breath and then started coughing, but she didn't wake up. He started praying as he picked her up and put her in the passenger seat of his car, then kept it up the whole way to the hospital.

It was the most he'd talked to the Man Upstairs in years.

Lise came to as he was carrying her into the Emergency Room. Her eyes were bloodshot and unfocused, like she'd been on an all-night bender.

"What's happening?" Her voice was scratchy and still a little slurred.

"Carbon monoxide poisoning."

She blinked at him, her face a blank. "What?"

"Exhaust fumes were getting into your car somehow. You breathed in too much CO."

"I felt tired, thought it was making love instead of sleeping," she slurred, as her head lolled against his chest.

"No."

"Glad."

"You're glad you've been poisoned?" he asked incredulously.

"Didn't want to give up making love."

He squeezed her tight, making her cough. "My chest hurts."

"I'm sorry, baby."

He stopped in front of the nurse's station, ignoring the admitting desk entirely. "She needs to be put on oxygen imme- diately."

The duty nurse looked up, her expression harried. "Is she breathing?"

"Yes."

"Then you'll have to take her to the admitting desk."

"Like hell. She's suffering from carbon monoxide poison- ing and we've got to get it out of her body right now."

Joshua was used to being obeyed and whether it was the tone of voice he used in the field or the look in his eye that promised retribution if she denied him, the duty nurse did not argue again. She called for a gurney and oxygen, stat.

"Joshua . . ."

"What?"

"I'm going to be sick."

He looked at the nurse. She pointed to a doorway across the hall and he sprinted. He made it just in time.

"How is she?"

Joshua turned his head at the sound of Nitro's voice. "Better."

She'd been on oxygen for a couple of hours now, and he was finally starting to breathe easier himself. A lot of people did not realize the brain damage that exposure to carbon monoxide could cause, but he did and he'd been worried spitless for her.

Lise went to take the mask from her face and he grabbed her hand. "No."

She kept trying to talk and he'd told her to keep quiet or he was going to leave and wait in the hall outside so she wouldn't have anyone to talk to. She needed to concentrate on breathing only, clearing her body of the CO.

She glared at him now, still mad about the threat.

He wasn't the most diplomatic man around, but she'd get over her irritation.

"I feel fine," she said through the muffled cup of the oxygen mask.

Right. She looked like she'd fall flat on her face if she tried to stand.

"You're keeping the mask on." And he put his hand on her cheek, his finger pressed gently against the elastic band that held the mask in place to make sure.

"You're worse than a mother hen," she grumbled.

"And you're too damned complacent about your own well-being. Now stop talking or I'll have this conversation with Nitro in the hall."

Just as it had before, the threat worked.

Her mouth snapped shut and formed a thin line while golden sparks let him know she would exact retribution for his high-handed behavior later.

He almost smiled at the prospect, but he was a stubborn man, not a stupid one.

He turned to Nitro, who stood at the foot of Lise's bed, eyeing Joshua and Lise with a knowing look.

He chose to ignore it. "Did you have the car towed?"

"Yes."

"Nemesis didn't make a play for the transmitter?"

"No."

Hotwire had kept her apartment under surveillance from the inside and would stay there, but Joshua had little hope of Nemesis falling neatly into the trap.

"Find the source of the exhaust leak."

Nitro nodded. "Watch over her," he said with a nod toward Lise, and then left.

"Do you think it was Nemesis?" she asked.

His thumb rubbed along her jawline and he was struck anew by the delicacy of her. "Yes."

It might be too soon to be making assumptions, but he knew what his gut was telling him. And it was telling him that she wasn't going back to her apartment again.

Dark circles marked the skin beneath her eyes and she looked a lot more fragile than she would admit to being. He still couldn't believe she'd balked at staying overnight, but he'd insisted and she'd given in. She hadn't thought she needed oxygen all night, but he'd known better.

So had the ER doctor who had examined her.

Her eyes drooped.

"Why don't you get some sleep, honey?" Rest and oxygen were the best things for her right now.

"Will you stay?" she asked.

"Of course." He couldn't believe she thought she needed to ask. Maybe she was still confused from the carbon monoxide poisoning.

Chapter 12

Lise's head hurt. She lifted her hand to her temple without opening her eyes. She was so tired, she didn't want to wake up, but nature called. She'd been telling a whopper of a fib earlier when she'd said she felt fine. The very idea of going to the bathroom on her own was daunting.

She felt like she'd had the flu for a solid week.

Her eyes slid open and she winced at even the subdued night lighting in her room. She hated being incapacitated, but she was grateful to be alive. Joshua had saved her, and true to his word, he sat dozing in a chair beside her bed, his strong fingers clasping one of her hands even in sleep.

It felt nice.

If he hadn't called her and told her to pull over, she would have run head-on into another car or a telephone pole, or maybe flipped her car over the guardrail and down the steep cliff.

She shivered from the thought, dropping her hand from her temple. Her fingers involuntarily squeezed Joshua's with a primal need for the reassurance of touch.

His eyes snapped open and he was instantly alert, making her wonder if he ever slept deeply.

"How are you feeling?"

She shifted slightly and urgent need made itself known in her bladder. "Like I need to use the bathroom."

"Okay." He stood up and stretched, then lowered her bedrail.

He even helped her take the oxygen mask off. She must have worn it long enough that he thought she could be without it for a few minutes at least. She was glad she didn't have to drag the oxygen machine after her on the way into the bathroom.

He pulled the covers away and she immediately realized her hospital gown had ridden up. It was an inch away from being indecent.

He gently tugged it down, his Hershey-dark eyes warm on her. "You are so beautiful."

Despite her headache and the pain in her bladder, she laughed huskily. Love was supposed to be blind, but apparently desire was, too. As nice as his words made her feel, emotional pleasure was not high on her list of priorities at the moment.

Making it to the commode before she wet herself was.

He guided her from the bed, making sure she was steady on her feet before allowing her to walk on her own toward the bathroom. He followed behind, pushing the I.V. stand.

When she got inside the bathroom, she went to close the door, but Joshua's body was in the way.

"Do you need something?" And couldn't it wait? She was getting desperate.

"You might faint again."

"I don't think that'll happen. I feel like I've been run over by a truck, but I'm not dizzy."

"I'm not willing to risk it."

He really was bossy sometimes. "That's unfortunate because I'm certainly not using the facilities with you in the room."

"Why not? We've done things a lot more intimate in the bathroom of your apartment."

"It's not the same thing."

He just looked at her with that expression that said she could argue until she was blue in the face, but he wasn't moving. She might be willing to go for blue if she wasn't so close to losing control of her bladder.

It hurt.

She frowned, wishing she could wait him out, knowing she could not. "At least come in and shut the door."

He did.

"Now, turn your back."

He did that, too, and she took advantage of the pseudo privacy.

"Nitro found a kink in the exhaust pipe."

"In my car?" she asked, feeling strange having a conversation on the commode.

"Yes. It was pressed up against the floor and there was a small hole that made it possible for the exhaust fumes to be sucked into the vacuum system. You had the heat on high, which increased the rate at which it came into the interior of your car."

"I was getting gassed by my heater?"

"Yes."

She finished, so she washed her hands and dried them. She didn't know if she could get used to talking while doing something so private, but she supposed that other couples did it all the time.

"I remember I couldn't breathe very well, so I turned it up."

He was facing her again. "You would have done better to open a window," he lectured.

"I was confused." She remembered that, too. "I couldn't seem to control the car."

"You were disoriented from the poison."

Yes, she had been, very. Another thing to lay at Nemesis's door. The sick jerk.

She scooted around Joshua and opened the door. "I assume it was something highly unlikely the police would detect in the case of an accident."

He ushered her back to bed and tucked her in, but when he tried to put the mask back on her, she stopped him.

"I'll put it back on when we're done talking."

"Okay." He sat on the edge of her bed, beside her thigh. "You're right, the exhaust leak would have been hard to discover and if it had been, it looks enough like normal wear and tear to be mistaken for it."

She shivered. "No evidence to take to the police, to convince them I'm not delusional or trying some publicity stunt." Again.

Joshua tugged her blankets up, tucking them more closely around her. "Right."

Nemesis had been very careful about not leaving footprints behind, except the bugs in her house.

"Is that why we haven't contacted the FBI?" She knew Joshua wanted to handle things on his own, but she wasn't sure she completely understood why. "Can't we tell them about the bugs and the camera? They'll believe that kind of evidence, surely."

"The police and the FBI are limited by procedure as well as strict adherence to laws. Hotwire, Nitro, and I are not."

He'd said that before, but it hadn't sunk in how seriously he did not want the authorities in his way during the investigation, which made her wonder what he planned to do that the FBI might object to.

"I'm not sure—"

He put his finger over her lips, gently cutting her off. "Don't worry, we'll bring them in eventually."

"After you've identified Nemesis?"

"When we're ready, yes."

"What do you mean, when you're ready?"

"I want a word with Nemesis before he seeks the sanctuary of jail." Joshua the nursemaid had taken a dive and the warrior was in full battle mode, his expression chilling.

The fact that he saw jail as sanctuary for Nemesis . . . from him, said a lot about Joshua's mindset. She shivered again, aching from tiredness and unaccountably emotional over his transformation to cold-eyed soldier of fortune.

It was a stark reminder that their lives might touch briefly, but he would leave her to go off and risk his life in a job few men could do and even fewer did with any integrity.

Then she considered what he might do in regard to her own situation and the coldness inside her grew. "I don't want you to do something on my behalf that could get you arrested."

He traced a gentle finger over her brow just as if he were any normal lover concerned for the welfare of his woman. "You've got a real thing about protecting other people, but I don't need you watching out for me. As you pointed out the other day, I'm a big boy."

Remembering what they'd been doing when she pointed that out made her cheeks heat and her body tense in places. "I can't help it. It's the way I'm made. Besides, you're a fine one to talk. You spend enough time worrying about me."

"You're the one in danger."

Yes, she was in danger, but so were the people around her. "You saved me." She reached out and laced her fingers with his. "Thank you."

His hand squeezed hers and his eyes closed. "It took ten years off my life waiting for you to pull over."

She wished that look meant something more personal, but he took his responsibilities seriously. She couldn't build dreams on a strong reaction to her being in danger. Joshua was the type who would feel responsible about what happened to her even if there was nothing he could have done to prevent it.

"I'm sorry."

His eyes opened and his thumb rubbed over the back of her hand. "It's not your fault." After a brief but poignant kiss, he slid the oxygen mask back on her face. "Go back to sleep. We'll talk in the morning about where we go from here."

But when morning came, Joshua had plans.

He surprised Lise by waking her very early and telling her he had to go for a little while. He left Nitro in the room with her, promising he'd be back in about an hour. She wasn't sure she needed a bodyguard. With the heightened hospital security, she didn't see how Nemesis could get to her room without revealing himself, but she didn't mind Nitro's quiet presence all the same.

An hour and ten minutes later, Joshua walked back into the room, carrying a suitcase and a bag, his expression grim.

He handed the bag to Nitro. "All set."

"Good." The other man walked into the bathroom. He came out ten minutes later, his hair tucked under a trucker cap and looking uncannily like Joshua. "Is my Lise ready?"

"Yes."

"*Your* Lise?" she asked, staring at Nitro, not quite able to get over how much he looked like Joshua just then.

"The decoy."

"What decoy?" she asked Joshua.

"I'll explain in the car. We've got to move fast if this is going to work."

She wasn't about to argue, but she couldn't help commenting, "I don't suppose it matters to either of you that it's my life we're dealing with here and I'm the one in the dark."

They both stared at her blankly.

Lord, save her from arrogant men.

She threw up her hands and flopped back against the bed, regretting the action when her headache, which had been much more low-level this morning, increased. She glared at them both, irritably blaming them for her discomfort.

Nitro winked at her, shocking her silly. "Where's the decoy?" he asked Joshua.

"In a wheelchair in the hall. I explained the situation to the duty nurse and she's going to have an orderly wheel our decoy to the front with you. My car is parked in the Emergency parking lot." He handed Nitro a set of keys. "Good luck."

"Got it." Nitro went to the door and stopped, turning his head back so he could look at both Joshua and Lise. "Take care of her. She's good people."

Touched and even more stunned than when he'd winked, Lise gave Nitro a shell-shocked smile before he turned around and disappeared through the door.

Joshua pushed the call button for the nurse. "We need to get you dressed and out of here."

"I still don't understand."

"I said—"

"I know. We'll talk in the car." She sighed. "You're awfully stubborn, not to mention bossy sometimes."

"You've said that before."

"It's still true."

He shook his head, a small smile playing at the corners of his mouth, and stepped back as the nurse came into the room to unhook monitors and remove Lise's I.V. shunt. She left and Lise got up to take a shower so she could dress.

When she came out of the bathroom fifteen minutes later, wearing a fresh pair of jeans and a sweatshirt over her t-shirt, Joshua handed her a set of scrubs. "Take off your sweatshirt for now and put these on. We're leaving anonymously."

She'd gotten that impression with the decoy, but what she still didn't understand was why. How could it matter if

Nemesis followed them back to the apartment? Wouldn't that be one more chance to catch him? Maybe Joshua was feeling overprotective after yesterday.

Despite not understanding his motives, she did as he said and peeled out of the sweatshirt to don the scrubs.

He made her wear a green shower cap-looking thing over her hair and a surgical mask that covered her face.

"This is all very cloak and dagger, but I don't see the point," she grumbled on the way to the elevator.

"Don't talk until we get outside."

She sighed heavily and frowned at him, but complied. Though how much of her frown he could see behind the dumb mask, she didn't know. He wasn't even looking at her, anyway. His attention was on everything and everyone around them.

Which should make her feel safe at the moment, but annoyed her instead. *Good night!* She was really in a cranky mood. Was it the aftereffects of the CO poisoning?

He took her out behind the hospital, tucked her into another nondescript-looking rental car, and left.

"Can I take the mask off now?"

He looked in the rear-view mirror and executed a couple of swift turns before saying, "Yes."

She yanked it off. "After wearing an oxygen mask all night, having something against my face right now is about the last thing I want," she said, trying to explain her impatience.

He pulled his off, too, and tossed it in the back seat. "I imagine so, but the oxygen was necessary."

"Thank you for insisting I stay. I wasn't really with it enough to make good decisions last night. I hate being confined, but staying over in the hospital was the best thing for me."

"You're right, it was."

"Hasn't anyone ever told you that saying *I told you so* is tacky?"

"My sisters may have mentioned it once or twice."

She found herself grinning in spite of her bad mood. "I bet they did."

She rubbed her temples, trying to dispel the lingering headache. "So, what is going on?"

"Nitro and a female operative named Josie McCall, decoying as you, left the hospital in my original rental car to drive to Vermont."

Maybe her brain wasn't working properly yet, but that didn't clarify one tiny thing. "Why?"

"Because we want Nemesis to follow them."

"Why do we want him to follow the decoys?"

"It will give us a chance to get there ahead of them and set a trap."

"Why Vermont?" Wouldn't Texas make more sense if they wanted to set a trap for Nemesis to fall into?

"My home is there."

"You're taking me to your house?"

"Yes."

"I thought you told Jake you were moving in with me, not vice versa."

"Things changed."

Yes, they had. "Is that where Jake and Bella are?"

"No, they're staying at Nitro's place."

"Fewer people to keep track of when you spring your trap."

"Exactly."

It made sense.

"I thought about sending you to stay with Jake, but I figured you had a right to see this thing through."

She was glad he'd worked that out on his own. "How would you catch Nemesis if you sent me away? I'm the bait."

"Not anymore. The decoy is now the bait."

"How do we know Nemesis will follow them?"

"He put a transmitter on my car last night."

"He did?"

"Yeah, and if I'd thought of it, I could have been having my car watched and we'd have the bastard nailed already."

"You can't think of everything."

His expression said, *Want to bet?*

"Well, you didn't this time and it's no use getting all excited about it. What's done is done."

"I don't get excited."

"Sure you do." He liked to pretend he was all dead inside, the standard hardened mercenary, but Joshua cared too much about other people, even if he didn't realize it.

The look he gave her was one-hundred-percent masculine sensuality. "Yeah, I do, but that's not what we're talking about here."

She swallowed. "So, how does having a transmitter on your car guarantee Nemesis will follow?"

"You've got to try to think like he does."

"I'm not the stalking type," she said with acerbity, cursing the headache that made every tonal change feel like a pounding hammer in her head.

He didn't take her to task for her crankiness, but said, "If he doesn't follow, he risks the possibility of losing track of you. I don't think he'll do that."

"But he's following a decoy. Don't you think he'll figure that out?"

"He's not going to risk getting close enough for visual because it goes both ways. If he can see you, then you can see him and he risks becoming a familiar face to you. Remember, he can follow his transmitter from enough distance that he'd never be spotted as a tail."

"But . . ."

"If he does get close enough for a visual, he's nailed anyway because we know who he is now and Nitro will be on him like a nitrate burn on your trigger finger."

"What?" she practically screamed.

They knew who Nemesis was? "Who is it? When did you find out? Why can't we find him without leading him into a trap?" She glared at Joshua, wanting to brain him but not willing to risk it while he was driving. She'd had her limit of near death experiences in the car for the week already. "I can't believe you didn't bother to tell me until now!"

"Hotwire made the I.D. at four this morning. I told you as soon as it was safe to do so."

"In the hospital—"

"It wasn't a secure environment."

"It was secure enough for you to tell the duty nurse about Nemesis and leave Ms. McCall waiting in the hall as my decoy."

"Do you want to harangue me some more or hear what I know?" He sounded willing to go either way and it was all she could do not to growl like a rabid dog.

Arrogant men and cranky women were not a good combination.

"Tell me how Hotwire traced him. I thought none of his e-mails were written from his home computer."

"They weren't, but Hotwire traced the source of an e-mail you had in your archived folders that he had a hunch about. It was written a few months before the stalking started. A woman who thanked you for finally getting through to her mother with your book."

Lise had forgotten all about the e-mail because it had been so brief and the reader hadn't even signed her name. "How did Hotwire trace that e-mail to my stalker?"

"He connected the dots and everything in Ed Jones's life fits our perp."

Joshua pulled the car onto the freeway, dragging the surgeon's cap off his head, and Lise followed suit.

"He's originally from Southern California, but he moved to Texas almost a year ago. He disappeared when you moved to Seattle. We haven't been able to locate his current address in the city. It could take weeks to do so and in that time he could do something a lot worse than setting you up for CO poisoning. Trapping him is faster and more certain."

"I don't recall ever meeting an Ed Jones."

"You probably haven't, at least not before he started to stalk you. Your guess that his wife left him and he was unemployed was right on target. She had him arrested for assault about seventeen months ago and pressed charges. He got out pretty damn fast, but he lost his job because of the arrest and his wife filed for divorce."

"Do we have a picture of him?"

Joshua tilted his head toward the back seat. "The file is back there."

She scrambled around and grabbed it. She flipped through the information Hotwire had found on Ed Jones. He was a former program manager in computer software and always paid his taxes on time. According to Hotwire, he'd never even had an overdue library book, but he was deranged enough to abuse his wife and stalk Lise. The pictures in the file were not very clear, but they made her shake because she recognized him.

"He was the handyman at my apartment complex in Canyon Rock. He was soft-spoken and pleasant." She'd spoken to him almost every day for months—just pleasantries, but still, it had been contact and she never would have guessed.

"That's a piece of information Hotwire can use. Do you remember seeing him anywhere else?"

"Not since I came to Seattle, but then he wouldn't have risked that, would he? And the night of the Seahawks game, there was more than one man wearing a ski mask because of the cold."

"All along he's been very careful not to take a lot of risks. Which is why I'm sure he won't risk getting a visual of our decoys."

One thing was good. "At least now I know he didn't sit at a restaurant table next to me on my trip from Canyon Rock to Seattle. I would have recognized him. He must have followed at a distance."

"Exactly."

For some reason, that consoled her, made her feel like he wasn't so in control. He had his limits, too.

"I still don't see how you can be so confident of leading him into a trap. Now that he knows I'm with you, he's bound to suspect something is up."

"I don't think so. He thinks he's safe in his anonymity. Even knowing about me, he doesn't know about Nitro and Hotwire and he has no reason to believe I've got the necessary skill set to find his bugs. If he knew we'd tampered with his equipment, he would not have risked putting a transmitter on my car."

"That makes sense, I guess." But it seemed too easy. "You're a mercenary with a background in the Special Forces. He'll assume you've got some level of advanced knowledge and he could guess at the rest."

"If he digs into my identity, and I'm sure he already has, he'll only find that I live off my investments and like to travel. Even finding a record of my Special Forces tour in the army will take a lot more effort than it did to hack into your system or some medical records he knew he was looking for."

Joshua still wasn't making a lot of sense. "But people know you're a mercenary."

"It's not top secret, but it's also not documented. The company I took over is one that never advertised. All of our business is by word of mouth and very few of my clients know my real name."

"But your family . . ."

"Don't make it a habit of telling other people."

That was true. Bella had never told her about Joshua's job. Lise had figured it out on her own.

"If he did private dick work, that would be one thing. But he's staying too low-key for that and it's pretty obvious, he relies heavily on the computer. I'm betting he's doing all his investigation via the Internet. At least now. Most likely he watched you for a long time before he started the recognizable events."

She'd figured that out, too, and it gave her the creeps. "So, what happens after Nitro and Ms. McCall lead Nemesis to Vermont?"

"His ass is mine."

"If you use your home as the base for the trap, he'll know where you live. What if he turns his anger on you?"

Joshua laughed out loud, the sound filled with genuine mirth and no little diabolical self-assurance.

"It's not funny. You aren't invincible."

"As far as he's concerned, I am. The only thing saving him is his anonymity and that's been compromised. We'll find him and when we do, I'll make sure he's damn sorry he ever fixated on you, sweetheart." He gently forced her hand open and laced his fingers with hers. "Stop worrying."

"I'll try." She watched out the front window for several minutes in silence.

He flicked her a glance before doing that thing he did, looking in all the mirrors. Probably checking for a tail. "What's wrong, honey? That is not an *I'm not worrying anymore* look."

She smiled at his belief that she could dismiss her concerns in the blink of an eye because he said so. He really was one very confident man. She was trying, and that was the best she could do, but no matter how hard she tried, she could not dismiss a growing certainty in her heart.

"I think Nemesis means to kill me."

The time he'd shoved her into traffic, she could have been badly hurt or killed and this thing with her car's exhaust had been even more dangerous.

Which is what she said to Joshua.

"Most people start vomiting before they pass out when they're exposed to carbon monoxide."

"So?" Was that supposed to mean something to her? She swore, sometimes talking to Joshua was like coaxing honey from a turnip.

"If you'd reacted classic textbook, you would have pulled over sooner."

"Before I got so disoriented I drove over the guardrail?"

"Yes."

"So, you *don't* think he's trying to kill me?"

Joshua's hand on the steering wheel tightened until his knuckles were white. "*Not yet.*"

Chapter 13

Suddenly cold, she reluctantly tugged her hand from his so she could pull off the green cotton top and put her sweatshirt back on. "Not yet?" she prompted.

"He's too cavalier with your life. There have been two incidents now that could have been fatal. Both times the chance of injury was greater than that of death, but you can't get around the fact that he was willing to risk it. I think he has plans for the future."

The need to vomit Joshua had mentioned earlier hit her now. "You think he's on some sort of timetable, or that he just wants to taunt me sufficiently before killing me?"

"It could be either, but I wondered if yesterday's incident wasn't engineered so he could kidnap you."

"Why kidnap me?"

"Honey, that's a question I'd rather not answer."

As one terrifying and soul-sickening scenario after another started flying through her imagination, she realized it was a question she wished she hadn't asked, either.

Joshua's takeoff was smoother than any commercial flight she'd been on, but the change in pressure still affected her head. She took some painkillers with a long drink from the water bottle he'd given her after belting her into the co-pilot's seat.

He sent her a concerned glance. "You okay, Lise? Maybe we should have waited until tomorrow to fly out."

"I'll be fine."

"I wanted to get you out of Washington."

Because he'd been worried about her even though he would never admit it. The knowledge did more to dispel her headache than any pain reliever could.

"Did you fly in the Rangers?"

He nodded. "Choppers. I didn't learn to fly a jet until the year after I went independent."

"Why did you leave the army?"

The thing that had fascinated her the most when she'd been interviewing mercenaries for her books had been their varied reasons for becoming what they were. They had ranged all the way from wanting to do what they did already, but with no red tape limiting the success of their missions, to simply wanting to get paid more for risking their lives.

Joshua had a lot of integrity. She'd bet his reasons for going independent were good ones.

But when he didn't answer at once, she began to wonder if his reasons had been painful as well. "You don't have to answer if you don't want to."

He turned to look at her, the plane on automatic pilot now that they were flying at altitude. "I got married the second year of my tour in the Rangers."

"*You've been married?*" The news shouldn't have come as such a shock. After all, she'd been divorced. But it did.

His eyes reflected faint humor at her surprise. "Most men over the age of thirty have, at least once."

"I guess you're right, but I never pictured you as the domestic type." A warrior, yes. A hearth and home man, no.

"It wasn't a craving for domesticity that prompted my marriage. I was a nineteen-year-old kid who wanted a little softness when I wasn't in the field. Melody was soft—at least, her body was."

"Did you love her?"

"I thought I did, but I learned that kind of love is more illusion than reality."

He couldn't have meant his words the way they sounded, but she had to ask to make sure. "Are you saying you don't believe in the love between a man and a woman . . . at all?"

His jaw tightened, his expression hardening. "No."

She inhaled air into lungs that hurt with the effort it took not to protest the wound his words inflicted. If he did not believe in love, it was a safe bet he did not love her and that news was about as welcome as a snakebite in the desert.

"What about Jake and your sister, what about your parents?" Bella had told her that their parents were happily married and had been for decades.

"Lee is not my real father."

"So, he's your stepfather, but that doesn't negate the love he feels for Myra. He adores her." Even if Bella hadn't told her that, it had been obvious at both the wedding and Genevieve's christening.

"No, it doesn't." He adjusted something on the instrument panel. "I should have said that I don't believe in it for me. What Jake and Bella have is unique."

"You don't think you're capable of experiencing those feelings?"

"No."

"Because of your marriage?"

"What I thought was love turned out to be nothing more than sexual infatuation." His dark eyes bored into hers, letting her know he believed everything he was saying. "When our marriage ended, the only thing I missed about Melody was the sex and holding someone at night."

Was that all he would miss about her when she moved back to Texas and he went on to his next assignment? She'd miss the sexual intimacy, too. The passion between them was beyond anything she could ever have imagined, but for her it was so much more. The pain in her chest grew and she wondered if broken hearts really did shatter.

She could not force herself to say anything, even the inane, but apparently he wasn't expecting an answer because he went on.

"Melody and I played at marriage. Looking back, I realize our relationship was nothing more than a series of intense sexual encounters. We didn't talk. We didn't want to buy a house, or do any of the things married couples interested in becoming a family do."

"You mean like having children?"

"That was one thing. She didn't want kids and I didn't want to try to be a dad when my life was dominated by my job in the Rangers. I'd seen too many marriages split, leaving kids devastated."

"You got married thinking you might get divorced?"

"The divorce rate in the Rangers is eighty percent. I had to consider the possibility."

"Even so, that's a pretty cynical attitude."

"I was right."

She couldn't exactly argue with that. "What happened?"

"I came back from assignment and found my wife having sex on the coffee table with one of my Ranger buddies."

"On the coffee table?" The image was mind-boggling.

"Yeah. They were going at it so hot and heavy, they didn't even realize I'd come into the room until I dumped a bucket of ice water on them. I never got so lost in sex with Melody that I didn't know what was going on around me. To tell you the truth, it pissed me off that he was getting something from her I hadn't managed to find. Complete oblivion."

She put the rest of his comments in the back of her mind to dissect later and focused on how he'd handled the situation. "You dumped ice water on them?"

"It beat taking my Ranger brother apart until there was nothing left."

"Brother?"

"*Brother*. Being in the Special Forces is an intense way of life. If you can't trust your buddies absolutely, you can't do your job." He sounded like he was reciting incontrovertible truth. "You believe they'll cover your back no matter what it takes, and you'll risk your life to cover theirs. You learn to trust them more than your own family."

"And your *brother* betrayed you?"

"Yes." Joshua's expression hardened and she could almost feel sorry for the other man. "Melody's betrayal hurt. I won't pretend it didn't. I was still a kid with illusions about love."

And those illusions had been smashed to little bitty pieces, both by his ex-wife's betrayal and his own less-than-consuming emotional reaction to it.

"But my buddy's betrayal made me reevaluate my priorities, who I trusted, and what I wanted to do with the rest of my life."

"And you decided you'd rather be a soldier of fortune than an enlisted man."

"I didn't trust my buddy anymore. I wondered how many of the other Rangers would let me down in the right set of circumstances. It was a bad mental attitude. Dangerous. When it came time to re-up, I chose to go it on my own."

"But you still wanted to be a soldier?" Amazing how she could carry on a conversation with her heart a dead weight within her.

"Yes, but I decided that if I couldn't trust my companions, I might as well be in a situation where I knew that was the case than one in which I had a false sense of belief in their integrity."

"You trust Hotwire and Nitro." If he denied it, she'd call him a liar.

The bond between the three of them was extraordinary.

"We were buddies in the Rangers. They stuck it out for another tour, but they both had their own reasons for leaving and when they did, I talked them into joining me. I trust them because they've each proven themselves in numerous ways."

"It goes both ways, though, doesn't it? They trust you, too."

"It's more than any of us ended up having in the Rangers."

"So, your marriage convinced you that you weren't capable of romantic love?" she said, going back to the aspect of the conversation that concerned her most deeply.

The one that was tearing her apart on the inside.

"It convinced me that *erotic love* rarely lasts."

Funny, she was pretty sure the love she felt for him would last for the rest of her life. There was a big dose of erotic love in there, but he got to her on a level that went much deeper, too. If she told him, he would probably deny it, but she knew that even if she never saw him again, she would not be able to forget him or stop loving him.

Clearly, he didn't feel the same way toward her, and as much as she wanted to blame him, she couldn't. He'd never once implied anything more on his part than physical desire. He'd said it was more than sex, but she now realized he was most likely talking about the friendship that had developed between them and his willingness to help her for Bella's sake.

They had a family connection, but not a heart connection, and hers was bleeding to death because of it.

"I can't believe you let one bad experience convince you of something so important."

He let out an impatient breath. "It didn't, not completely. I've been divorced for over a decade. I've had some very satisfying sexual relationships, but I've never found anything like what Jake and Bella have."

Which told her in unequivocal terms just what his feelings for her were.

He could not have the same intense tenderness and need growing inside him toward her that she felt toward him and deny his ability to feel true love.

She turned her face away, her eyes closing on the tears she was not about to give in to. "I think I'll take a nap."

He reached out and brushed her temple.

She flinched, his touch hurting in a way that had nothing to do with the physical.

"Are you still in pain, Lise?" Concern deepened his voice and she fought the urge to latch onto it.

"Yes." It was the truth, even if she wasn't talking about her head.

He didn't say anything else and eventually her body relaxed into sleep.

When she woke up they were flying directly toward the side of a mountain.

She sucked in her breath and then opened her mouth in a silent scream as Joshua tilted the plane on its side and they flew into the crevice of a ravine. The next few minutes were harrowing as he expertly guided the plane through twists and turns that made her stomach flip with each dip of the wings.

Then there was a landing strip in front of them and he was bringing the plane to a smooth stop.

"Is that how you land your plane every time you come home?" she asked, her stomach roiling.

"Yes, but it's nothing compared to landing in Hong Kong. There, you're maneuvering between skyscrapers."

She didn't even want to imagine it and made a mental note never to fly into Hong Kong. "Whose bright idea was it to put the landing strip in a ravine?"

"Mine." He grinned at her, the smile stopping the breath in her chest. "You wake up cranky."

She certainly had today, anyway, both that morning and just now. "Not always," she defended herself.

"No, not always." And the look he gave her left no uncertainty about what he was remembering.

The way she woke up in his arms.

Cranky could not begin to describe her attitude then, but that wasn't something she wanted to dwell on right now.

"Stop that," she grumbled.

One dark brow arched. "Yes, ma'am."

"Why did you choose such a dangerous landing strip?"

"It's not dangerous if you know what you're doing."

"I think the people who die mountain climbing every year say the same thing."

"You really are in a bad mood." His brows drew together. "Are you feeling okay?"

She closed her eyes and sighed before opening them and forcing a smile that was a little ragged around the edges. "I'm fine, I just don't get why you built your landing strip this way unless you like the testosterone rush it gives you pitting your skills against such a harrowing takeoff and landing."

He searched her face as if trying to decide whether or not she was telling the truth about feeling okay. "Being in the ravine makes it virtually impossible to detect from the air. The locals don't know it's here because there's a town at the base of the mountain on the other side with a municipal airport, so the jet noise doesn't cause any suspicion."

She frowned, unbuckling her safety belt. "You've got a real thing for privacy."

He was already moving into the main cabin. "In my line of work, it can mean the difference between life and death."

Chilled at the reminder, she followed him.

In the main cabin, she grabbed the coat she'd bought after moving to Seattle and zipped herself into it. Even so, the frigid air outside about stole her breath when he released the plane's door.

He heard her gasp and turned to face her. "That's not going to do it."

He went to the rear of the plane, lifted one of the seats on top of a storage compartment, and came back carrying a big black parka. He put it on her right over her own coat, pulled the hood up and hooked clasps that kept it snug to her face despite it being several sizes too big.

"Tuck your hands up into it. I'll get the luggage."

She didn't argue, but followed him down the plane steps feeling like Nanook of the North.

They were standing on the tarmac, the only surface not covered in snow within sight, when she asked, "I presume there is a regular road to your home?"

There certainly wasn't one anywhere around the landing strip that she could see.

"On the town side."

"So, how do we get to your house now?"

They got there on the back of an oversized snowmobile, her clinging to him like a lifeline with her face buried against his back to avoid the cold sting of the wind and small snow flurries. Tucked inside the big parka, she was barely aware of the cold as the snowmobile carried them across the landscape.

About fifteen minutes later, he stopped the snowmobile, but did not turn it off.

She lifted her face from the security of his back and got her first look at Joshua's home.

All natural wood and lots of windows, it reminded her of something straight out of *Architectural Digest*. It soared toward the sky like an eagle ready to take flight.

"Wow," she breathed.

He didn't answer. He probably hadn't heard her over the high whine of the snowmobile.

She didn't know what she had expected Joshua's home to look like, but this incredible house on the side of a mountain was not it.

He guided the snowmobile into a large outbuilding she recognized as a garage when she saw an SUV and a black Jag, both parked inside the heated interior. It probably wasn't much above forty, but compared to outside, it felt like a sauna.

Once the noisy vehicle had been switched off and her ears stopped ringing from the cold ride, she said, "Your house is beautiful."

"Thanks." Joshua grabbed her cases and his duffel bag off the back of the snowmobile. "Nitro designed it."

"*Nitro?*" she asked, following Joshua around the back of the house to an entrance she hadn't seen from the garage.

Joshua unlocked the door, but didn't answer. He went inside and did a quick sequence on a keypad inside before turning to face her. "Yeah, you should see his house."

"He's got hidden depths." Which was an understatement. With that man, pretty much everything was hidden.

"Don't we all?"

She wasn't touching that with asbestos gloves.

She shrugged off both the oversized parka and her own coat. "You live here alone?"

"As you pointed out, I like my privacy." He hung the coats on hooks in the mudroom before leading her into the house proper.

"It's awfully big for a single man."

He shrugged. "It's a fortress."

She had a feeling he wasn't kidding.

That feeling was justified when she got her first glimpse of his bedroom, which could have doubled for command central. Video screens, what looked like a map grid with LED displays, and other impressive hi-tech equipment took up one corner of the huge room.

However, there was no doubt that it was a bedroom. A king-size bed dominated the center of the space, its charcoal gray comforter sporting a painting of a realistic-looking lone wolf in the middle. The animal's eyes were those of a predator used to traveling alone, like Joshua's eyes when she'd met him the first time. She wondered who had painted the wolf.

He dropped her suitcase and computer case on a large black leather recliner beside a standing lamp.

Apparently he expected her to share his room and that big bed under the lone wolf comforter. She wasn't sure how she felt about that.

He'd made no promises of love before making love to her in her own apartment and she had been okay with it. So, why did knowing he definitely *did not* love her make her feel odd about continuing their intimate relationship?

Hoping it wasn't something she'd have to deal with right away, she took in the odd characteristics of the room besides the command center. There were no windows, but the room was filled with natural light and, looking up, she saw why. A skylight the size of a plate-glass window took up a large portion of the ceiling.

"Is it made of bulletproof glass?" she asked, nodding toward his window in the ceiling.

"You know me well. Yes."

Skies as gray as any she'd experienced in Seattle made up the uninspiring view. She wondered how he kept the snow off the skylight, or the roof, for that matter. It hadn't really struck her until now, but the roof of the house had been free of snow as well.

When she asked him about it, Joshua shook his head. "I've worked with independent agents who aren't as aware of their surroundings as you are." His smile was one of approval. "The roof is heated with water-radiant heat. We don't get as much snow as some areas in the country, but we get enough that I built the house with that in mind."

"It must cost a great deal to heat the water."

He shook his head. "It's fed by natural hot springs that run underground. A section of the lower level of the house is built over one of the exposed pools."

"Is that how you keep the landing strip de-iced, too?"

"Yes. It prevents me from having to have domestic help to keep the walkways, landing strip, and roof free of snow."

"Ah, the privacy issue again."

He shrugged and she walked over to the bed, stopping to run her finger along the outline of the wolf. "How fitting."

Looking up, she found Joshua watching her.

The expression in his eyes filled her with conflicting emotions, none of which she wanted to deal with right now.

"What's with all the surveillance equipment?"

"I like to know what's happening in my environment."

"Your house is under video surveillance?"

"The entryways and passages between the rooms, yes."

"What's that thing?" She pointed to the grid map.

"No one comes up the road from town or within five hundred feet of my house without me knowing about it."

He pointed to a small yellow light on the grid. "This lights up when a car crosses my motion sensor halfway down the mountain." His finger moved to the red light next to it. "This one lights up when the car passes the turnoff for the forestry station. These others are indicators for weight sensors set in a random pattern in a circle around my house."

"With a radius of five hundred feet?" It was unbelievable. The characters in her books were never that thorough.

"The entire approach up the drive is under video surveillance as well."

"Remarkable." She couldn't think of anything else to say.

"You're safe here, Lise."

She didn't doubt it. No wonder he was so confident of setting the trap for Nemesis here.

"Thank you."

Joshua came over to where she stood by the bed and cupped her nape. "I mean it. I won't let Nemesis get to you."

"I believe you." She stepped back from his touch and ran into the bed. She had to grab his arm to steady herself, but then she scooted sideways, out of his reach. "I really appreciate all you're doing for me, Joshua."

His eyes narrowed. "I don't need your thanks."

"I know. The lone wolf who doesn't need anybody, not

even their honest gratitude." She hadn't meant to sound bitter, but the sound of her own voice echoing in her ears was enough to make her cringe in embarrassment.

Joshua didn't look angry, though; he just looked concerned. "What's the matter?"

Besides the fact that he didn't love her, "Absolutely nothing."

"Do you want to rest for a while? You're probably drained from the flight," he said, coming up with his own excuse for her inexplicable behavior. She usually stepped into his touch, not away from it. "CO poisoning takes time to wear off."

"I napped on the plane." Even as she said it, she realized he probably wanted a break from her.

Not only was she being unreasonably irritable, but they'd spent a lot of time together over the last few days. He was most likely going stir-crazy for some time alone.

"Why don't you lie down and see?" he asked, confirming her suspicions.

"I'm not tired, but you don't need to feel responsible for entertaining me. Really, you don't. I'll work on my book while you do whatever it is you normally do when you get home after a long absence."

He had said he'd been out of the country before coming to her apartment in Seattle and he hadn't left her side since. He probably had a lot of real life to catch up on and she was in the way.

"I'm not looking for an excuse to get rid of you. I probably should have left you in the hospital at least one more day, but I didn't want to risk Nemesis doing something that could hurt you, or the people around you."

"Don't worry about it. I'm fine."

He let out an exasperated breath and frowned at her. "I would feel a lot better if you'd at least try to rest. You were still in pain on the flight over here."

"Joshua, you've got the wrong build to be anyone's

mother, so stop trying to mollycoddle me, okay? If I say I'm up to writing, then that's what I mean." Cryin' out loud, couldn't she even *try* for diplomatic?

But then, the sublety of a Mack truck might be lost on this man.

"You're damn stubborn."

"I had a good teacher. Have you ever had an argument with Jake?"

"Yeah, over me staying with you. I won."

"Well, you're not going to win this one." She opened the side pocket of her computer case and pulled out the small Dana. "I'll just settle into your chair over there and write, okay?"

His eyes narrowed dangerously, reminding her he would always be more predator than patsy. "If you weren't so fragile, I'd convince you to stay in that bed with no problem."

She tucked the Dana under her arm and grabbed her notepad and pen out of another pocket in her bag. "If I weren't recovering from carbon monoxide poisoning, you wouldn't be trying to get me there in the first place."

He took two giant steps, closing the distance between them and shrinking her awareness of the room to the three square feet they occupied. She could smell the crisp air from outside clinging to his hair and skin, but also the indefinable pheromone cocktail that told her body her lover was excited.

Her gaze dropped to the front of his black jeans and she sucked in air, almost choking herself in the process. He wasn't just mildly excited; the tight denim of his pants tented away from his body from his straining erection.

Sliding his long, callused fingers around her neck, he cupped her nape.

His thumbs dipped underneath the crewnecks of both her t-shirt and sweatshirt to caress her collarbones, sending shivers of gooseflesh cascading over her breasts. "Are you sure about that?"

Chapter 14

Desire flooded her senses, adding to the volatile emotional cocktail traveling through her bloodstream.

Her only defense was in making it a joke, no matter how serious it felt. "Are you saying you *aren't* going to employ unfair tactics because of my recent brush with death?"

The color receded from his skin, leaving his usual tan vitality looking sickly; his eyes burned into her with disturbing intensity. "I'm sorry about that, Lise. I'd give anything to change what happened yesterday."

"It's not your fault."

"I'm supposed to be protecting you, and you could have died."

"You saved me."

"Because I didn't protect you well enough to begin with."

"There was nothing you could have done, Joshua."

She shook her head when he didn't reply and his expression remained stoically unmoved. "You told me the risks. I chose to take them."

"I wasn't expecting him to tamper with your exhaust. We checked your car for tampering with the brakes and other vital systems, but everything looked good."

"It's not your fault." She reached up and grasped his wrists, squeezing them. "You told me I couldn't blame myself for the problems Nemesis has caused for my family and you can't take responsibility for his desire to hurt me, either."

"Oh, baby." His face nuzzled hers until his mouth settled against hers, kissing her with tender sweetness.

His body vibrated with sexual energy, but his lips were as gentle as anything she'd ever known. He might not love her, but he cared, more than he was willing to admit to, maybe even more than she dared hope.

She was the one who turned the kiss into something more than comfort, opening her lips, tasting him with her tongue, nipping him with her teeth. His big body shuddered and he pulled her against him, devouring her mouth with a voracious hunger that she knew only she could appease.

For now.

He broke away from her, turning his head, his breathing heavy and erratic. "We can't, sweetheart."

"Yes, we can." She'd seen him pack the condoms in his duffel bag.

"You need to take it easy, to recuperate from yesterday."

"I need to make love with you." She emphasized her point by pressing herself against him and rubbing his hardness with her body.

He groaned like a man facing death. "No, Lise. We can't."

"Stop trying to tell me what's best for me, Joshua. Like you told Jake. I'm well past the age of consent."

"You're also sick."

"I am not."

It was getting harder and harder to say no. He'd never found it so difficult to do what he knew was right, but then he'd never had to turn away from the sensual promise of Lise's body when she was pleading with him to make love to her.

"We have all the time in the world to make love, but right now you need to focus on getting better."

"I am better, and we don't have all the time in the world. If things go according to your plan, you'll have Nemesis caught in less than ten days. I don't want to waste one of them playing sick when I'm not."

Was she saying she expected their relationship to end with the catching of her stalker? He had known their affair was temporary; mercenaries made poor husbands, but he hadn't expected her to be ready to boot him out of her life the minute she was free of Nemesis.

Even so, he couldn't agree that she was just pretending to be sick. He would never forget the way she'd looked, passed out in the driver's seat of her car, or her wan complexion throughout the night while her body rid itself of the carbon monoxide.

"You're too fragile right now, even if you're too stubborn to see it." He wished his sex would respond to the barely fading bruises under her eyes instead of the scent of her sweet skin so close and the feel of her under his fingers.

He jerked his thumbs out from under her shirt and dropped his hands away from her, but they tingled with the memory of her softness despite being clenched at his sides.

"I'm excited, not fragile, and if you'll just take your clothes off and get naked with me in that big bed behind us, I'll prove it."

The words and genuine feminine need swirling in her golden-green eyes were killing blows to his self-control. "All right, but damn it, no gymnastics or going down on me moving your head all over the place. I'm not going to be responsible for your headache coming back."

He lowered his lips to hers before she could say anything else, or start arguing his imposed limitation on their lovemaking into the ground.

He remembered how Jake and Bella had described Lise as a shy woman, an introvert who rarely fought with anybody. He had to wonder if they were talking about the same woman, because his Lise was more she-cat than shy.

Thoughts of brothers, arguments, and even proving anything to her melted into nothing as he got his first deep taste
of her lips in twenty-four hours.

He plundered the soft recesses of her mouth while his
hands slid of their own volition down her slender back to cup
her buttocks. He lifted her into intimate contact, shaking
with the need to make her his, to make her forget her plan to
break away from him after Nemesis was caught.

She moaned, a soft, sexy sound, and squirmed against
him. Just a small movement, but it was enough to make his
already hardened sex throb.

He started peeling her out of her sweatshirt and t-shirt at
the same time. She helped him, letting him break the kiss
long enough to get them off over her head. Then she tunneled
back into his arms and resumed the kiss with an intense ferocity that reminded him she matched him perfectly in every
way.

But his wild lover was temporarily fragile and no damn
way was he going to let her hurt herself.

He tempered the kiss to something this side of volcanic as
her small fingers went to work on the buttons of his solid
flannel shirt. She tugged it apart impatiently and the last
three popped off, pinging against the hardwood floor. Her
hands settled against the hot skin covering his tense pecs and
they both froze, savoring the contact.

One day could feel like a lifetime when it meant not touching the woman who turned a man's blood to molten lava.

She smoothed her fingers down his torso, making the muscles in his stomach contract and his dick throb.

He needed to feel her naked against him.

Sliding his hands around her back, he fumbled with the
clasp of her bra, shaking so much it took two attempts to get
the hooks to release. Then he peeled it away from her body
and gently crushed her against him. The rock-like tips of her

breasts pressed against him and his body jerked at the contact.

Pulling his mouth from hers, he gulped in air. "Damn, that feels good."

"It does," she gasped as she rubbed herself from side to side, abrading her hardened nipples with his chest hair and teasing him in the process.

He lifted her until one perfect, ripe berry was in front of his lips. She made a keening sound as he took her into his mouth and wrapped her denim-clad legs around his torso.

He wanted this to be gentle, but making love to her was like standing on the middle of the Golden Gate Bridge during an earthquake. He bent over and laid her on the bed, his mouth devouring her pulsing peak with tender violence.

She bucked up against him, her ankles joined behind his back. "Yes, Joshua . . ." Her hands locked to either side of his head, pressing him more firmly into her resilient flesh. "Suck me. Harder." She panted and squirmed. "*Now.*"

He would have laughed at her demanding tone, but he was too busy complying. She tasted so sweet and he could smell her arousal through the layers of her panties and jeans.

She lifted her pelvis, bringing both their bodies off the bed. "*I want you inside me.*"

She was losing control and so was he, but he couldn't let that happen. Not this time.

No matter what the sexy little tyrant wanted.

He released her nipple with an audible pop and unwound her legs from him despite her attempt to maintain intimate contact.

Sucking in air, he stood back from the bed.

She sprawled across it like an Amazon princess, her honey hair spread around her head in wild disarray, her skin flushed with excitement, her eyes burning gold with sensual demand.

She reared up on her elbows, pushing her swollen breasts

into prominence and nearly undoing his good intentions. "Come back here."

"In a second. Let me get my clothes off." And take a minute to get control of his libido.

She watched with parted lips, wetted by her small pink tongue, as he removed the remainder of his clothes.

She kicked out of her tennis shoes and toed off her socks while he shucked his pants from his body, but her gaze never wavered from what he was doing—and she left her jeans on. Thankfully.

His control was precarious enough as it was.

She licked her lips again, sending his temperature spiking into dangerous territory. "I read women aren't supposed to be visual, you know?"

"So they say." Where did she get the wherewithal to talk?

"But looking at you excites *me* so much I pulse between my legs like I've just climaxed."

He groaned, his knees damn near buckling at her words. "That's good to know."

She bit her lip, stunning him with a look of vulnerability. "I really seem to be more sexual than a lot of women."

"I like your rampant sensuality." Hell, he loved it.

"You do?"

He rolled his eyes and felt his cock bob. "Can't you tell?"

She seemed mesmerized by the sight of his throbbing erection. She licked her lips again and the muscles at the juncture of his thighs tightened. He'd meant what he said about her not giving him head, but he wasn't sure he'd have the strength to follow through on it if she took matters into her own hands—or mouth, as the case may be.

"Some men don't like forward women."

"So? Some men don't like a curvy ass, either. I'm not one of them."

She rolled onto her stomach and blinked at him over her

shoulder, jiggling her butt toward him. "Is my bottom curvy enough for you?"

If he touched it right now, he'd lose what was left of his brain function. "Yeah," he croaked.

She flipped onto her back and sat up, her hand going to the button on her jeans. "And I'm not too forward for you?"

He watched her fingers undo the metal fastening and then slide the zipper down, one slow tooth at a time.

"Not yet, but with the right kind of coaxing, I think we can get you there," he blatantly lied, unable to resist the urge to tease the she-wolf torturing him.

An expression came over her features that was equal parts mischief and feminine lust. "You don't think I'm aggressive *enough?*"

"Nah, but I'm sure you'll get there . . . eventually."

She kicked out of her jeans and panties at the same time, exposing the creamy expanse of her naked legs to his hungry gaze. He shook with the need to have her, but he was still a far cry from calm enough to give her the gentle lovemaking she needed.

After all, she was delicate.

But *weak* was the last thing she looked as she came up off the bed in all her naked glory, her breasts jiggling, her hips swaying, and her mouth curved in a sexy pout that would have done Mae West proud. She came forward until their bodies brushed.

Cocking her hand on one hip, she curled around his throbbing penis with the other. "Is this better?"

"It's incredible."

"But I could maybe be a little more aggressive?"

He wasn't answering. He had a feeling he'd dug himself into a pit with his teasing and when she dropped in front of him without warning, he knew he was right.

She took his head into her hot, sweet mouth.

They weren't supposed to do this, but she sure wasn't acting like a woman who had just gotten out of the hospital that morning. Working his shaft with her hands, she let her fingertips tickle his balls gently before rubbing up and down his hardness with the expert caress of a trained geisha.

Had *he* taught her that, or was it something that came naturally to her?

Her tongue swirled around his tip, drawing a long, low moan from him. "You're killing me, and we agreed you would not do this."

But if she stopped he'd really die.

She didn't. She made love to him with her mouth until his legs trembled with the effort of standing up, until he could feel the pressure of an orgasm building up.

He tried to pull her away. He wanted to prolong the carnal bliss, to give her pleasure before he took his own. She would have none of it, twisting her head out of his grasp, but not giving up her hold on him. Afraid that pulling on her could hurt her, he was powerless to impose his will on her. The suction inside her mouth increased.

Nothing else existed, but the feel of his sex in her mouth, the gentle touch of her fingers, and the insistence of her need to please him. The scent of her skin and her ardent arousal wafted up to him, exciting him beyond reason. His heart pounded in his chest.

He could barely withstand the sight of her head bent over him like a supplicant when he was the one who felt so desperate for what she could give him.

The pressure at the base of his penis grew agonizing, pushing, pushing, pushing until he started to come, his own warmth mixing with the wet heat of her mouth. His knees buckled and he sank to the floor, but she followed him, drawing his climax out to excruciating proportions.

His voice grew hoarse from shouting.

He was far from innocent in the art of sex, but he'd never known anything like this.

Still hard in her mouth, his muscles continued to spasm, but he had nothing left to give.

"Please, honey, I can't take any more." His voice came out guttural and harsh.

He'd never been this spent; his cock had never been this sensitive, and he had never once in his adult life acceded sensual defeat to a woman. Lise Barton did things to him that no other woman would ever be able to do.

And she thought she was leaving as soon as they caught Nemesis? No way in hell.

She withdrew her mouth, the sensation of her lips moving along his sensitized skin making his body jerk. She kissed him tenderly, on the tip, on his shaft and at the base of his sex. Her hands caressed his inner thighs and around to his butt, cupping him, soothing him.

Sliding them up the small of his back, she gentled the embers that still popped and sizzled, left over from the rage of passion that had exploded between them.

A breath from toppling sideways, he pulled her body up to press against his, needing to take possession of her mouth with primitive intensity. She gave him her lips with the same abandon she'd given him pleasure. The kiss went on and on, their bodies pressed close together, his heart hammering against his ribs with painful strength.

He finally broke his mouth from hers and buried his face in her hair, nuzzling the silkiness, kissing the soft, tender skin of her nape.

"What were you saying about aggressive?" she asked, her voice husky with desire and just a hint of laughter.

He closed his eyes and smiled against her skin. "I can't remember now. My brain has been turned to mush by a wanton she-wolf with elemental fire in her touch."

She choked out a sound and turned her head until their lips met again in a kiss of possession that shook him to his soul.

If things between them continued as they were, he was going to lose something he didn't think he had anymore . . . his heart.

Their mouths broke apart and he pulled away far enough to look into hazel eyes that glowed gold with desire and emotion. "Are you okay?"

"I'm fine. I told you."

But he hadn't believed her. "I was worried about you."

Something that looked like hope came and went in her eyes, but it was gone too fast for him to tell. "There was no need."

He looked down at her ruefully, shaking his head. "I wanted to be gentle with you."

"You were."

"How do you figure that?"

"You didn't push yourself into my mouth. You let me set the pace completely."

He'd barely restrained himself, but he hadn't wanted to force anything from her she wasn't physically up to giving. "I don't consider that the most noble behavior. I should have left the room when I had a chance."

"I like knowing I can make you go against your hard-earned self-control. It excites me and it makes me feel good deep inside."

"Well, you sure as hell succeeded."

She laughed, the sound so sexy, his cock twitched with renewed interest. Amazing. He was like a teenager who'd just discovered the joys of sex with her.

He swung her into his arms, renewed energy and sexual desire thrumming through his body. He knew what he wanted to do and where he wanted to do it. He turned and dropped her on the bed for a second so he could retrieve the condoms from his duffel bag; then he picked her up again and started out of the bedroom.

"Where are we going?"

He'd had a lot of erotic dreams about this woman, but none of them more tormenting than one particular fantasy. "You'll see."

The almost diabolical sound of Joshua's voice sent delicious shivers of awareness skittering down Lise's spine. Apparently, he'd gotten over seeing her as a sick little waif he had to take care of and saw her again as his woman.

Satisfaction bubbled through her veins along with the unquenched desire he'd ignited in her.

He carried her out of the room, along a hallway and down a staircase she had not noticed earlier. When they reached the bottom, she was momentarily startled out of her complete preoccupation with him.

The lower level of his house looked like a weapons arsenal for a third-world country. Guns, launchers, knives, even swords filled the locked glass cases covering the walls from floor to ceiling. One end of the room boasted a lathe and some other machining equipment. In the center were two different work benches, both tall and pristine in their appearance.

"Do you make your own guns?" she asked, feeling some trepidation about what he wanted to do with her in this room.

Yet, she could not deny the thrill of wanton desire inside her. She yearned for untamed intimacy with him.

"Not usually, but I like to modify them myself and make my own ammunition."

He went directly to one of the tall, narrow tables and laid her on it. The smooth, polished surface was chilly against her skin and she shivered.

"Cold, honey?"

"A little." She trusted him not to hurt her, but that didn't mean he wouldn't push her beyond her comfort zone.

This time the shiver had nothing to do with the cold table.

"I'll warm you up." He arranged her arms above her head and then brushed her nipples with the back of his forefinger, going from one to the other with seemingly random movements.

"I fantasized about having you here, in my workroom. Ever since that damn kiss that ended too early, I couldn't get you out of my mind, even when I was working down here."

She arched toward his gentle touch, her heart contracting at his words. Not love, but something more than mere sex.

"So this is by way of exorcising some ghosts?" she asked.

"More like living out a fantasy gone wild. I have a feeling once I've made love to you in here, I'll never be able to forget it."

"Or me."

His eyes were almost black, but she could still read the disbelief in them. "I could never forget you."

"So, you'll miss more than just the sex with me after I'm gone?" she asked.

His eyes registered remembrance of what he'd said on the plane. "You're more than just a body to warm my bed, Lise."

They weren't words of love, but they definitely implied more than he'd had with his ex-wife. "I'm glad."

He ran his hand down her side, tickling her with the light touch, but not so much that she lowered her arms. "I would be polishing a gun and thinking how much I'd like to have my hands on your delectable body."

"You really fantasized about me?" *While he was awake?* It was one thing for his subconscious mind to play tricks on him, another entirely for him to voluntarily think about her.

"I really did." He was touching her the way he said he'd

wanted to, his fingers dipping into every crevice, sensitizing every nerve ending.

"This is better than a fantasy," she gasped out between suddenly dry lips.

"Much better." He lowered his mouth to her body and covered the same skin his fingertips had seduced with pleasure.

When he moved to rock his mouth over hers, his hand skimmed down her stomach and over her thighs, playing at the juncture just a little before moving down to touch the back of one knee with a knowing stroke that made her body swell with feverish longing. Her legs separated of their own volition, her body greedy for the feelings he could evoke.

His fingertips trailed back up the inside of her legs, closer and closer to the heart of her. "You're soft, like Chinese silk," he breathed against her mouth.

Then his fingers were there, on her most secret place, and she was arching up toward him, eager and needy.

As his fingertip slipped inside of her, his eyes burned with near-black fire as he possessed her more completely with his hand.

It felt wild, amazing, and beautiful.

When she was shaking with the need to climax, he positioned her so that her bottom was on the edge of the table.

He stood back and looked. "Yes, just like that."

"Joshua?" Her legs dangled at an uncomfortable angle, but she didn't move them, did not want to detract from the look of utter eroticism on his face.

He rolled a condom over his huge erection and then came to her. He gently lifted her legs onto his forearms, alleviating the discomfort and opening her completely to him.

For several seconds, he did nothing but look, a thunderstorm of yearning in his eyes. Then he lined his sex up with hers in total intimacy and pushed the head inside. He took long minutes effecting complete possession, refusing to increase his pace beyond the tender wooing his intimate flesh was giving her own. When he was completely inside her, he set up a rhythm that drew forth her passion in one drenching wave after another.

They'd done this many times in the past few days, but it felt new, more intense, more powerful, and when she climaxed, she sobbed out her ecstasy and then just sobbed.

Dark and fathomless emotions swirled through her, devastating her senses and leaving her with no reserves to combat the tears.

He picked her up again, wrapping her tightly in his arms. "Shh, Lise, don't cry."

"It's too much, Joshua."

"No, it's not. What happens when we touch is very special, but it isn't too much."

"It's like a hurricane that leaves me wrecked in the aftermath." She wasn't complaining—far from it, but she was trying to help him understand why she couldn't stop crying.

"I know, sweetheart—me, too."

She savored the admission like the declaration of emotion she would likely never get.

He didn't take her back up the stairs, but through a door in the back of his workroom.

Suddenly she was in a different world. Green plants grew wildly under special lights and steam filled the air, created by a dark, heated pool in the center of the space. The floor and walls were hewn from natural rock. The scent of damp earth, flowering African violets, and steaming mineral water surrounded her. It was an underground jungle paradise.

Incredible that it could exist in the Green Mountains of Vermont.

She was in awe. "The hot springs."

"Yes, this pool is cool enough to bathe in, but there's another behind that rubber tree that you could boil eggs in."

Probably the one that fed his radiant heat for the roof and walkways.

She looked at the pool, her heart skipping a beat. "It's dark and very mysterious."

"It's safe."

"It doesn't look safe. It looks magical."

He smiled at that. "Do you trust me?"

"Yes." Always. With everything.

"Then relax and enjoy." He lowered them together in the pool.

Steaming water, hot but not unbearable, covered her body.

Keeping her in his lap, he settled on what must have been some kind of seat because her feet dangled over the side of his bent legs without touching the bottom of the pool.

They rested in silence for several minutes, content to let nature's hot tub soothe their love-wracked bodies. She didn't feel the need to speak, but reveled in his nearness. He dropped gentle kisses on her temple and cheek and then nuzzled her ear.

Familiar feelings began to curl through her as his tongue traced the outline of her ear.

Was her capacity for pleasure infinite? It felt like it. No matter how much their earlier lovemaking had taken from her, her body was preparing for him again.

"This is kind of scary."

He didn't say anything, but she knew he understood.

She cuddled into his body. "I like it all the same."

"Me, too."

He kissed her, claiming her mouth with a leashed control that felt different from anything they'd shared. Emotions swirled around them with the hot, fathomless water and she wrapped her arms around his neck, allowing him complete freedom to touch her.

Anywhere he wanted.

Any way he wanted.

He used the hot water as a lubricant to slide his masculine hands over the soft dips and hollows of her body. He built the pleasure inside her with skillful caresses until she was trembling with the need to climax.

She tried to touch him, but he caught her hand and put it on his shoulder. "Give yourself to me."

Chapter 15

The words were dark and as magical as this secret place, demanding a surrender that she wasn't sure she understood. All she knew was that he wanted to pleasure her while she sat in his lap, doing nothing but accepting his touch.

She made a small assenting noise and did not balk when he slid her thighs farther apart so he had complete access to her secret place. He touched her with his fingertips, light caresses that gave pleasure and demanded nothing in return.

His ministrations had her squirming, but again he broke his lips from hers. "Relax."

How could she relax when he was touching her like that?

But she forced her body into stillness and experienced something amazing. It was as if she was in her body, but out of it. Each glide of his fingers increased the burning fire inside of her, bringing her closer and closer to orgasm, but her body did not tense for it.

She didn't know if it was his adjuring to be still or her own body's exhaustion, but she felt her climax build inside with unstoppable escalation while her body remained pliant against him. His mouth possessed hers with tender but absolute control. His tongue tasted her, his lips molded hers.

And all the while her womb tightened and her inner flesh throbbed around the fingers invading her. Her breath splintered as a climax of amazing depth shook her inner core, sending her into a black oblivion.

When she woke, Joshua was laying her carefully onto his bed. "You'll sleep now, won't you, honey?"

She looked at him, her tongue refusing to work.

She didn't know what had happened down there in his tropical paradise, but it had been life-altering.

He didn't seem to expect a response and left the room after kissing her, with aching sweetness, on her lips.

She woke later, feeling refreshed, and all of the aftereffects of the CO poisoning gone.

She sat up to find Joshua reading one of her books in the big black recliner in the corner. Her stomach growled before she even said anything, and his head came up with a snap.

"Hungry?"

She nodded. "What was your first clue?"

"Other than the wild animal sounds your stomach has been making for the last half-hour while you were sleeping, nothing . . ."

She grabbed a pillow from behind her and threw it at him. He caught it and stood up, letting the book drop onto the chair behind him. "Want to play?"

She tried for a look of innocence, but he wasn't buying it and they ended up wrestling the covers off the bed before he bullied her into getting dressed so he could feed her.

"Most men want women to take their clothes off," she grumbled as she pulled on the thick socks he'd insisted she wear when she told him she hadn't brought a pair of slippers with her.

"It's either get you dressed or take you back to bed and you need sustenance to keep up with me later tonight."

"I like that," she mocked.

"Yes, you will," he promised in a dark voice that sent shivers of anticipation along nerve endings she'd discovered only since becoming Joshua's lover.

They cooked together in his huge, state-of-the-art kitchen, though he did most of the real preparation.

"You really do like to cook, don't you?" she asked.

"Yes." He dropped the fresh noodles he'd just rolled and sliced into thin strips in a pot of boiling water. "It helps me relax."

She stirred the sauce he'd put her in charge of. "You're also very good at it."

"It's a lot like making your own ammunition. You've got to know how to read a recipe and augment it for the best results."

She laughed at the analogy. "That's a very interesting way to look at it, but I still think cooking is a unique hobby for a professional soldier."

"Life can't all be about warfare."

She thought that was an even more unusual attitude for a mercenary to have. "Is that why Nitro designs houses?"

"Uh-huh."

"What about Hotwire?"

"He paints."

"Your bedspread," she breathed, remembering the realistic wolf and how much it resembled Joshua.

"He's got a gallery in New York interested in his work."

"So, y'all have careers to fall back on when you're too old and decrepit to run around saving the world."

Joshua put his arms around her and nuzzled her neck. "We've got plans for leaving the business long before the word *decrepit* becomes part of our everyday vocabulary."

She quivered as his lips brushed the sensitive skin behind her ear. "You do?"

"Yeah."

"When?"

He kissed her and stepped back. "We don't have a definite date."

She stirred the pesto sauce with a great deal of concentration. "I guess it depends on what other things you want from life."

"Right."

"So, what do y'all plan to do?"

"Security consultation. We've got a lot of experience breaking through security, which should make us the best at designing systems that work."

She couldn't argue with that. "It's probably not as exciting as being a professional soldier."

"No, but it isn't as likely to get a person killed, either."

"You could probably retire early without having another job to go to." He owned a plane and his house bespoke a man who had done very well with his career.

Joshua nudged her out of the way and started adding last-minute ingredients to the sauce. "Too boring."

She tried to imagine life without her writing and agreed. "I don't ever want to retire," she admitted.

"Good. I love your books."

She smiled, feeling warmed clear through.

Joshua set the sauce aside and put two chicken breasts on his range-top grill. The fragrance of seared meat and spices mingled with the pesto sauce, filling the kitchen with yummy odors. "Why don't you make some coffee for after dinner?"

She noticed he had an espresso maker. "I could make cappuccinos. I took an evening workshop on the fine art of making coffee right after I moved to Seattle."

"Sounds great."

The perfectly foam-capped cappuccinos smelled rich and decadent when she was done, and she put them on the table with the dinner plates Joshua had served up while she was busy with the espresso.

He'd lit a candle and turned the overhead lighting off; the room glowed in soft amber light.

She looked around as he helped her into her chair. "This is awfully romantic for a mercenary's pad."

His smile was sensual and tender. "You bring out things in me that I didn't know were there."

He didn't think love was there, either, but she was seriously hoping he was wrong and that she could bring that emotion out in him. Because if she had to say good-bye to him, she didn't know how her heart was going to survive.

The dining room looked out on the snow-covered forest— her gaze was drawn to the stark beauty of the landscape over and over again while they ate. "This is an amazing place to live."

Joshua nodded, relaxing back in his chair. "There is no place I would rather spend my downtime."

"Your family doesn't mind that you live so far away?"

He shrugged. "It isn't that far from Massachusetts."

"It might as well be, you living practically on top of a mountain and all."

He slipped his arms over the back of her chair and brushed her shoulder with his fingers. "They don't mind."

She shamelessly scooted her chair closer and snuggled into his side, resting her head back against his chest.

"Not even Myra?" Lise had no experience of mothers, but she'd always heard they were somewhat possessive of their children, even the grown ones.

"She understands. I left home to join the army when I was still a teenager and haven't been back except for visits since then. I like my privacy more than the rest of my family."

"Do they visit you here?"

He sipped at his cappuccino, his silence thoughtful. "I haven't invited them yet."

Despite his penchant for privacy, that surprised her. "Your family is so close-knit. Don't you want to?"

"Someday."

"You have a lot of solitude up here. It's wonderful. I can understand you not wanting to spoil it."

"Most people wouldn't like it."

"I would love it. It would be even better than the ranch for writing outside in uninterrupted privacy." Once the words were spoken, she realized how they sounded—like she was angling for an invitation to live with him, or at least come for a very long visit.

Embarrassed, she didn't know how to back-pedal without swallowing her foot up to her ankle.

"You'd get a lot of work done in a place like this, wouldn't you?" He didn't sound offended, or worried about her motives.

"With you here?" She had to laugh. "I give it a fifty-fifty chance for the writing. You're a pretty good distraction, even better than the whole city of Seattle."

He dipped his head and spoke against her skin. "Am I?"

"Yep." And how.

"In what way?" he asked in a voice laced with sensual promise.

She turned her face so their lips met and let her mouth answer the question silently.

When they broke apart, they were both breathing heavily and his expression was indecipherable.

She stood up and began clearing the table, feeling more at peace than she had in a very long time. "Can we go for a walk in the snow?"

No Nemesis lurked outside to threaten her, or watch her. Just a forest filled with snow-crusted pathways, trees missing their leaves for winter, and a star-filled sky she longed to be out under.

The freedom of breathing non-city air and tramping through trees, the only sound that of wind and wild animals, was an irresistible siren's call to her psyche. "Please."

He picked up the remaining dishes from the table and followed her into the kitchen to drop them in the sink. "It's ten below freezing out there."

She turned to face him, her heart skipping a beat at the sheer beauty of her wolf in relax mode. "Don't tell me you're too much of a hothouse flower to want to go tramping in the woods during the winter."

He gave her a look that doubted her sanity. "*You* don't have proper winter clothes."

"So, lend me some of yours."

That made him smile. "They'll swamp you."

"We'll make do."

And they did. He lent her a thermal shirt to wear over her own layers and another oversized parka that he once again insisted she wear over her own coat.

"I feel like a snow mummy," she complained as he led her out of the mudroom onto the crunchy white nature's winter carpet.

"You look like a stubborn woman who insisted on taking a walk in subfreezing temperatures when most people would be thinking about getting ready for bed."

She arched her brow at him, realizing the gesture was probably futile, considering how little of her face was exposed to the air. "The only people thinking about bed at nine o'clock at night are cowboys on roundup and men who have libidos with more surges than the Rio Grande."

"Don't pretend you're all sweetness and light, Ms. Barton. Who was it that went down on me after I specifically said it wasn't a good idea?"

"It didn't hurt me."

"It about killed me."

"Want to get close to death again later?"

Her only answer was a low groan. She grinned, feeling pleased with herself.

She loved every second they spent outside, even though her nose turned red from the cold and her lungs felt frozen from the frigid air. The heady freedom of open space and no peering neighbors was a fizzy cocktail to her system.

*   *   *

Joshua carried Lise back inside over his shoulder.

He'd realized he had no choice the third time he suggested returning to the house and she answered with a request to investigate just one more *little ole path*.

She pounded his back, laughing. "I just wanted to see where the rabbit tracks led."

He patted her bottom, caressing the curve with a lot more interest than he felt for following any rabbit tracks. "If you'd had your way, we would have hiked all the way back to the landing strip."

"Could we? It seemed like a pretty long ride on the snowmobile."

"The footpath is more direct. The snowmobile is too wide to fit between some of the trees."

"Oh. Can we walk down there tomorrow?"

He shook his head. This woman was a nature baby to her sexy little pink toes. "We'll see."

"You sound like somebody's cranky grandpa."

He squeezed the pliant flesh of her bottom. "I don't feel like a grandpa."

She squealed and reared up, trying to wiggle out of his arms. "Stop that."

He tightened his grip on her legs at her knees and let his other hand slip between her legs, so he could tickle her inner thighs.

She squirmed and laughed, now pounding his shoulders. "You stop that."

"Can't help myself. I like touching you."

"You're tickling me!"

"Am I now?" he asked, imitating her Texas drawl.

Whatever she was going to say got lost in the moan she gave when he caressed the juncture of her thighs with sure fingers.

He let her body slide down the front of him until she was

cradled against his chest, oversized, puffy coat and all. Nuzzling through the fur lining of the parka hood, he found her lips and kissed her. The feelings thrumming through him felt a hell of a lot more tender than lust.

When they got back to his bedroom, he took a long time peeling away the layers hiding her body from him and made love to her with all the softness and slow touching he'd wanted to earlier. This time, she made no effort to go wild, but trembled and shook with a need that went too deep for words.

So they were silent.

He kissed and caressed her, his body vibrating with torrents of desire that her touching released while the room seemed to whisper with their breathing, the words going unspoken.

But when he reached for a condom, she shook her head. "Not this time, please. I want to feel all of you."

The mere thought of entering her without barriers was enough to make his groin ache. "I could get you pregnant."

"It's the wrong time of the month."

"There's always a risk." As he'd told her before, they were so physically compatible, he wasn't sure hormonal cycles would matter if she let him pour his sperm into her womb.

"Life's full of risks, but some of them are worth taking."

There was a deeper message in her words than a simple invitation to enter her body unprotected by a condom, but he wasn't going to analyze that right now. He wanted to feel that naked, hot, silky sheath all around him as much as she wanted to accept him without barriers.

He slid his finger into her pulsing wetness, teasing himself with the possibility. She clutched her vaginal muscles around him and whimpered. "Please, Joshua."

He pulled his finger out and brought it to his mouth to suck the essence of her off of it. She gasped and watched him, her mouth moving as if she wanted to talk, but couldn't.

"You taste good, honey."

He touched her again, just lightly and then put his finger against her lips. "Here, taste."

She let him slide it inside her mouth and as she sucked on it, he settled between her thighs, nudging the head of his penis into contact with her slick and very swollen opening. Her eyes glazed over and he pulled his finger from her mouth to kiss her. She responded with a white heat that burned him to the depths of his being.

And he made love to her, drawing each thrust out until they were both shivering with the need for release.

When they climaxed it was like a supernova engulfing them both, showering their senses with the heat of an exploding sun.

"I love you, Joshua." She clasped his body with her arms, her legs, and her woman's flesh. "*I love you.*"

The words went through him like white lightning, finding a way into a heart he'd thought impervious to a woman's love.

Afterward, they collapsed together, panting and sweaty.

She didn't repeat her avowal of love and he didn't say anything, his mind too numbed by what had just happened between them.

Nemesis closed the laptop, satisfaction coursing through him.

Joshua Watt thought he was so smart, but he wasn't as intelligent as Nemesis. Not even close.

Nemesis knew more about him than he would ever begin to guess. Like that he was former Special Forces. He'd left the army after one tour, but it had been a tour as a Ranger. He was an adversary Nemesis would have to outsmart.

Brain over brawn.

Not that Nemesis wasn't strong, but only an idiot faced a trained killing machine in an equal battle. He had to stack the odds in his favor. He picked up his copy of *The Anarchist's Cookbook* and flipped it open to the section on napalm.

It was a well-read section, but he couldn't risk forgetting anything important.

It would be so much easier if he could take his vengeance now. He had surprise and anonymity on his side. But he could not kill Lise Barton until his marriage was officially dead. An eye for an eye.

There was still a chance for a reprieve.

He'd called his wife last night and reminded her that marriage was supposed to be for a lifetime, that even though she had betrayed him, he still loved her. She had cried.

He didn't like remembering his marriage, his life as Ed Jones. There was too much pain there. Too much loss, but justice was not justice without the letter of the law being adhered to. Until his divorce became final, he could not follow through on his plans for Lise Barton.

His wife had seemed softer toward him last night. Had even said she missed him, but she had not agreed to come back home. She'd said she didn't know when the divorce would be final. Perhaps that meant she was considering withdrawing the petition.

If she didn't, he would have the right to do to Lise Barton's life what she had done to his.

Destroy it.

Then he would have to consider what to do with his wife. She could not be left free to marry another man. It would be wrong. No matter what the legal decrees said, she was his. Could only ever be his.

Should he let Lise Barton know he knew where she was?

The thought tempted him. She thought she could get away from him, that she could run away with Joshua Watt and disappear, but he would always be able to find her.

Nemesis could not be escaped.

* * *

Before dawn, Joshua climbed out of bed, careful not to disturb Lise. He'd woken her up several times in the night to make love and she deserved her rest.

She'd told him she loved him twice more.

The first time she'd said it had about poleaxed him, and each subsequent time hadn't been much better.

The sex between them was better than good—it was the most amazing thing he'd ever experienced. Could she be confusing the overwhelming physical pleasure with something much deeper?

Much like being the first man a woman made love to, he'd been the first one to give her real pleasure. Her marriage had not been a passionate one, but their relationship gave the word new definition. They were more than sexually compatible; they were combustible, and how much of the feeling she had for him was wrapped up in that fact?

Women often mistook sexual love for the real thing. Hadn't his ex-wife? For that matter, hadn't he?

It made sense that Lise would think she loved him. After all, she'd been in love with the only other man she'd ever had sex with.

But he knew how impossible that scenario really was. Unlike a lot of people, Lise actually knew what it meant to be a mercenary. Because of her interviews, she understood the shadow world he lived in better than even his family did, but she'd been living inside of a tight box of fear for months.

He'd made it possible for her to break out of that box. Wasn't it far more likely that she was grateful to him than that she had fallen in love with a hardened mercenary?

A man who had killed, who had seen things he would never tell another soul about.

With her imagination, she might have created a hero in her mind and pasted it over the true man. However, she was too discerning not to see through the illusion eventually and realize what she'd thought was love was only gratitude mixed with intense desire. He would be setting them both up for heartache if he took her declarations at face value and let himself believe in a fairy tale he'd given up as fiction long ago.

Determined to forget Lise's words and the sweet sensations they evoked deep in his soul, he sat down in front of his computer in the surveillance center and logged onto his company's personal server. Hotwire had installed so many layers of security that it would be harder to hack into than the Pentagon. A lot harder.

He checked his e-mail. Hotwire would arrive tomorrow. Part of Joshua mourned the imminent loss of the privacy he shared with Lise. The other part thought it was probably for the best. The more she saw him around his team, the clearer her vision of him would become.

The better chance she would come to her senses before he got seduced into the emotions swirling in her golden-green eyes whenever they were together.

Nitro had e-mailed him, too. Nemesis had not made contact with the decoys. There was no way of knowing if he was following them or not.

According to Hotwire's e-mail, Ed Jones had not used his credit cards since leaving Texas.

The man believed he was anonymous, but he still wasn't taking chances. That fact interested Joshua because it spoke of a mind that was slightly paranoid.

He wished he could be *sure* Nemesis had taken the bait, but his instincts were clouded by his concern for Lise.

If he still had a heart, it would belong to that woman.

Chapter 16

Lise put the Dana down and stared off into space for something like the fifth time in an hour. Somewhere in this house, Joshua was working.

The man she loved.

She'd honestly believed after her divorce that she would never fall in love again. Mike had betrayed her though he had loved her with a commitment she had believed unshakable, if not a passionate desire. She'd spent two years focusing on the worlds she created in her books, worlds she could order, where emotional pain was always assuaged and the heroine always won the day.

In the space of weeks, everything had changed. Both inside herself and in the world around her.

She was no longer alone facing her stalker. She was not alone, period. She'd gotten out of Seattle, a beautiful city, but one that had been choking the life out of her body just the same. She'd taken a lover, discovered she was way more sexual than she'd ever thought possible, and experienced pleasure beyond anything she had ever fantasized.

She'd even told Joshua she loved him.

He hadn't responded in kind, but there was a freedom in the telling that had released chains on her heart she hadn't even known were there.

She jumped to her feet. She wasn't going to get a lick of work done on her book while her body burned with need to be close to Joshua. It wasn't hunger to make love, though she wouldn't turn him down if he asked, she thought with an inward smile.

It was a simple desire to be in the same room with him. To breathe the same air he was breathing. To know he was there, where she could see or touch him.

She went looking for him, carrying her Dana.

She found him in his workroom. He was packing shells on the same workbench he'd laid her out on to make love to the day before.

He looked up when she came in. His gaze traveled over her, as if he could see right through her jeans and long-sleeved t-shirt. Maybe he could. Feeling wanton and free, she'd left her bra off at his request that morning, and could feel her nipples hardening against the snug fabric now. If he couldn't see them, he needed his eyes checked.

The dark glow in his gaze said he saw just fine. "Hi, honey."

She smiled. "Hi." She loved it when he called her honey, or sweetheart.

It felt warm and intimate.

"I was hoping you wouldn't mind if I worked down here with you." She lifted her Dana so he could see it.

"Not at all. It won't bother you to have me in the room while you're writing?"

She shook her head. She was fast growing addicted to his company, but when she looked around her, she realized she hadn't planned very well. She supposed she could sit at one of his workbenches.

"Here, let me get you something to sit on."

"Okay."

He left and was gone several minutes. When he came back,

instead of carrying a kitchen stool like she expected, he had a comfy-looking brown armchair and padded footstool.

And he was carrying them like they weighed about as much as the kitchen stool she'd thought he would be bringing.

He set them up close to where he was working and smiled at her. "Will this do?"

"Yes." For some reason she found it difficult to speak past the obstruction in her throat. "It's perfect."

"Hey, are you okay?"

"Yes, it's just that you always do more than I expect. I whined about needing to get out of the apartment and you took me to an island where I could experience Native American culture up close. I wanted to go tramping in the woods and you took me, even though it was dark outside and below freezing. You spoil me."

"I like doing it."

She shook her head, wondering if she could even explain the emotion overwhelming her at the moment. "I was an extra person in my dad's life, one he would have been real pleased to see gone, and I always felt like a weight on Jake. Dad was nuts, but ninety percent of the problems my brother had with him were because of me and his desire to protect me. Ever since my divorce, I've been very careful not to rely on anyone too much, but you just step in and take care of me."

She did not want to cry. He probably thought she was an emotional basketcase already. "You are doing more for me than any human being should be expected to do, but you don't act like it's any big deal. You won't let me pay you, and you . . . and you . . ."

She couldn't go on without making an idiot of herself, so she just waved at the armchair, indicating the last item in a long line of things he'd done for her that made her feel special.

Joshua shook his head and pulled her to him for a long, satisfying kiss. "It's easy to do things for you because you're so damn sweet."

Then he released her and patted her bottom, pushing her toward the chair. "Now, write."

She sank into the chair and got comfortable, putting her feet up and her Dana in her lap. "So, why do you make your own ammunition?"

"Because I know I can trust it."

"Oh. In my books, my heroines do it because they want to customize the velocity of the bullet and charge of the explosion."

He laughed. "There is that as well. Now stop stalling and get back to work."

She mock saluted. "Yes, sir."

She spent the next couple of hours working while Joshua made ammunition and then started cleaning guns.

After finishing a scene, she needed to stretch, so she got up and went over to Joshua, watching him sharpen a short knife. If she remembered correctly from her research, it was the kind that went into a belt and looked like a buckle, but could be pulled out in less than a second.

Come to think of it, he'd probably been wearing something similar pretty much every day since she met him.

He looked up, his expression not in the least impatient. "Did you need something, honey?"

"I thought I'd soak in the spring for a while. My muscles are cramped from sitting."

He cupped her nape and pulled her closer so he could reach her back and then he started massaging her muscles, making her groan. "Do you want some company?"

"I'd love it."

The underground jungle was every bit as impressive on the second visit as it had been on her first.

"This place is incredible. I can't believe you have it."

"I like the jungle, but usually when I'm there, relaxing is the furthest thing from my mind. I wanted my own private sanctuary where I could be a man, not a mercenary."

She sensed he'd surprised himself as much as her by the open admission, but unlike many men would do, made no effort to cover it with a bunch of excuses or a subject change.

He just started taking off his clothes, which she guessed could be considered a change in subject because it certainly took her attention away from what they were saying. She began undressing as well, sliding her shoes off and toeing off her socks while she watched his body come into view.

He was in the water first, but she took her time climbing into the pool, enjoying the sensation of being naked in the steam-warmed room, almost drunk on the simple freedom of being a woman.

He settled back against the wall of the pool, his gaze centered completely on her. "You're teasing me."

She stood on the side, feeling her nipples grow hard and her breasts swell under his intense scrutiny. "Am I?"

He stood up and moved across the pool until he was right in front of her in the water. He was eye level with the apex of her thighs and he reached out and brushed through her curls with probing fingers. "Yes, come in here. The water feels good, but you'll feel better."

She grinned and obeyed, sliding into the water and his arms at the same time. "This is such an incredible sensation."

He hugged her body to his. "Yes, it is. You're an incredible woman."

She would have said he was the amazing one, but he kissed her and she lost touch with reality. Just that quick.

Their passion grew incendiary in seconds and she was panting and straining against him when his hand slid between her legs to check her readiness. She yelled a demand for him to take her and other demands that turned them both on. When they actually joined, she was so lost to the consuming firestorm of desire he ignited in her that she came almost immediately.

So did he.

Her climax overpowered her completely, leaving her wrenchingly drained. Combined with the lack of sleep the night before, she could barely keep her eyes open. She must have dozed, because when she woke up, he was toweling her dry. She hovered between sleep and wakefulness as he took her back to his bedroom.

He smiled down at her. "You need a nap. I wore you out."

He sounded awfully pleased with himself, but she couldn't work up any energy to be bothered by that. And why should she be? He should be happy with himself. It wasn't every day a man could wear out a she-wolf. She snuggled into him.

However, when they entered his bedroom, he stopped in his tracks and swore, using words she'd never even heard of and she was positive were in more than one language.

"What is it?"

"I forgot Hotwire was coming." He made it sound like a federal crime.

She'd thought one of his indicator lights had shown that Nemesis was there, or something equally negative. Hotwire's arrival hardly seemed something to spark that kind of reaction. "Is that all?"

"It's enough."

"Does he need you to pick him up, or something?"

"No. He's already here."

That didn't make any sense. "How do you know? I haven't seen him."

Joshua inclined his head toward his surveillance center.

Duh, she thought.

"Hotwire is here," she repeated, still not taking it in completely.

"Right."

Joshua's friend was in the house, had arrived while they were occupied in his private jungle.

The thought of what he must have heard, might even have seen, woke her up real fast. She'd been screaming like a banshee, all sorts of lascivious demands of Joshua there toward the end.

"He heard me, I'm sure he did." She hit Joshua's chest with the side of her fist. Not hard, because she didn't want to hurt him, though he was solid and she wasn't sure it wouldn't take a Sherman tank to do that. "Why didn't you tell me?"

He laid her on the bed, pulling back the comforter and tucking her underneath. "I forgot."

"You forgot he was coming? How could you? You don't forget anything."

"When I'm with you, I forget my own name."

For some reason one of the things he'd said about his marriage breakup came back to her. His first wife had not been able to give him complete oblivion.

"You mean nothing else exists for you when we make love?" she asked, just to clarify.

"Exactly." He didn't sound pleased by the fact, but she was overjoyed.

Joshua frowned. "It's a damn good thing Hotwire is a friend. If it had been an enemy, he would have been on us without advance warning."

Considering the tight security of his home, she doubted it, but she positively beamed at the idea that making love with her was more involving for him than it had been with Melody. Maybe the feelings he had for her would be more long-lasting and encompass more than just his dick as well.

"What has you grinning?"

"Nothing."

He leaned over her, blocking her view of anything but him. "Something has you smiling."

"Making love with you always makes me smile."

"But first it makes you cry."

Sometimes it did. "It overwhelms me."

He bent down and kissed her fiercely before standing up. "Rest, I kept you up too late last night. I'll go find Hotwire."

"Okay."

"Okay?"

"Yes."

He felt her head. "Are you all right?"

She laughed. "Better than all right, but I *am* tired." She yawned just to prove her point and because she couldn't help herself.

She also wasn't keen on the idea of facing Hotwire, not knowing what he'd seen or heard. It might be cowardly, but she was more than content to let Joshua deal with the initial awkwardness all on his own. After all, Hotwire was his friend.

Joshua stepped back from the bed. "Be good."

She snuggled under the wolf comforter. "Put some clothes on before you go looking for Hotwire. He might not find the sight of your naked body as appealing as I do."

He laughed at that. "I'm not the only bossy one around here."

She merely smiled.

Hotwire was working on his laptop at the kitchen counter, munching on some popcorn when Joshua found him.

Joshua slid onto a stool next to his buddy and grabbed a handful of popcorn. "When did you get in?"

Hotwire looked up from his computer screen, a knowing gleam in his eye. "A couple of hours ago, not that *you* noticed."

Damn it, Joshua had never been shy, but he didn't know how to ask his friend if he'd come downstairs while he and Lise were making love. What disturbed him the most was knowing that he wouldn't have noticed if Hotwire had come into the jungle room and said something.

He'd been that far gone.

Making a stab in the dark for what he hoped was the case, he said, "You didn't come looking."

"Didn't need to. The surveillance equipment showed two warm bodies in the jungle room."

While Joshua did not do video surveillance in the rooms of his home, his sensors could pretty accurately pick up the number of people in each room.

"I thought you might be a tad upset if I interrupted your afternoon hot tub." The Georgia twang was liberally laced with wry humor.

Joshua didn't bother replying. His friend was right and he was glad the other man's sometimes off-the-wall sense of humor hadn't prompted him to knock on the door. He didn't want Lise embarrassed. "What's the latest word from Nitro?"

"He and Josie are making good time, but they're still two days out."

"No contact from Nemesis yet?"

"No, but Nitro says he's being followed."

When you lived a great deal of your life relying on your instincts, you learned when you could trust them. Joshua trusted Nitro's as surely as he trusted his own. "Good."

Hotwire took a long drink of beer from the bottle at his elbow before talking again. "I did some more digging and you're not going to like what I found."

"What?"

"Ed Jones belonged to a fringe militarist group, the kind who pass out *The Anarchist's Cookbook* as Christmas gifts."

The perp was getting more irritating by the minute. "How heavily involved was he?"

"I'm not sure, but it looks like he did some computer hacking for them. He quit the group a couple of years ago."

"Do you know why?"

Hotwire nodded his blond head. "According to some e-mail correspondence I found on their server, he was offended when he wasn't given a leadership position among them."

"Because of his hacking?"

"Yeah. Apparently, he thought he was more important to the cause than the rest of them did."

"Sounds like an egoist."

"That's only part of the picture." Hotwire popped a couple of kernels of popcorn in his mouth and chewed. "His employee records also indicate dissatisfaction with his career growth. He saw himself as more key to the company than management did. Losing his job would have been a huge blow to a guy like that."

Joshua's face tightened. "Nothing like the blow I'm going to deal him when I get my hands on him."

Hotwire's expression said he understood and agreed. "How's Lise holding up?"

"She's fine, but I want that jerk off her back."

"Considering how much time you two spent in the jungle room, I'd say she's more than fine." His eyes mocked Joshua.

"That's none of your business."

Hotwire's lips quirked. "Nope, it sure isn't, but I've got to say I'm glad I wasn't the enemy."

"Anyone but you, Nitro, or I would have a helluva time getting through my security."

"True."

Joshua ran his fingers through his hair. "I know I should leave her alone."

"But you can't?" Hotwire asked with interest.

"No."

"That's different."

"*She's* different."

"Are we going to be moving up our plan to go into security consultation?"

They'd been talking about getting out of the merc business for the last year. Although they'd been soldiers for almost two decades, none of them had been ready for the switch just yet, particularly Nitro. He still had a lot of the restlessness that drew men to their line of work.

He got up and started putting things away, tossing his friend's beer bottle in the recycling container. "Lise deserves better than a merc with my past and no emotions to speak of."

"You don't look like your emotions are dead when you're around her."

Joshua was beginning to believe that, but that didn't mean he had a future with her. "She's innocent and so damn sweet."

"And?"

"I've done and seen things that would make it into most people's nightmares."

"Haven't we all? But I don't think she minds."

"That's because she's made me into something in her mind that I'm not. Once reality hits, she'll want to move on."

"I don't think so."

"I heard what you two were saying that day in the apartment about how this was like an adventure in one of her books. It's a fantasy for her, not reality."

"You just keep telling yourself that, Wolf, but I'll flip Nitro for the best-man slot at your wedding."

The next couple of days went by quickly with Joshua and Hotwire coordinating the trap for Nemesis, Lise trying to meet deadline on her current book, and she and Joshua making love each night in the privacy of Joshua's bed.

Nitro and Josie McCall arrived late in the evening. It had been snowing softly for a couple of hours and Lise had been fretting about driving conditions. Joshua laughed at her. "Nitro has driven in full-scale blizzards on balding tires.

Don't worry about him and Josie making it up the mountain."

Lise had nodded, but bit her lip. The relief she felt when the decoys made it safely to Joshua's home was palpable.

Nitro parked outside, a ways from the house. He and Josie crossed the snow-covered ground and cleared walkways to the front door.

"I can't believe how much she looks like me," Lise commented to Joshua as Josie followed Nitro into the house.

Josie smiled at Lise, though the smile looked strained to Joshua. "Makeup and a wig will do wonders, but I'll be glad to get them off."

"I can imagine." Lise's voice was typically warm with understanding, and Joshua put his arm around her waist as he led them all into the primary surveillance room where Hotwire continued to monitor the equipment.

She smiled up at him and for a second, he forgot about the other people crowding into the room.

"I'll leave Nitro to give you the report." Josie's voice brought him back to the present. "It isn't much, really, and I'm going to go turn back into me." She turned to Hotwire. "You want to show me the way to a bathroom?"

"The report can wait—I'll show you," Nitro said before the other man had a chance to answer.

He went to take Josie's arm to lead her off, but she sidestepped his touch. "Just show me the way, Hotshot. You don't need to manhandle me to do it."

Nitro's expression didn't change, but the sense of leashed intent emanating off of him rose several notches.

However, he spun on his heel without a word or further attempt to touch her and stalked away. Josie followed, her expression readable if Joshua's buddy's was not. The female operative looked ready to chew nails.

A half an hour later, they all congregated in the primary surveillance room off the entryway again.

Lise had been surprised when Joshua had showed it to her the first time. "Why do you have two of them?" she'd asked.

"It's convenient."

"It's overkill, if you ask me. How many monitors can one man possibly need?"

"I'm the security expert," he reminded her and she stuck her tongue out at him, which led to a long, drawn-out kiss when he showed her more effective uses for it.

"A car followed you onto the road, but it didn't go past checkpoint two," Joshua said now to Nitro.

"Nemesis."

"There's no way of knowing that," Lise said.

"I feel it in my gut. He was following us." Nitro looked at Josie. "You felt it, too."

She nodded, her gaze nowhere near meeting Nitro's. She focused on Lise. "I'm sure he was there. It was like I could feel him watching."

Nitro made a sound that could have been taken as agreement, or something else.

It made Josie stiffen, but she didn't look at him. "I'm a damn good operative and my instincts have never let me down. Regardless of what some pigheaded, chauvinist, badass mercenaries of this world might think."

"If I didn't think you were the goods, I would never have brought you into the case," Joshua said, knowing she wasn't talking about him, but wanting to pull Nitro's chain.

"I think you're one of the best operatives I've ever known," Hotwire said, his Georgia drawl very pronounced and his blue eyes filled with mischief.

The smile he turned on Josie was all Southern charm, and Nitro looked ready to kill someone.

Josie wasn't looking at him, so she didn't see it, but everyone in the room knew who *her* glare was for. "*I wasn't talking about you two.*"

Nitro said something that made Lise gasp.

"Are you two going to have a problem working together?" Joshua asked, not altogether just to push his friend.

He didn't want the mission screwed up because of a personality conflict.

"Yes. *I'm* a professional." Josie turned to give Nitro the benefit of her filthy look this time.

"It's not a problem," he said, his eyes narrowing as they took in Josie's hostile stance. "I survived four days on the road with nothing but her company—I can last out the end of the mission."

Josie's eyes clouded with pain before she turned her body so that her back was to Nitro. "What do you want me to do?" she asked Joshua.

He felt sorry for her. Nitro *was* a badass, and if Joshua's emotions were on ice, his buddy's had been burned right out of him. Something was obviously going on between them, but Josie would be smart to cut her losses, because Nitro was not a man to give a woman emotional power over him.

"When I'm not with Lise," Joshua said to the female operative, "I want you with her. Nitro, Hotwire, and I will split the surveillance watch and the outside reconnaissance, but I don't want Lise alone ever, okay?"

"Are we bunking together?" Josie asked.

"No, she's staying in my room."

Surprise contorted Josie's features. "*On a job?*"

"This isn't a regular mission."

Josie shook her head, comprehension dawning in her eyes. "I thought you'd never fall. You always acted so immune."

Lise turned six shades of pink and tried to move away from his arm. "He didn't fall, he's just . . ."

"Not going to talk about it." He reined her back in, keeping her small body close to his own.

Josie smiled, her whole stance relaxing. She even laughed. "That's great. It really is, but I'm mum on the details from here on out. Sorry," she said to Lise, "I wouldn't have said *anything* if it hadn't come as such a shock."

The sound of disbelief that came from Nitro really had Joshua wondering what was going on between the two of them, but nobody pried into Nitro's life, not even his friends.

It was a way of being Joshua identified with well, despite having two sisters and a mother who didn't know the meaning of the word *privacy*. Which was probably one of the main reasons he'd never invited them to visit his sanctuary. There were big chunks of his life they knew nothing about. Stuff they could not handle if they did.

Chapter 17

Lise's body convulsed with pleasure, her heart exploding with emotion, and she cried out, "I love you, Joshua!"

She couldn't keep the words inside. She didn't even try anymore. Not when they made love.

His mouth slammed down on hers, marking her as his while at the same time sealing her words of love inside her. He came, his whole body shuddering over hers while he threw his head back and shouted her name over and over again.

Interspersed with her name were words of need, of approval, of volcanic pleasure.

But no words of love.

And Lise's heart contracted with pain, even as her body knew a satiation that left her totally drained.

Afterward, he got up to take care of the condom and she tried to regain emotional perspective in the brief solitude, but hot wetness burned the back of her eyes.

He was the perfect lover, burning her up with his passion and yet patient when she needed him to be. Her love for him grew more powerful every time they came together in physical intimacy, but that was only part of it. Unquenchable emotion also consumed her on each occasion he exhibited the bone-deep character that made him who he was.

Not to have her feelings returned shredded her insides. But how could any man be so tender and caring for her every need, when he felt no real emotion for the woman in his arms?

When Joshua came back, he pulled her against him like he always did after making love.

She searched his eyes for some indication of deep emotion as their breathing returned to normal, but his chocolate gaze remained impenetrable.

She stifled a sigh and said good night, unwilling to break their rapport with questions she wasn't sure she wanted the answers to.

Warmth flared briefly in his expression as he leaned forward to kiss her lips and whisper, "Good night," before tucking her head under his chin.

Emotion beat around her in the ensuing silence, and she would swear on her publishing contract that it wasn't all coming from her.

Hope flooded her and she took his hand in hers, bringing it to her mouth to kiss his palm, her love for him pulsating on her lips and through her fingertips.

She pressed his hand against her heart and nuzzled his chest. "I do love you, Joshua."

He didn't say anything, though he hugged her more closely to him. It definitely wasn't a rejection, but could it simply be physical consolation for his lack of emotional attachment to her?

"Joshua?"

"Shh, Lise. Go to sleep, honey."

She tried to do as he said, but inexplicably, despair grew second by second until she could stand their intimacy no longer.

It was too much of a reminder of what she needed that he couldn't give and she turned from him, scooting away so their bodies no longer touched. The immediate sensation of being cut off from something infinitely precious and necessary swept over her in a drowning wave, and she had to bite her fist not to cry out at the pain of it.

His big hand settled on her naked shoulder. "Lise, is something wrong?"

Nothing she wanted to talk about, so she shook her head.

He didn't ask why she'd pulled away, but he tugged her back into his arms and she let him. Even this false sense of emotional intimacy was better than nothing.

Only a small voice in the back of her head said she was doing it again, hiding from a reality she didn't want to face, but one that wasn't going to disappear.

Joshua took his turn at monitoring the surveillance equipment late that night while Nitro performed physical reconnaissance outside. His attention on the monitors, Joshua's mind worried a problem he wasn't sure how to tackle.

Lise had told him she loved him again.

Like the other times she'd said it over the past few days, not knowing what to say, he had not replied.

If he returned the vow, and he admitted it wouldn't be that hard, would that be fair to her? Was the witch's brew of emotion filling his insides love, or a very complicated form of physical desire? And if it wasn't love, did it matter?

He was sure that whatever it was, it was a permanent condition, so would it really hurt to tell her he loved her?

It definitely hurt her that he didn't. He could see the pain in her soft hazel eyes, feel it in the stiffness of her body against him when the words would not come.

They had gone to sleep that night with an emotional distance between them that had not been there before, and he didn't like it.

His eyes flicked from monitor to monitor and across the

grid. Nothing. No activity to get his mind off the emotional upheaval he hated acknowledging, much less concentrating on.

The hair on the back of his neck stood up and he knew immediately what that meant. Lise was awake.

No sound came from behind him, but he could sense her watching him. It was like a wire connected them, sending a buzz through his body when he became the focus of her concentration.

What was going on inside her head?

Was she trying to come up with a way of telling him that she didn't want to sleep with a man who was too damn hardheaded to acknowledge a passion that eclipsed the physical?

After several seconds of silence, the sound of rustling bedclothes told him she was moving.

Then she padded across the floor in her bare feet and he had to swallow down an admonishment to put on some socks. It got cold at night and neither of them liked a very warm room for sleeping. Where this nursemaid side of him came from, he sure as hell didn't know, but Nitro and Hotwire would laugh their asses off if they knew about it.

He flicked a quick glance at her when she stopped beside him before resuming his vigilant observation of the equipment.

She'd pulled on his white t-shirt. It hung down to her thighs, but her dusky nipples showed through the thin cotton and he had no problem picturing the silky, perfectly shaped body beneath it. He tried not to.

He needed to keep his full attention on the monitors and indicator grids in front of him, not let his mind wander down salacious paths that would send his thinking to his other head.

"I think Nitro's in love with Josie."

Whatever he'd been expecting Lise to say, that wasn't it.

"They're at each other's throats."

"Anger can often mask other strong emotions." She wasn't touching him, but she might as well have been, her presence was so indelibly printed on his psyche.

His whole body contracted in reaction to her nearness.

"Nitro's a loner, honey. Whatever he feels for Josie, it's not love."

He had to admit that the past couple of days with the two of them around had been interesting ones. The tension was so thick between them, it was a surprise they didn't spontaneously combust.

Several seconds of silence greeted his comment.

What was Lise thinking?

He wished he could turn and look into her eyes, see what their clear depths would reveal. Something had started her on this train of thought and he wanted to know what it was, afraid his lack of love words earlier might have been the trigger.

"I think you're wrong," Lise finally said. "He never takes his eyes off of her when they're together and it makes Nitro really mad when Hotwire touches her, even when it's just to grab her attention."

Joshua had noticed that, too, but he didn't think it meant love. "He wants her."

"You think *lust* and only lust explains the way they lock onto each other like heat-seeking missiles when they're in the same room?"

"Yeah."

The quality of her silence changed and he couldn't resist a quick glance at her. She was looking at him like he'd crawled out from under a rock.

Damn it, why *had* he said that? He wasn't even sure it was true. He was too used to thinking in terms of the physical and denying the emotional. He hadn't given her theory even minimal consideration and now he'd put his foot in his mouth and was choking. Boot leather tasted like crap.

She sighed, the sound sad and discouraged, but her hand hooked into his waistband and she stepped closer. "Just because you don't think romantic love exists doesn't mean the rest of the world is handicapped by your cynicism."

So, this *was* about what had happened earlier. She'd been using this whole thing about Josie and Nitro as a blind to talk about what she wanted to know . . . what he felt.

It was damn good battle tactics, but her timing stank.

He wasn't good at subtlety when it came to the emotional side of life. Feelings were problematic enough without getting all cagey about them.

"This is not a good time for this conversation." He needed to be able to give her his undivided attention because he didn't want to screw this up, but he had to focus on the surveillance equipment right now.

"I'm sorry. I didn't realize talking about your friend's love life was a taboo subject." Sarcasm dripped like water from a melting icicle in her voice.

He reached back and found his t-shirt. He used a fist of it to pull her around in front of where he sat on the tall swivel stool. Tucking her between his legs and her head under his chin, he kept them both facing the surveillance equipment. She struggled, but he wouldn't let go and finally she settled against him.

He rubbed the top of her head with his chin. "But we're not talking about Nitro, not really. This is about us and I don't want to discuss our relationship when I can't look in your eyes, much less give you my full attention."

Even now, he had to keep his gaze locked on the monitors and merely holding her didn't feel like enough. Not by a long shot.

"*We don't have a relationship.*"

His body tensed with the same battle-readiness he experienced before going through with a mission. "Like hell."

She snorted. "We've got sex and a living arrangement you'll want to end as soon as we catch Nemesis."

She talked as if *she* didn't want to move out of his house any more than he wanted her to leave.

Now was not the time to make decisions about their living arrangements, though. Not when the threat of Nemesis might be influencing her feelings for him as well as what she'd once called *the sex thing*.

He put his hand over her stomach and pressed her more firmly against him and decided to address *the sex thing*. "Calling what happens between us mere sex is like calling the crisis in the Middle East a family squabble."

"Okay, so it's a *great* screw, but it doesn't mean anything to you. You've made that clear."

She was really intent on pissing him off, wasn't she?

"I never once said it didn't mean anything to me."

"You never said it did, either."

His arms tightened around her convulsively. "I said it was more than sex."

"What does that mean, Joshua?"

For the first time that he could remember, thoughts and emotions fought for supremacy in his mind. He didn't like the out-of-control feeling it gave him, or all the conflicting judgments that vied for supremacy in his head.

Women said they wanted honesty, so he gave it to her. "I don't know, and I really don't think this is the time to dissect our relationship."

She went completely still, not even breathing, and then let out a long sigh.

Turning, she pressed her face against his chest and kissed him right over his heartbeat. "I'm sorry, Joshua." Her soft voice tugged at something deep inside him. "I know you never made me any promises and my feelings aren't your responsibility. I don't have any right to get all bitchy with you because you don't share them."

Who said he didn't share them? He wasn't sure what he felt, but did she have to dismiss it all without even a hearing?

He opened his mouth to demand just that when the first checkpoint light began to glow.

He rubbed Lise's neck and shoulders, trying to soothe the tension in her as he waited to see if checkpoint two lit as well, but his instincts said it was going to.

"You can get as bitchy as you want, not that I think that's what you're acting like," he hastened to assure her, "but, honey, your timing sucks."

"We don't have to talk about this at all." She was trying to sound huffy, but her words were muffled against his chest and it spoiled the effect. "I shouldn't have brought it up."

He tightened his hold on her, allowing a small smile to curve his lips. "We'll talk about it, all right, but *later*."

"Why later? Why not now?"

"Because checkpoint two just lit up."

He reached for the Comm button and pressed it. "Recon One, come in."

He released the Comm button and a second later heard Nitro's voice. "This is Recon One. Go Comm Center."

"We've got an eagle on the mountain."

"Stats."

"Passed C-Two eleven seconds ago."

"I'll move in for visual."

"What is your location?"

"L-P path thirty meters out."

Shit. Even moving as fast as Joshua knew Nitro could do, he wouldn't be able to make visual of the approach to the house from his location near the launch pad in less than five minutes.

Nemesis could make the gate at Joshua's entry in that time if he was traveling fast enough. They had disabled the electric field on the gate and fence because the idea had been to catch Nemesis, not keep him out.

Lise broke from his arms as he signed off with Nitro, her expression not easily read. "*He's here?*"

"We can't be positive until we have visual, but yeah, I think he is."

She moved behind him while he called Hotwire and Josie. When he put the comm unit down, he realized she was wearing jeans and tying her tennis shoes.

"You're staying in the house."

"I'm not an idiot, Joshua. I won't get in your way, but I'm not helpless, either. I was raised on a Texas ranch."

"And you refused to learn to shoot a rifle or a handgun. Jake told me."

"So?"

So, she wasn't getting any closer than a gunshot to that sick bastard and since she couldn't shoot a gun, she wasn't going in at all. "You're staying inside. Got it?"

She rolled her eyes. "I didn't say I was going outside."

"Promise me, Lise."

"I won't get in your way," she vowed.

He'd tell Josie to keep her inside, no matter what.

Joshua left Lise and Josie manning the surveillance and comm center downstairs while he and Hotwire left the house via an exit in the weapons room. They went in opposite directions around the house so they could take parallel paths to the drive and stay out of open visual range.

Joshua came around to the front under cover of the trees. He was in position on his side of the drive, his eyes scanning both the woods and the open area, when the comm unit in his ear beeped.

"The intruder is on foot," Josie said, her voice flat and professional, "three meters northwest of the drive, point five kilometers from the drive entrance, headed toward the house."

That put Nemesis on the opposite side of the drive from Joshua. He took off toward the location Josie had given, knowing Nitro and Hotwire had received the same information and would be approaching Nemesis from their positions as well.

Joshua had visual within seconds.

Wearing snow camouflage and a backpack, the intruder carried a folded M-16 over his shoulder. His parka covered his hair, but Joshua had no doubt that it was Ed Jones.

Several meters from the perp, the crisp white snow hindered a completely silent approach, and because of it, the speed of Joshua's movements. He pulled his own standard M-16 into firing position, the selective fire mechanism set to semiautomatic.

He was still too far away for a flying tackle when Nemesis stopped, pulled his gun off his shoulder, and then his pack off his back. He dug in the pack for a couple of seconds before pulling out two grenades and setting them on the ground. He flipped his M-16 open and set one of the grenades into the grenade launcher on the barrel.

Ed Jones lifted the gun toward the house and Joshua fired.

A second report followed closely on the first, and Nemesis spun, lifted, and then fell to the snow, motionless.

Joshua was already approaching at a dead run. He and Hotwire converged on the perp at the same time.

Joshua carefully turned the man over while Hotwire examined the pack.

No crimson wetness stained the pristine white of the snow.

Joshua checked for a pulse at the neck. "His heart's beating." He unzipped the parka on the intruder and noted the steady rise and fall of the man's chest. "Kevlar."

"Uh-huh," Hotwire said noncommittally. "He awake?"

"No. Out cold, and he'll probably stay that way for a while after taking two hits."

"Too damn bad."

The tone of Hotwire's voice made Joshua look up from the man who had caused Lise so much grief. "Why?"

"He's got an armed bomb in his pack."

The unmistakable odor of napalm confirmed the type of

bomb before Hotwire carefully pulled it out and Joshua whistled low when he saw it. The timing mechanism was connected to a detonator with two sticks of dynamite strapped to the bomb casing.

"Nitro, give an ETA," Joshua said into the mike of his comm unit.

"Thirty seconds."

"Good. We've got an armed napalm with two sticks and a detonator cap."

"Shit."

Joshua's thoughts precisely.

Nitro jogged up seconds later and dropped to his knees beside Hotwire, immediately beginning to check wires. "This guy is serious about his explosives."

"Yeah." He'd been even more serious about killing Lise and anyone with her.

"*There's a bomb?*" It wasn't Josie's voice coming over the comm unit. It was Lise's.

And she sounded upset.

"Don't worry about it, honey. This is Nitro's specialty."

"*Don't tell me not to worry.* You're down there at risk while I'm sitting in safety up here, and Nemesis is *my* problem."

Didn't she realize yet that her problems *were* his? "He's nobody's problem anymore."

What sounded distinctly like a snort came across the Comm unit. "I heard you. You said the bomb is armed."

Joshua grimaced. Too bad she'd heard that, too. "It is."

"What kind?" This time it was Josie's voice, sounding slightly less no-nonsense than usual.

Nitro gave the details through his comm unit while Joshua secured the perp's wrists and ankles with plastic ties. He wasn't risking Ed Jones waking up and trying something stupid.

"Is it a simple setup, or complex?" Hotwire asked.

"Looks pretty textbook for someone who's read *The Anarchist's Cookbook* one too many times." Nitro spoke without looking up. "I like a fastidious nutcase."

"How long is the timer set for?"

"Don't know the initial time, but we've got less than six minutes . . ." Nitro's voice trailed off and then he swore, loudly.

"What's the problem, buddy?"

"Never trust a man who makes his own napalm. He's got a trip wire on the timer and the connectors between the detonator and the dynamite."

"How stable is the big bomb?"

"It's homemade." Which meant Nitro didn't trust it for transport.

He sliced through black tape holding the dynamite to the napalm and carefully set the bomb on the padded snow.

"Check it for a second detonator." Josie's voice held all the authority of a woman who knew exactly what she was talking about.

Nitro didn't answer her, but he did open the bomb. "Shit."

"There's a second one, isn't there?" Josie didn't sound smug at being right. She sounded worried.

"Yes. It doesn't have near the explosive capacity of the dynamite, but it's enough to set the napalm off." Nitro's eyes burned with frustration. "The tape had a foil lining. Cutting it started the second timer. Ninety seconds and counting."

Lise watched on the video cam as Nitro revealed the double bomb threat and then she turned to Josie. The other woman's eyes were glued to the cam and she was talking to Nitro, but not into the comm unit. "Don't cut that wire. Damn it, I need to touch it . . ."

"Do you know something about disarming bombs?"

"Yes."

"Shouldn't you be out there helping him?"

"Wolf's orders were to stay with you inside."

"The mark of a good recruit is knowing when to ignore your commanding officer."

Josie laughed. "You'd have had a rough time in the army."

"Were you military?"

"No." The expression on Josie's face said there was a story behind that *no*, but Lise would have to wait to hear it.

Lise said, "Nemesis is incapacitated. I don't need your protection, they do. Go."

Josie was already moving.

Lise put the camera nearest the men on zoom and watched in horrified fascination as real life played out like a movie in front of her.

Josie came sprinting up and then fell on her knees, facing the camera, beside the big bomb. "Let me feel it."

Lise could hear everything, including each person's breathing patterns, through the communication units attached to them.

"I've been disarming bombs for years without your woowoo help." Nitro's voice vibrated with irritation and what sounded like disgust across the comm unit. "Go back to the house."

Josie's face tightened, but she started running her fingertips over the wires, an intent expression on her face.

"I think it's this one." Josie's voice held an odd quality.

Nitro was frowning to beat the band, but he nodded. "I agree."

Joshua waited silently by. Why didn't he come up to the house? Because he trusted Nitro so implicitly to disarm the bombs, or because some macho mercenary code said you couldn't run away from danger, even if there was nothing you could do to fix it? Where was Hotwire?

Something told her he hadn't done the sensible thing and come back to the house.

She stayed where she was, terrified for them all and determined to do nothing, not even gasp into the comm unit, that might distract Nitro at a crucial moment.

Nitro snipped the wire.

Nothing happened.

But there was no time to rejoice because they'd disarmed the big bomb—Nitro still had to disarm the dynamite. If it went off, everything within a thousand feet would be blown, including the napalm. She wished now that she hadn't researched some of her books so well.

Josie started touching wires, but before she said anything, Nitro set his snips on one. "This is it."

His almost imperceptible pause was followed by a clear snip when Josie nodded her agreement. He disconnected the detonator from the dynamite. It was only as Nitro tossed the cap toward a clear area that it sank in to Lise that nothing had happened from snipping the second wire, either.

Her mouth stretched in a huge grin and she laughed out loud. Joshua was okay. Everyone was okay.

No one would pay the ultimate price for helping her.

The relief was enormous and her knees buckled, but she pushed herself up and went running outside.

She skidded to a stop beside Josie. She reached out to hug the other woman. "You were right, *both times*."

The female mercenary simply nodded, her eyes holding none of the joy of a job well done. Her body was turned perceptibly away from Nitro.

Lise didn't have any time to ponder that because Hotwire arrived with a bomb kit and Nitro went to work stabilizing the napalm.

Joshua grabbed her and kissed her, his lips fierce. When he lifted his head, she felt more than weak-kneed—she felt dazed.

"Get back into the house. I don't want you out here."

She glared at him. "Why not?"

"The situation isn't stable yet."

She rolled her eyes. "The bombs are disarmed."

"They're homemade."

She didn't respond to that bit of nonsense. If Nitro could disarm a bomb, he could surely handle it without setting it off.

She stood in the frigid cold, feeling the strangest sense of incompletion. She should be elated, jumping around with joy, but all she felt was numb.

"You don't suppose he had a partner, or anything, do you?"

"No." Joshua glared at the still-unconscious Ed Jones. "He was a loner."

She considered the trussed-up man and the two disarmed bombs. "It seems almost too easy."

Nitro shrugged. "Wolf always gets his man."

She opened her mouth to say something when a large flash and small explosion came from her left.

Chapter 18

Lise jumped, her heart doing double-time. Joshua wrapped her up against him, hugging her tight, and she leaned into his big body, clinging to his warmth and strength in a way she would not normally allow herself to do.

His hand rubbed up and down her back. "It was just the detonator, honey."

"I wasn't expecting it," she mumbled into his coat.

"I didn't feel like risking the odds again when I could let it go off without hurting anyone or anything."

Nitro's explanation made sense and she pulled from Joshua's arms to tell him so, along with giving him her thanks. "You risked your life for me." Her watery smile encompassed Hotwire, Josie, and Joshua, too. "You all did. *Thank you.*"

Hotwire shrugged, his blue eyes twinkling with Georgian charm. "It's all in the job description, ma'am."

Nitro's dark face came as close to smiling as she'd ever seen it. "I disarm bombs in my sleep. It was no big deal."

Lise could not quite tell, but she thought maybe he was actually kidding her. She grinned. "I'm sure you do."

"No doubt," Josie drawled, her anger with Nitro as obvious as a Brahma bull in the middle of a herd of Hereford steers. "And you didn't need my help, either. You don't need *anyone.*"

She turned to Joshua. "I'll go back to the house and call the authorities while you wrap up out here."

"I'll go with you. I've got buddies in the FBI that we should call. Jones crossed state lines to perpetrate his stalking and attempted bombing and that puts him under federal jurisdiction."

Joshua nodded. "Good—take Lise with you."

She wasn't sure if she was going to argue or not.

He didn't give her the chance and pulled her to him for another quick but mind-numbing kiss. "It's cold out here. I want you inside."

She didn't argue that he was no more impervious to the cold than she was because in this case it was just possible he was right. She was shivering despite wearing her winter coat, and he didn't look chilled at all.

"What about him?" She nodded toward Ed Jones, who still had not awakened.

"Nitro and I will bring him in when we're done."

"Okay."

The next few hours were harried ones.

The bombs had to be disposed of.

Afterward, Ed Jones was transported to the hospital because when he finally did wake up, he complained of pain in his chest. It could be bruising from the hits through the Kevlar, but his skin tone had been pasty and she wondered if it was his heart. Lise had learned that he'd made a full confession on the way to the hospital, apparently feeling the authorities would believe he was justified in his hatred of her.

Although Hotwire's friends helped to deal with the local law enforcement, there was still a lot of red tape and questioning to get through. Joshua had to explain why he hadn't brought law enforcement in to begin with and from the looks on the officers' faces, Lise didn't think they liked his reasoning.

After answering questions for hours for two sets of authorities, she was finally able to relax. She curled up in an armchair in the living room to wait for Joshua and the others to finish, too.

He found her there and scooped her into his arms without a by-your-leave.

"Your caveman tendencies are showing again."

He smiled down at her. "I'm beginning to think that's a permanent condition when I'm around you."

"Hmm . . . Where are the others?"

"Nitro left with the bomb unit—he'll be back later. Josie's packing and Hotwire is still talking with his FBI buddies."

"I'm glad it's over."

"Me, too, sweetheart. I've never had a job that stressed me out so much."

She laughed even as her heart filled with hope. Earlier, he'd said he wanted to discuss their *relationship* and now he was telling her that protecting her had impacted his emotions. Those were two very good signs. Certainly making it worth sticking around to find out if they had a future.

She floated through the next few days in a strange sort of limbo, not wanting to discuss her future with Joshua until the present was more settled. She and Joshua spoke to the FBI twice more and the prosecutor's office once. They slept together and made love, but by tacit agreement, they didn't talk about their feelings or their future.

She finished her book and sent it off to her editor, hoping what she'd been through while she was writing it had made the book stronger, not a jumble of incomprehensible words. That done, she decided the time had come to confront Joshua about their relationship.

She was soaking in the hot springs, celebrating making her deadline, when Joshua walked into the jungle room. "You're not writing."

He sounded puzzled and she grinned up at him. She had spent pretty much every daylight hour, and plenty of the dark ones besides, working on her Dana and laptop Hotwire had brought with him when he'd come.

"I finished the book and sent it off to my editor a little while ago."

"Are you going to take some time off before your next one?"

Was he going to invite her to stay in Vermont with him while she did? "That's my plan."

"How long?"

"I usually like to take off a week or so, but this time I want a real break. I'm not starting anything new for a month."

He started peeling out of his clothes. "That sounds about right."

For what? Did he think their relationship would have run its course by then? Her thoughts splintered as he finished undressing and she sucked in air at the sight of his naked body.

"I don't think mercenaries are supposed to blush, but if you keep looking at me that way, I'm going to."

She laughed softly. "I can't help it. You're so sexy."

He looked down at his body and then at her with a grimace. "I've got more scars than a Hollywood stuntman."

She waited until he'd joined her in the water to answer and then she traced a mark that had obviously been a knife wound. "Call me nuts, but I like it. It's all part of what brought you to be the man you are."

He shuddered at her touch, his eyes turning to dark fire. "Whatever turns you on."

She leaned forward to lick the thin ridge of white flesh she'd been touching, loving the scent and heat of him. "I get a definite charge out of knowing you got these marks defending and saving people."

He made a sound of pure masculine pleasure and pulled her into his lap, their naked thighs sliding against each other.

She felt an immediate response in both her heart and her inner flesh at the sensation.

He leaned down and kissed her.

Slowly and thoroughly.

When he lifted his head, his expression was so serious it would have scared her if the warmth in his eyes wasn't just as intense. "Will you find a security consultant as sexy as a warrior?"

Her heart tripled its beats per minute. "*You're retiring?*"

Joshua's smile was as gentle as the hand caressing her hip. "Nitro, Hotwire, and I think maybe it's time."

She could barely believe what she was hearing. They had to be talking about the future here.

"Security is a much safer profession than being a soldier of fortune," she said with deep approval.

"There's still some danger, but nothing like rescue operations."

"Or catching bomb-wielding stalkers."

Ed Jones was still in critical condition. His heart had an arrhythmia and the stress of no sleep and eating convenience foods while he stalked her had exacerbated the problem to deadly proportions. Other tests had shown he was suffering from liver cancer, too, most likely linked to inhaling the fumes while making napalm. The advanced stage of the cancer indicated that even if they got his heart stable again, he probably wouldn't live long enough to go to trial.

To her way of thinking, the most ironic thing about the whole mess was that the Joneses' daughter had been so concerned about her mother, she'd given her Lise's book to read. While Mrs. Jones had called one of the crisis numbers in the front, Lise had no doubt that her daughter would have found another way to get through to her mother if Lise's book had not worked.

Ed Jones had brought about his own demise . . . in more ways than one.

Lise shivered. "He could have gotten counseling, been willing to change. He didn't have to lose his marriage and his family."

"He made the choice," Joshua said, proving he knew who she'd been thinking about. "We all do."

"Like you choosing to retire before you're maimed," she said with definite satisfaction.

"It's not exactly retirement."

"It's close enough." And she kissed him to show how much she liked that.

When she was done, he rubbed his cheek against hers. "I always figured a husband and father should put his family first. A mercenary can't do that."

"Husband?" she asked, breathless, her eyes now glued to his while her heart beat a nervous tattoo. "*Father?*"

"I know I'm not the best investment you could make when it comes to picking out a mate."

The man really did see things in very primitive terms. *Mate* indeed.

"I've done and seen a lot that I wouldn't wish on another person, but I need you, Lise, and I don't think I can let you go. I'm hoping you feel the same way."

From going full throttle, her heart seemed to stop beating altogether and she could barely breathe. "*You want to get married?*"

"Yes."

"But . . ."

"You said you love me. Did you mean it?"

After all the times she'd said it, she couldn't believe he had to ask that. "*Of course I meant it*. What do you think, I go around saying that kind of thing to lots of men?"

Under the circumstances, she could be forgiven a little sarcasm. Her feelings had never been in question.

At least not to her.

"No, but have you considered that it could be gratitude?"

Did he really think she couldn't tell the difference between sincere thankfulness and love? "If it was, then I'd have a case on Nitro and Hotwire, too, not just you."

He did not like hearing that, his whole body tensing around her while his eyes burned down at her with censure. "I'm not just talking about the Nemesis mission, but a lot of women think they love the first man they have sex with."

And he thought their circumstance was the same? Man, he had a lot of insecurity she would never have guessed he was capable of feeling.

"Most of them are right. Just because the relationship doesn't work doesn't meant they didn't love those men. Anyway, you *weren't* the first man I made love with."

"In a way, I was."

She knew immediately what he was getting at. He was the first man to give her the kind of pleasure most women would kill for. "I hate to break it to you, but it's really not the same."

"Are you sure about that?"

For such a smart, logical, and usually rational being, he was certainly leading with his emotions on this one.

"I don't think so, and if you were thinking more logically, you wouldn't, either." But he wasn't thinking completely reasonably because his heart was involved.

She wanted to sing hosannas and shout the "Hallelujah Chorus."

"Joshua, a woman doesn't have to sleep with ten different men to know when the right one comes along. I've never felt about another man the way I feel about you."

"You loved Mike."

"Yes, I did, but what I felt for him was so shallow compared to what I feel for you that there's no comparison."

"Are you sure?"

She stared at her sexy, badass mercenary and shook her head with exasperation. "Cryin' out loud, Joshua. What do I have to do, write it across my forehead? Yes, I'm sure. I love you and it isn't just because making love with you is so awe-some. I love the deep well of integrity inside of you, I love being with you. Believe it or not, you're peaceful to be with . . . for me, anyway. We fit on a level that has nothing to do with the physical. But most of all, I love the man your past has made you to be, the man who looks at the present with the eyes of a protector and the heart of warrior."

Dark brown eyes turned suspiciously bright and he nuzzled her neck. "So, let's get married. You've got a month off. We can take a long honeymoon, maybe travel to a jungle as tourists for once, or something."

She wanted it more than anything she'd ever desired, but if he didn't love her, wouldn't he grow bored with their marriage?

"Are you sure you want *marriage?*"

"Yes." He kissed her again, this time his lips hard and insistent, but she fought losing herself in a sensual daze.

She needed answers to tough questions and she wasn't hiding from asking them anymore.

She pulled away, her breathing as rapid as her pulse. "Joshua, do you love me?"

He took so long to answer that she began to despair it wasn't going to be the right one.

When he started talking, his voice was low and furred with feeling. "For a long time I thought you were making up an image in your head of someone I wasn't, someone you could fall in love with, but you saw me more clearly than anyone ever has."

She was glad he realized that. "I don't love you for who you could be, but for who you are."

"Yes. That's an incredible feeling, sweetheart."

"I'm glad."

The question was, did he feel something similar?

"The first time I saw you, I wanted you."

She smiled in memory. "I could tell. You were intense."

"You were scared."

"I didn't want to lose myself again."

"Loving someone shouldn't make you less than what you are, it should make you more."

"It does." She'd finally figured that out.

"I know."

Her heart stopped and then started beating so fast, she felt faint. "You do?"

He cupped her face, the hot water lapping around them. "I love you, Lise Barton. Please say you'll marry me because letting you go would mean tearing my heart out."

Emotion choked her and she could barely get the word out of lips stiff with joy. "Yes."

His kiss was filled with the promise of every tomorrow.

They made love there in his underground jungle paradise, using love words they'd kept locked deep inside.

Afterward, they called Jake and Bella to tell them the good news. Her brother wanted them to get married on the ranch and Lise agreed without a murmur of protest.

She didn't care where she got married so long as she got to spend the rest of her life with her Wolf.

Two weeks later, she walked out of the bathroom in their honeymoon hideaway located in the heart of the Brazilian jungle.

The bedroom was lit with candles, soft drums played outside the window, and an array of exotic orchids and other flowers filled the room with their scent. Joshua was lying on the bed, propped up on his elbow and wearing nothing but a wolf's smile.

"Come here."

She shook her head. "I've got something to give you."

"I know you do, but I can't have it with six feet separating us." Then, apparently too impatient to wait for her, he came up off the bed in a rush and pulled her into his arms, into his body, into his love.

They fell together on the bed and she forgot about her present until he made a noise of surprise and grabbed the small, rectangular box from where it had fallen under his muscular butt. "What's this?"

"Open it and see."

He undid the ribbon and lifted the black lid off the gold box. She knew what was inside. A small white stick with two blue lines.

He looked up at her. "Is this what I think it is?"

She licked her lips. "What do you think it is?"

"A pregnancy test."

"Yes."

"The blue lines mean it's positive?" he asked, his voice giving nothing away about how he felt, but the throbbing erection against her thigh was another story.

She nodded. "I'm going to have your baby."

She found herself flat on her back and he loomed above her, the biggest smile she'd ever seen on his face, his eyes molten ingots that burned her with his pleasure. "I was right."

She smiled up at him, her heart so full, she was afraid it would overflow in happy tears. "Yes. Our bodies are very compatible."

"So are our hearts. I love you, Lise."

She whispered the words back into his mouth as he kissed her with passion and tenderness that made her glad she'd taken a chance on loving a badass mercenary with a tendency to boss other people around.

As she'd told him once, some risks in life were worth taking.

And here's a first look at
Gemma Bruce's sexy whodunit
WHO'S BEEN SLEEPING IN MY BED?
available now from Brava . . .

Nan's heart skittered to a stop, seized up for a moment, then banged back to life, hammering at her rib cage. Okay, just one little backslide, just one night. She deserved it. And besides, Delia had eaten three doughnuts.

It didn't have to be a backslide. Damon Connelly might be the kind of man who liked to talk after sex. She could find out a lot of information that way.

Who was she kidding? She was rationalizing. She knew it and she wanted to ignore it, but she made a last-ditch effort to control herself.

"I'm not having casual sex these days."

Damon's eyebrows twitched. It was such a turn-on. "It won't be casual. I promise."

He stepped toward her. She stepped back against the table. His hands slipped around her waist. He lifted her up and sat her down on the top.

Nan reached back to steady herself. Her hand squashed into the baguette, but she was beyond caring.

He eased a hip bone between her thighs, then stepped between them. Pulled her forward until she was straddling him. Her skirt rolled up her thigh. She locked her ankles behind him and pulled him even closer.

He groaned as body parts came together in a teasing

dance. Then his mouth covered hers so violently that she fell backwards. He grabbed her around the shoulders and held on, assaulting her mouth with thrusts of his tongue. Mashing his lips against hers, driving her teeth against her lip, drawing blood.

He eased up and ran his tongue along her teeth and lips, licking the blood away. "Sorry," he mumbled and went in for a second offensive.

This time he was gentler. It was even better, knowing that he was holding himself back. It gave her a chance to reciprocate.

She was vaguely aware of her cell phone ringing; a faint echo from inside her purse that she'd hung over a chair back. She briefly considered reaching for it, but couldn't let go of Damon.

His hair was soft and just the right length for wrapping around her fingers. She did and pulled. He groaned again and deepened the kiss. This time she fell backwards onto the tabletop, taking Damon with her.

The French bread went down for the count. Neither of them noticed. Damon's hands were everywhere, roaming at will, his touch hitting every spot but the one that needed it most.

"Not a table, either," he said against her ear. And suddenly she was lifted up. And being carried across the room, her legs still locked around his waist.

He shouldered the door open and stepped into the hall.

"Bedroom," he said.

"Yes," she answered. Didn't understand why he laughed.

He started down the hall with her clinging to him. Paused and threw the first door open. It was the closet. A muffled expletive and he started up again. The bathroom.

"And behind door number three . . ." she said breathlessly.

"Aha," said Damon as he opened the door to the bedroom.

Anticipation rushed through her. Just one little backslide, she promised. He'd be gone in twenty minutes—forty, max. But until then . . . Shit. He'd stopped just inside the door. Why was he just standing there?

"Hmm?" she asked.

Damon jerked. "Just looking." Then he moved again, across the room, and they fell on the bed together. He loomed over her, expression stark, eyes glittering with something scary.

A part of her brain, the part that was still trying to think rationally, was clamoring for her attention. She didn't know anything about Damon Connelly. She was nuts to let this man into her house, much less into her bed. And then the part of her that was responsible for her being sent to Camp Wilderness spoke up. *You'll get information this way. And have a hell of a ride along the way.*

She consigned her rational self as well as her good intentions to the bottom of Long Island Sound and reached for the buttons of Damon's shirt. It made the tussle in the parking lot look like an amateur sting. This was a fight to the finish. They groped for each other, getting in each other's way, but neither yielding ground.

Finally, Damon pushed her to her feet. His shirt hung by one arm. His trousers were halfway unzipped. Her dress was up by her waist. He steadied her on her heels, then pulled the dress over her head in one smooth movement. She stood before him in nothing but four-inch heels and a beige silk thong.

A sharp crack of sound, somewhere between a laugh and a cry, escaped from deep in his throat. He was breathing hard and taking her in.

He yanked the sleeve over his wrist and tossed his shirt past her. She started to reach for him.

"No," he said. "Stay right there. Just like that." His eyes were feasting on her. Scrutinizing every inch of her. While her insides were tugging with desire, with impatience, and with shear physical need. Her thong was wet with anticipation.

Damon shucked off his trousers, boxers, shoes and socks. Then he stood before her.

She licked dry lips and his cock jumped in response. What a sense of power. So why didn't he come to her or draw her toward him?

They stood facing each other, not more than four feet away, discovering everything they could by sight, but Nan was eager to get to the touch and taste part. And so was Damon if she knew the signs. And she knew the signs.

Then he moved and she was in his arms, their bodies pressed together, sharing heat, exchanging desire. He didn't kiss her this time or suckle her, but scooped her off the ground and laid her gently across the bed. He lifted her leg, slipped off her shoe, and held her bare foot in his hand.

His tongue flicked across her toes. Nan wriggled. Jesus. The man even made feet erotic. He nibbled each toe, then slid his tongue up her instep leaving a heated wet trail to her ankle.

Oh, boy. She didn't think she could wait for him to make his way all the way up her leg. She reached for him again, but he pushed her hand away. Continued to lick and nibble his way up her calf and thigh. Exquisite torture. It was time to reel this baby in.

"Damon," she whispered.

"Soon." He nuzzled the crease at her hip, just inches from where he needed to go. She wondered if he needed a road map. She shifted under him, trying to give him a clue. His breath puffed out over her belly, making her shudder. He was teasing her.

Nan's whole body clenched in anticipation. Okay, she was going to die without ever getting to the really good part.

Finally, his tongue slipped beneath the tie of her thong. He followed the string to the triangle of fabric. She felt the rasp of his tongue on her skin, now just centimeters to the left of home.

"Damon."

He kept moving, bypassing where she needed him, then coming back a little closer and skirting off to the side again. She was squirming beneath him. Out of control, helpless to make him hurry.

Then his tongue slipped out of her thong and he moved away. Nan felt a wash of disappointment.

But he moved back to her, his mouth inches above the fabric. His head dipped, his teeth closed over the silk triangle, soaked from both their body fluids. He jerked his head. The fabric ripped as the thong came away in his mouth.

He tossed it to the side and dove to his final destination.

Nan whimpered. She never whimpered, simpered, or whined. But she felt like doing all three. She fell into a vortex of pleasure. The movements of his tongue, the nip of his teeth diffused waves of heat through the rest of her body; drove an acute tightening deep inside her.

She was caught up in the moment, yo-yoing between trying to guess what he would do next, and not caring at all as long as he kept going. She was turned on by the unpredictability of it all, and totally helpless to reciprocate. Finally giving up, she succumbed to the escalating rhythm of his tongue and her response to it.

She grabbed his hair, pulling him into her. He urged her toward the brink, winding her tighter and tighter, until the spring uncoiled and she rocketed through space. Damon hung on all the way, riding her until the last contraction subsided.

He followed his tongue up the center of her body.

"Can't wait," he said and thrust into her, before she could even say "condom."

Don't miss this super-sizzling sneak
peek at Diane Whiteside's
THE RIVER DEVIL
available now from Brava!

Hal Lindsay yanked her down across him and kissed her. Fast and hard, his tongue diving between her teeth.

She stiffened, affronted by the unexpected familiarity.

His mouth gentled. His tongue delicately caressed her lips as he rumbled something persuasive.

She sighed, captivated, and her jaw relaxed, admitting him. Then it was too late for objections as her sanity fled under his expert attentions.

He kissed her like a devil intent on sweeping a woman's soul away. His neat goatee caressed her cheeks and chin as his tongue claimed hers. He tasted of bourbon and sugar . . . and man. She moaned and her fingers caressed the whisker stubble on his cheeks. He was warm, and real, and infinitely better than any lonely dream.

Lindsay growled something and stood up, lifting her into his arms as if she were a petite demoiselle, not an overly tall Amazon. Fire flowed down her spine, from her throat to her core, at his easy mastery of her.

"What the devil do you think you're doing?" Rosalind gasped, stunned by how easily he carried her. Her breasts firmed, all too aware of the heat of his big body.

"What do you think?" Lindsay wasn't even slightly winded.

"Put me down!" she protested, trying to deny her own reaction to him.

"Not yet."

She considered shouting for help but decided against it: only his servants could hear her. Besides, the warmth building between her legs made it difficult to argue with him.

The terrier limped after them, his tail wagging jauntily. The undershirt was now just a distant lump on the carpet, an inconsequential oddity in the magnificent hallway.

Hal pushed open a door and dropped her on his big carved mahogany bed, taken by his grandfather from a British merchantman during the War of 1812. The crystal lamps and brocade coverlet had come from France by way of New Orleans during the last war; legally paid for, unlike the bed. Winds from an approaching thunderstorm set the Irish lace curtains to dancing at the windows. Lightning sparked the sky in nature's fireworks.

But his prize was more unique than anything captured by his ancestors. He'd beguiled her into his house as neatly as he'd grabbed that last pot at Taylor's house with an unexpected bluff. And now he could savor her to the fullest.

She fascinated him. He had a million questions for her, ranging from how she'd managed to disguise herself to her opinions on lower Mississippi riverboat traffic. But none of them came to his lips, not once he'd felt her lovely ass as he carried her. He needed more of the woman hidden inside that far too concealing frock coat.

His cock lengthened at the prospect.

Hal caressed her jaw lightly, surprised at how his fingers trembled. "Where did you get the name Frank Carstairs from?" he asked hoarsely.

She tilted her head slightly to consider him. Hal smiled inwardly; of course, his little poker shark would want to think first. He'd enjoy burning all that cool consideration out of her. Damn, he'd like to see her knocked off balance and into overwhelming lust, after watching her icy control at the poker table.

"My mother's maiden name was Carstairs," she answered slowly. He continued to fondle her, wondering how he'd ever mistaken cheeks this smooth for a man's.

"And Frank?" His fingers trailed through the fine locks of hair at her temples.

"My second name is Frances." Her head turned slightly to follow his touch.

"Mine is Andronicus." Hal traced the outer curve of her ear and knew he deserved a medal for making conversation when his cock was this hard. But he needed to wait, needed to seduce her, his little poker shark who was all too comfortable with the guns at her waist. Damn, she was a better challenge then piloting the *Belle* through the great rapids before Fort Benton.

"Henry is your first name?"

Hal's mouth thinned briefly. No one, except his father, had ever addressed him as Henry and he'd never accepted that hated name from a lover.

Rosalind's breath caught as his fingers teased the pulse point under her jaw.

"Indeed. But you'll call me Hal tonight." He breathed the last syllables against her lips before he kissed her again.

And he'd wager a year's profits that this lady wouldn't bore him within the hour, unlike every other respectable woman he'd ever met.

Rosalind's willpower fled as soon as his lips met hers again. Her body had even less interest in maintaining sanity this time than it had exhibited on the stairs. Months of loneliness fled, banished by the hunger racing through her blood, fueled by his demanding mouth and hands.

His hands fondled her back and swept down over her ass, cupping it and pulling her close. She moaned and wiggled against him, driven half-wild by the first feel of his magnificent hard cock, outlined by his trousers' rough wool. The scent of lilacs spilled into the room from the garden beyond, like a call to sensual delights.

He growled something and slid his hand inside the back of her waistband.

Rosalind jerked and stared up at Hal, panting for breath. How had he known she loved to have her backside fondled? Her breasts ached for his touch, her pulse thundered through her veins, and heat pulsed and melted and pooled between her thighs. "Hal," she moaned.

He stared down at her, his chest rising and falling rapidly. His eyes blazed blue fire, like a pirate gazing at golden treasure. "Damn, I need to see you."

Fire seared her at the hunger in his blue eyes.

Don't miss Amy J. Fetzer's
ultrahot and supersexy thriller
NAKED TRUTH
coming in August 2005 from Brava . . .

Killian flinched, slapped his hand over his gun, instantly awake. The drapes leading to the deck blew inward and he slid to the floor, tracking shadows and moonlight. The remaining door was still locked, traps in place, and he rose slowly, moving to the open door, then relaxed when he saw her. She stood at the low rail, the east China breeze pushing her hair back with the folds of the silk robe.

Hell of a sight, he thought, like a fantasy played out; hair flying, the thin fabric whipping and molding her body in the moonlight.

"Alexa." She didn't open her eyes but knew he was there.

"I didn't mean to wake you."

"Are you nuts to be out here?"

"Maybe."

He came to her, leaving the gun close. "How'd you get past the traps?"

She smiled softly. "I have my talents," she said, staring out at the port.

There was something different about her, her expression was more relaxed than before, almost serene.

"Isn't it beautiful out here?"

He glanced; the city and harbor lights sparkled on a sea of black. "I guess."

Alexa smiled. "Spoken like a true warrior," she said.

Killian was still, tempted to reach for her, but if he put a single finger on her, it was a mark he could never erase. Alexa could be programmed, a traitor, even if she didn't know it or had no control. That he hadn't updated his men said he was bending the wrong way in this battle, yet she'd proven to be his ultimate temptation. Everything he desired in a woman. He faced that somewhere around the witching hour, yet knew it long before, probably from that first kiss in the jungle. Halfway through his third shot of whiskey, he went macho, telling himself she was the best fuck on the planet and that's all it was. But he wasn't into lying, even to himself.

He didn't want just her body, he wanted her soul.

He took a step, crossing a line, and moved behind her, sliding his arms around her waist.

"Oh, I was hoping for that." She sighed back into him, closing her hand over his.

Just to feel her soft length against him was enough to make him rock hard. The sleek curve of her throat beckoned him and he pressed his mouth there, feeling her pulse beneath his lips. It nurtured something in him, this need to close the distance between them, and when she twisted enough to kiss him, pushing his hands where she wanted, Killian wanted her more than ever. He pulled at the sash, exposed her warm flesh to the moonlight, circling her nipple with his thumb, his free hand sliding down to lay flat on her belly. She wiggled in his arms, pushing his hand, deepening his touch. He slid slower, his finger diving between her warm folds, becoming coated with her liquid. She moaned, a delicious purr as she pushed back into his erection. She turned, sliding her hand under his shirt and pushing it off over his head. Then her mouth was on his nipple, lips tugging.

"No clothes this time," she whispered.

"I thought you said there wouldn't be a next time."

"I lied." She slicked his nipple and Killian felt his world shudder. "Aren't you glad?" She opened his jeans.

"You have no idea."